STOLEN MOMENTS

New Haven Series (Book 2)

Samantha J. Ball

Cover photo designed by Racool_Studio/Freepik

ISBN-13: 9798521030026

For my dad. I miss you.

Chapter One

NEW HAVEN, CONNECTICUT, 2016

Alexandra Masters walked along the sidewalk with a spring in her step, her stomach fluttering in excitement as she navigated her way around an array of pumpkins. For the first time in ages, she'd be spending the holiday with special people. People who were more like family than friends.

The late morning sun blinded her, forcing her to shield her eyes with her hand, and a smile spread across her face. She had a good feeling about today's celebrations. Maybe it was the effect of the sunlight? Whatever the reason, she was looking forward to seeing her best friend Melanie Danvers and her seven-year-old daughter Sophie.

Admiring the russet-colored wreath on Melanie's front door, Alex smoothed down her blue skinny jeans and rang the apartment doorbell. She didn't wait long for the door to open.

"Wow, you look stunning, Alex!" Melanie said.

"Thanks, Mel. Happy Thanksgiving."

"To you too."

Alex offered up a hamper of hand-selected coffee pods, maple syrup, and candy.

"You know you didn't need to." Grinning, Melanie checked out the contents of the gift basket. "But it's perfect."

"You're welcome. Thanks for inviting me."

Melanie stepped aside, and Alex entered, strolling toward the kitchen.

"Mmm, I smell pancakes." Breathing in the familiar aroma, she picked up her pace and called out, "Sophie? Your mom didn't leave you alone in the kitchen again, did she?"

"Um, it isn't Sophie..."

Alex didn't stop to wonder why Melanie sounded worried. Instead, she rounded the corner and skidded to a halt, her pulse skyrocketing. Zac, Melanie's brother, was in the kitchen. He was also the last person she'd expected to see today.

Melanie could've warned her!

The first and only time Alex had ever seen Dr. Zachary Danvers had been at Sophie's christening over a year and a half ago. She still remembered his hurtful words about his sister's choice of a godmother: 'A teacher?' and 'Near stranger'. He obviously hadn't realized Alex—said godmother—was right behind him in the church when he'd said those words to Melanie.

They'd been imprinted on Alex's mind ever since.

Even so, when they'd first come face to face, she'd felt attraction like a bolt of lightning. His clear blue eyes had stared into the depths of her soul, mesmerizing her. His strong jawline and muscular appearance, evident in his formfitting white shirt, hadn't gone unnoticed either. Her body had hummed. Since then, she'd tried not to conjure up his image too regularly.

She hadn't succeeded.

"What are *you* doing here?" she blurted at him, mortified when her voice sounded harsh in her ears.

"Nice to see you too." Zac's voice dripped with sarcasm while his enigmatic smile didn't quite reach his eyes.

"I didn't mean—" she began, her face heating. Why hadn't she thought before she'd spoken? Of course, he took it the wrong way! Why did he have to be so rude?

"Miss Alex, you're here!" Sophie barreled into her from out of nowhere, just as Melanie entered the kitchen and paused.

Alex bent down to hug her goddaughter. "Where else would I be but with my favorite little person?"

"Uncle Jack's?" Sophie asked innocently.

"Uh, no," Alex said, straightening, "but he'll be at your grandma's later." Ignoring Zac's curious gaze, she helped herself to a tumbler from a top cupboard, tipped in some juice, and took a long drink.

In the meantime, Melanie and her daughter claimed barstools at the island, and Zac sprang into action. He deposited an extra plate and silverware onto the stone surface, then occupied the seat beside his sister, leaving Alex to partner with Sophie.

"Let's eat before this all gets cold," he said gruffly, lifting a pancake with the spatula and plating it for Alex.

She rolled her eyes. Did he think she couldn't serve herself?

As Zac spread syrup on his pancake and added cut banana and walnut pieces, Alex struggled to keep her eyes off him. When he stabbed a portion of food and lifted it to his mouth, his gaze collided with hers. Heat rose up her neck, and she grabbed her knife and fork to cut into her plain pancake.

"So, Alex, I take it you and Jack are an item?"

Her knife slipped, scraping the plate and making her wince. Why was it any of Zac's business who she was dating?

Melanie jabbed her brother's side, and Alex bit back her response.

"What?" He peered between them with raised eyebrows. "Just making conversation."

"It's okay, Mel." Alex glanced at Zac. "We're sort of seeing each other."

"What does 'sort of' mean?" His furrowed brow and interested tone confused her. Why did he care?

"Well, uh, we've gone out for drinks a few times." She shot a pointed look at Melanie, expecting assistance. None came, so she explained huffily, "We're taking it slow."

"You look cute together, Miss Alex," Sophie piped up, in between mouthfuls, "but I think you and Uncle Zac suit each other better."

"Sophie!" Melanie sounded horrified.

Feeling her face heat up hotter than a pizza oven, Alex dipped her head fast.

"Isn't Jack much younger than you, Alex?"

Huh? She glowered at Zac, her blood pressure rising at his patronizing tone. Did the high and mighty doctor grill everyone he came into contact with, or just her?

"You're thinking of Brad," Melanie corrected him.

"My mistake."

If Alex hadn't been looking forward to sharing Thanksgiving with everyone else, she'd leave. The less she had to do with this insufferable man, the better! She couldn't wait to see Jack at Melanie's parents' later. At least *he* was a gentleman, even if he didn't make her pulse race.

"Mommy, why isn't Mr. Steven here?" Sophie asked, creating a welcome distraction.

"He's picking us up later to go to Grandma's."

"Oh. I wish Mr. Steven was here now," Sophie said glumly, then perked up. "He promised to do stuff with me, Uncle Zac, so he's kinda like my daddy now."

Melanie visibly paled, and Zac spluttered, spilling orange liquid over his T-shirt.

Without thinking, Alex leaned over and dabbed at the damp patches on his shirt with her napkin. Her breath caught in her throat at the feel of his taut muscles under her hand.

"It's fine, don't worry." He swatted her hand away, apparently unaffected by her touch. His shrewd gaze shifted to his sister. "Care to elaborate, Mel?"

Well, well. Alex smirked. So Zac knew nothing about Steven.

"Steven offered to do 'dad type' things with Sophie," Melanie explained.

"I see." He stuffed another bite into his mouth and asked nothing further.

Alex frowned. Why didn't Melanie want to tell Zac the truth? It was bad enough keeping Steven in the dark, but her brother too? Though, going by his earlier interrogation about Jack, she was certain Zac was only temporarily dropping the topic.

Hey, at least she was off the hook.

***

Once breakfast was over, Melanie disappeared to the bathroom, and Sophie went to the front door to wait for Steven, leaving Zac alone with Alex. The same floral scent he remembered from the first time they'd met lingered in the air. He watched her hovering around the sink, wiping the kitchen counters for the third time.

"Is there a problem, Alex?"

She faced him, cloth in hand, her eyes narrowed. "What do you mean?"

"Between you and me?"

"No." She pursed her lips. "Why would you think that?"

"You seem uncomfortable around me."

"I am not!" she said, her voice rising a few notches. "Best you get over yourself, Zac Danvers."

The sound of a throat being cleared stopped his cutting response. A second later, a man strolled into the kitchen with Sophie trailing him.

"Hi, Alex," the man said, kissing her on the cheek. "Happy Thanksgiving."

"To you too, Steven."

Sophie eyed the adults, shrugged, then wandered off into the living room.

Zac wasn't sure what kind of guy he'd been expecting. He hadn't seen any photos, but this good-looking, spiky-haired man with facial hair would definitely turn heads. Particularly with his distinct footballer build. He sneaked a peek at Alex and gave an internal fist pump—no blushes there.

"Hello. Nice to meet you, Steven...my sister's current boyfriend." Zac stuck out his hand in greeting, hoping the man would go easy on his doctor's fingers. "Though, I can't say I knew anything about you before yesterday," he added wryly, matching Steven's intense gaze and refusing to look away.

"Good to meet you, Dr. Danvers." Steven took hold of Zac's hand and tightened his grip, his expression seemingly neutral.

Okay, Melanie's boyfriend had balls. Maybe this one was a keeper. Either way, he had every intention of making sure this guy didn't hurt his sister, like Sophie's father had.

Melanie waltzed in just then, gorgeous in a short, leafy-colored dress and wearing killer heels. Her appearance broke the tension, and Zac caught a glimpse of Steven's appreciative expression. At least he wasn't leering at Melanie the way Zac had seen other men do.

After a sickening display of PDA from the couple—one which elicited a romantic-sounding sigh from Alex—Zac muttered, "Why don't you two just get a room?" He cast another glance at Alex, who snickered when Steven and Melanie broke apart, looking slightly abashed.

"Zac, I assume you've met Steven?"

"Yep," he answered, keeping a straight face and his tone serious. "I told him he'd better not hurt you, Mel, or else he'd answer to me."

Melanie's hands flew to her mouth. "You didn't!"

Alex chuckled, her eyes glinting with amusement. About to join in, Zac caught her scathing look and stopped. "He didn't," she said. "But I wouldn't put it past him."

Ignoring Alex, and Melanie's glare, Zac opted to let them all think the worst of him. He meant what he said. Melanie had been left alone and pregnant once before, and that must never happen again.

"Okay, well, I'm starving," his sister declared unexpectedly, followed by, "Everyone in the truck."

Suited him—he couldn't wait to taste his mom's home-cooked food again. New York takeout couldn't compare.

Outside, Zac held open Steven's rear passenger door for Alex. But what did she do? She promptly rounded the vehicle to the other side and opened that door.

"Unbelievable!" he muttered to himself. Their journey hadn't even started, yet already it was proving to be anything but harmonious.

How ironic, given it was Thanksgiving.

The minute they reached their destination, Alex jumped out of the truck like she'd been stuck in a trash can and couldn't wait to escape. Melanie and Steven exited the vehicle more sedately while Zac stayed seated, tracking Alex's hasty progress up the gravel path to his parents' house. Did she hate him that much that she had to rush off so fast? Enough to risk getting caught by her seat belt?

The tension between them during the short trip had been palpable. Yet, if he wasn't mistaken, the attraction he felt was reciprocated. Even Sophie's constant chatter failed to provide any distraction.

Jack Carrington, Alex's 'sort of' boyfriend, was waiting on the front doorstep, smiling broadly. The couple shared a loving embrace, and Zac's stomach tightened. Sighing, he turned to the one other person left in the truck. "I guess I'll help you out, Sophie."

"Thanks, Uncle Zac. You're the best." She blew him a kiss, and his heart melted.

As they made their way toward the group gathered outside the house, he clasped Sophie's hand in his and forced himself to admire the holiday pumpkins decorating his mom's front porch. Anything to keep him from making a fool of himself by staring at Alex. Her beauty drew him in like a magnet to metal. Looking at her could never be a hardship, but restraining himself was an issue.

"Happy Thanksgiving, Uncle Jack. Look who's here —my Uncle Zac." Sophie's cheerful voice brought him back to the conversation.

Stepping forward, he shook Jack's hand. "Great to see you again, Jack."

"Yeah, you too. You here for long?"

"Until Sunday." His gaze darted to Alex's beautiful face, and his breath hitched. Her lips were pressed together. Why would she have a problem with him conversing with his sister's friend and colleague? Jack was a good man and, if circumstances were different, they'd probably be buddies. It wasn't like he wanted to date the man!

He focused his attention back on Jack. "So you and Alex—"

"I think we should go inside," Alex interrupted, grabbing Jack's hand and whisking him away.

What was wrong with the woman?

For a moment, her skittishness made him want to chuckle until a thought occurred—she wanted time alone with Jack before lunch. Suddenly his palm and jaw hurt from being clenched.

"Uncle Zac?" Sophie tugged on his hand. "Are we going in?"

"Yep. Let's go find your grandma," he said, faking a smile.

In the kitchen, his mom was finishing off the food prep for their Thanksgiving lunch. Zac hadn't been home in a long while, and seeing her again made him realize how much he missed her calm demeanor. After catching up for a few minutes, Mom got Sophie to peel some carrots and suggested he make the gravy.

Feigning ignorance, Zac left for the living room, where he stopped in the doorway. Dad was chatting with a woman he didn't recognize, so his gaze gravitated across the room to Alex—a vision of beauty—standing next to Jack. His heart rate doubled. How could one woman take his breath away, even from a distance? If only he could touch her porcelain skin and the silky blonde strands falling gently around her jaw. How would they feel if he ran his fingers through them?

"Zac, you gonna say hello to your old man or stare at Alex all day?" Dad's deep voice was laced with mirth.

Heat crept up his neck as he tore his eyes away from the woman who was occupying way too many of his thoughts lately.

"Hi, Dad. Happy Thanksgiving," he said, greeting him with a hug while willing his skin to cool down fast.

"Glad you're here, son." Dad turned to the stranger in the room. "I'd like to introduce you to the lovely Julie Rolland," he said, admiration clear in his voice.

Zac's gaze took in the voluptuous woman's short, green dress, which showed off her hourglass figure to perfection. It was unusual seeing Dr. Danvers senior being bowled over by someone. But Dad sure knew how to spot a fine specimen, and he was right–the woman was lovely, no, stunning.

"Gorgeous." Zac stepped sideways, taking her hand in his. "Nice to meet you, Julie." He pressed his lips to her peach-scented hand.

Pleasure shone in her eyes. "Why thank you," she said, revealing a perfect set of teeth. "Coming from such a handsome man, that means an awful lot."

He smiled at her, then glanced over at the other couple. Jack's jaw twitched as he stared at a piece of Dad's artwork–a portrait of their old family dog, Dex–Zac's favorite. Either Jack wasn't a fan of watercolors, or something else was up. Not bothered to figure it out, Zac's gaze drifted to Alex, whose narrowed eyes were trained on him. She wore a curious expression he couldn't work out.

Melanie, strolling into the room with Steven, diverted his attention.

"Happy Thanksgiving, Dad," she said brightly. "You remember Steven?"

Dad grinned as he pumped Steven's hand. "I do, except you're a strapping fella now, Steven. About time someone decent claimed my girl."

Steven looked uncomfortable, so did Melanie.

Wow, Dad certainly was in a generous mood with his praise today. To do with Thanksgiving, perhaps? A perfectionist and not a sufferer of fools, it was a near-impossible task to please him—at least in Zac's opinion. He recalled a recent phone conversation they'd had.

"I take it things are going well at the practice since you haven't come crawling back to New Haven and asked to work with your old man yet."

"They are," Zac had answered through gritted teeth, suppressing the annoyance he felt at his dad's opening words.

"And, I assume working with your partner Dr. Wilson must be easy. Otherwise, you'd have gotten rid of him already."

"I couldn't ask for a better business partner, Dad. Dan Wilson's a true professional. I completely trust and respect him."

"Those high standards I demanded from you when you were younger paid off then."

"I guess they did." He hated admitting it, but his drive and ambition were all due to his father's pushing over the years.

"Don't forget, Zac, being the best scholar possible, then the best student enabled you to become the best doctor in your field."

"I know."

His dad's approval and respect were all he'd ever really wanted. Except, he needed to earn them through hard work and dedication, not because he had the same blood running through his veins or the same surname. It was a big part of why he'd jumped at the chance to go to New York—to gain experience in a doctor's practice there, instead of joining his dad's practice in New Haven. Not that Dad had seemed eager for him to do that anyway.

"Zac? I'd love to hear about your work in New York." A warm hand on his arm and Julie's soft voice drew him out of his thoughts. She was gazing at him intently, her mouth curved up playfully.

Now, *this* he could get used to. Maybe Julie would become a friend, someone willing to visit him in the city? She was here alone and, therefore, single—as far as he knew.

"I'm going to see if I can help Mom and Sophie in the kitchen." Melanie's comment reminded Zac that there were others in the room. "I'm sure you guys can sort out drinks," she added, waving in the direction of the drinks cabinet.

"I'll come help too." Alex glared briefly at him as she passed by.

What was *that* about?

Her absence left him feeling alone and strangely empty inside. Crazy, considering all the men remained. And Julie.

Chapter Two

The delicious flavors of Mom's Thanksgiving dinner lingered in Zac's mouth as he escorted Sophie to his parents' basement for some fun and games. Melanie and Steven followed behind them while Julie opted to visit the bathroom first, saying, "I'll join you guys shortly."

Apparently, Jack and Alex 'wanted a moment to themselves'.

Whatever. Zac refused to think about why.

He swung open the heavy door, rubbing his arms as he stepped inside the large, mostly undecorated space. The heating was on low—useful because things were about to heat up. He loved healthy competition, and if he remembered correctly, Jack was a pretty competent ping-pong player. He had no idea about Steven.

Spotting bean bags across the room, Zac led Sophie toward them, and together they shook out the casual seating. As the dust settled and Sophie got situated, he wondered about Steven again. How would the star quarterback fare, playing this very different game?

Swiveling on the balls of his feet, he was confronted by Steven—standing an arm's throw away—with his hands full.

"Here you go," Steven said, his lips curving up as he handed over a couple of paddles and some ping-pong balls.

"Thanks." Zac returned Steven's smile, as best he could. He still wasn't entirely sure about the guy. Probably just his overprotective nature kicking in. Melanie was a grown woman, and he needed to trust her judgment. But sometimes he forgot his sister was no longer a scared, pregnant eighteen-year-old with no partner to support her.

Melanie trod over to join them, holding a pad of paper and a pen. Her gaze remained fixed on Steven as he sank onto the bean bag adjacent to her daughter.

"You ever played ping-pong before?" Steven asked Sophie.

"Every time I visit." Her eyes twinkled. "Grandpa used to beat me all the time. But ever since I started winning, he says his back's acting up."

Zac chuckled. His niece sure was a firecracker.

"I see," Steven responded, his tone serious. "I'll make sure you're on my team then, Miss Sophie."

Her delighted expression touched Zac. The usual weight of guilt he carried, for not being around the way a godfather should be, lessened. Having a father figure in the picture, like Steven, would be beneficial for Sophie. He only hoped the man wouldn't leave the minute his contract was up. The three of them came across as a perfect family unit.

A jolt of unexpected jealousy came out of nowhere. *He* was the older brother. It should be *him* with the wife and child. Fat chance when he didn't even have a girlfriend!

Oh sure, plenty of women threw themselves at his feet. Beautiful, intelligent women who were generally after his money, position, and looks, but none of them held a candle to Al—

Animated voices, announcing the arrival of the others, interrupted his train of thought.

Julie strode right up to him, gripping his shirt where he'd unbuttoned it earlier to remove his tie. Batting her long eyelashes, she smiled seductively. "You'll be my partner, won't you, Zac?" Her quiet voice dripped with honey.

He grinned. Two could play this game.

"If your strokes are as beautiful as you, then absolutely," he said, covering Julie's hand with his and staring into her sparkling green eyes. Funny, his heartbeat remained steady despite this incredible woman being up close and personal. Yet thinking about Alex, right behind them, spiked his pulse something terrible.

"Cut the charm, Zac." Jack's disapproving tone was crystal clear as he handed a paddle to Alex. "I'm looking forward to beating the pants off you, just like my football team."

Alex snorted, quickly covering her mouth. Her very cute mouth. Trying hard not to be distracted by it, Zac transferred his attention back to Jack and scowled. He may not have had control over his team on the field, but he definitely had control on home turf.

"Brave words there, Carrington," he said, giving Julie a paddle before focusing on Alex. "You'd better hope your girlfriend knows how to swing a paddle."

Adorable red patches appeared on Alex's cheeks. "I'll have you know—" she started, in her best school teacher voice, but Jack covered her mouth with his hand and whispered in her ear. Closing her eyes for a second, she nodded, then swung away from Zac.

He sucked in a breath. What made him say that? He hadn't meant to embarrass her. Anyone who knew him would agree he was an even-tempered person, a perfect gentleman. Normally.

Jack glared at him. "Ready, Zac?"

Ignoring him, he quirked a brow at his sister. "You scoring, Mel?"

She waggled her pen and paper at him.

Okay then. "Let the games begin," he growled.

During the rather lively game, Melanie had to remind him a few times about their impressionable young audience. By the time the final point was scored, his eyes were throwing daggers at his sister.

Shrugging her shoulders, Melanie congratulated Jack and Alex. "Better luck next time, Zac."

"I want a rematch." He knew he sounded like a petulant child, but he couldn't care less. After all, his competitive nature made him one of the leading medical doctors in New York.

"How about you swap partners," Melanie suggested.

His heart leaped at the idea of partnering with Alex. He could do that.

"I'll play with Jack. If he's up for it?" Julie looked across at Jack, who nodded in agreement.

"Zac, will you play nicely with Alex?" Melanie asked, arching a brow.

He peered at Alex. Worried eyes stared back. Maybe it wasn't wise to show his enthusiasm. "If I must." Her beet-colored face and taut lips made him immediately regret his blasé response.

"You know what, Zac?" she said fiercely, "I've had enough of your attitude. Find yourself another partner." Dropping her paddle to the table, Alex turned and stormed out the room.

While Zac steeled himself for his sister's reprimand, Jack made a move to follow Alex.

"Wait," Melanie said sternly, stopping Jack's departure with an arm across his body. She grabbed Zac's wrist with her other hand and glowered at him. "Go apologize right now, Zac. Whatever your problem is with Alex, sort it out." Disappointment showed on her face, and guilt assailed him. The last thing he wanted to do was hurt his sister. "Alex is right," she added, "you've been an absolute jerk to her."

"Fine. I will."

Shoving his hands in his pockets, he headed out the room, overhearing Melanie as he went. "So, Jack and Julie against Steven and me. Everyone happy?" The cheer in her voice sounded forced.

Fantastic! That's what he got for being an idiot. Now he'd have to apologize to two women.

After Zac left the basement, he pondered Alex and Jack's relationship. It made sense, he supposed. Jack was a good-looking guy. Kind and trustworthy, with an admirable job. Apparently, his sister's husband, Mark, worked away a lot, so being the family man Jack was, he often helped Charlotte with her three kids. Alex deserved a good guy like him, someone who would treat her well and certainly seemed to be into her.

Yet, for some inexplicable reason, he still had a major crush on her. To him, she was an angel—beautiful and graceful. If she were attracted to him, she had never given him any indication, not even a little. Never mind two major obstacles: he lived in New York, a four-hour round trip away, and she had a boyfriend.

It drove him crazy hearing about Alex during his sister's periodic phone calls or his infrequent family visits back to New Haven. Thoughts of Alex were continuously mulling around in his head. The more he saw of her, the more his attraction grew. Time and distance had made no difference at all.

When she was around, he found it increasingly difficult to refrain from moving physically closer and wanting to touch her. Instead, he chose to be a jerk. He couldn't help it. Alex hating him would make it easier to go back to New York. Easier to put ideas of them ever being together out of his mind so he could move forward with his life. Thankfully, moving back to New Haven wasn't an option. The idea of seeing Alex on the arm of a great guy like Jack, potentially married to him, wasn't one Zac could stomach. No matter how much he missed his family.

So, New York it was. He just had to sift through the women wanting to be trophy wives and find a genuine one he actually felt attracted to. Up until now, that hadn't happened, but it was possible. He hoped.

In the meantime, how was he going to be alone with Alex and not kiss her? A tightness, comparable to a wound-up corkscrew, gripped his gut, and his heart thumped in his chest.

Nearing the end of his search of the house, he stopped inside the TV room doorway. Dad sat in his lazy chair with a book in his lap. "If you're looking for Alex, son," he said, "she went outside onto the patio. She didn't look happy."

"Thanks, Dad."

French doors led outside to where Alex leaned on the handrail overlooking the garden. Zac picked his way toward her and heard her heavy sigh.

"Alex?" he called quietly, not wanting to scare her.

She glanced over her shoulder. "Great," she muttered. "Just the person I wanted to see."

The animosity in her voice cut into his heart, not that he'd expected a welcome mat. Guess he'd really done a number on her. Shoving his hands deep into his coat pockets, he cleared his throat. "I've come to apologize."

She swung around fully, hands on hips. "You mean Mel sent you to apologize."

Kicking the gray stone paving with his shoe, he raised his eyes to her angry ones. "Busted."

"Don't bother, Dr. Danvers," she said, turning away from him again. "I'll tell her you said sorry."

Frustrated at having to speak to her back, he huffed out a sigh. Melanie wouldn't be happy if he didn't actually apologize.

"Alex? Will you *please* look at me?" He tried not to sound desperate.

Shuffling around, she crossed her arms. Her glower rendered him powerless to open his mouth for a few seconds.

"What?" she demanded.

Taking a step closer, he caught a whiff of her subtle perfume and had to remember why he was out there. Her floral scent complimented her beauty perfectly. He sandwiched his palms together and licked his lips.

"Listen. I *am* sorry for my behavior. It was wrong. You don't deserve to be treated that way."

She tilted her head, searching for what, he had no idea, but her scrutiny disarmed him nonetheless.

"I'm not sure I forgive you," she said, her brow furrowed. "Maybe if you explained why you've been a jerk to me all day?"

He eased near enough to touch her. "Honestly? It's easier than doing what I want to do."

She shot him a skeptical look. "And what is it you'd

rather do, Zac? Because I'm sure it's preferable to you being inexcusably mean."

"This," he said, cupping her left cheek with one hand and lowering his mouth to hers. Finally, he tasted her sweet lips. They were exactly as he'd imagined they'd be, soft and pliable and glorious. He kissed her the way he'd dreamed of from the first time he'd laid eyes on her. It only lasted a few seconds but was deep and passionate.

A sudden resounding smack across his cheek shocked him, and Alex's angry expression confronted him. "How dare you?" she hissed before pushing past him and retreating back into the house.

Left with a stinging face and injured pride, Zac uttered a four-lettered word.

Fool!

Why had he been kidding himself thinking she might be 'the one'?

Sinking onto the porch swing, he rested his head in his hands, a niggle settling at the back of his mind. Alex *had* kissed him back, hadn't she? Shaking his head, he groaned. Maybe he'd imagined it.

The whoosh of the door opening made his heart jump. *Alex?*

Disappointment rose as he looked over his shoulder to see Julie. Of course. Why *would* Alex return after branding him the way she had? Except, he'd hoped. Hoped she'd reacted instinctively when she realized it wasn't Jack kissing her. That after having had time to think about it, she wanted to explore the strong connection between them.

Keep dreaming, Zac.

"I thought you might like something to warm you up," Julie said, giving him a small smile as she handed him one of the steaming mugs she carried.

Why couldn't he be attracted to her instead? She was gorgeous *and* single.

"Thanks, Julie." Cradling the mug in his hands, he blew across the top of the hot liquid and peered up over the rim. "You're very kind."

She gazed down at him, regarding him curiously. "Would you like some company? You look like you might need some comfort."

He frowned. Why would she think that? Being alone was normal for him. As a doctor in New York, getting a date wasn't a problem, but seeking out company he actually enjoyed, now *that* was a different story.

Julie pointed at his throbbing cheek. "I take it someone wasn't happy with you."

"I haven't exactly been a good male role model today." He twisted his lips and patted the empty spot next to him. "Join me, please. If you dare?"

She sunk gracefully onto the seat and faced him. A chuckle escaped his lips at her obvious concern, causing him to wince. Alex's hand was sure to be stinging too. A vision of him kissing her palm better flittered through his mind.

"Do you want to talk about it?" Julie asked. "I promise I'm a good listener and won't gossip." Keeping her eyes trained on him, she took a sip of her drink. "If you need a reference, just ask Steven."

"You and Steven are close?"

"Yes."

"How does Mel feel about that?"

"Believe it or not, she's cool with us being friends. Besides, I'm not a threat."

"Really?" He quirked a brow. "Why not?"

"My heart belongs to another."

He studied her. Would she spill if he waited?

She didn't.

"Let me guess," he said. "The man in question hasn't a clue."

"Exactly."

"Jack."

Alarm filled her eyes, and she nearly spilled hot liquid as she raised her hand to object. "No! Yes. How'd you guess?"

"He's the only one you don't flirt with. In fact, if I were him, I'd think you didn't like me at all."

"Am I that obvious?"

"To me, yes." He smirked. "Lucky for you, Jack's oblivious. Though, unless you want him to continue being unaware of your feelings, you might decide to pay him some attention."

Julie peered into her mug, then up at the night sky. Did she see the one bright star framed by millions of specks of light like he did? Her faraway expression hinted she was blind to the beauty of creation she gazed upon. Her focus came back to him.

"I'm not sure that's a good idea, Zac. In case you hadn't noticed, Alex isn't exactly fond of me. If I flirted with her boyfriend, she'd quickly ensure I got excluded from this tight-knit group." After another sip of her drink, she added, "To be honest, I'm only here because Steven invited me."

"I see." He pressed his lips together. "I'm not sure what to advise then."

"It's okay; I'm a big girl. I can take care of myself."

"I've no doubt."

Finishing off her drink, Julie popped the mug under the swing. "So why did Alex mark your cheek?"

Not willing to admit anything, he sent her a challenging look.

"I put two and two together." She grinned, cute lines creasing her pretty eyes. "And Alex stalked past me, looking very angry."

"I kissed her."

"What?" She laughed briefly, then realized he wasn't joking. "Yeah, that would do it. I take it she wasn't a willing participant?"

"No. Not really."

Julie laid a hand on his thigh. "We're a sorry pair, aren't we?"

"Hey! Speak for yourself," he said with mock indignation. Setting aside his empty mug, he nudged her closer and slung his arm across her shoulders. "I'll be your friend if you'll be mine?"

Her head bobbed up and down. "Deal."

After a minute of comfortable silence, she asked, "Does this mean I can visit my new friend in New York sometime?"

"Anytime." He chuckled. "Just give me a few days' notice, and I'll clear my schedule so we can hang out."

Chapter Three

Furious, Alex stared down at her red, throbbing hand. Why had she let Zac kiss her? As if he had a right! And why had she kissed him back?

Talk about mixed signals. Now she just felt so guilty.

For some reason, Zac had been determined to rile her up, and it had worked. From the first time she'd been introduced to him, she'd felt a strong attraction. Today had been no different. He'd never given her any indication he liked her before—the opposite, in fact. Her strategy of studiously avoiding him as much as possible and appearing disinterested had protected her fragile heart.

Until now.

How had she read the situation so wrong?

She'd been stunned when she realized he intended to kiss her. For a few seconds, she'd felt all her dreams come true, and excitement had bubbled inside her—Zac felt the same way she did! Then, common sense prevailed. If he really felt anything for her, his treatment of her wouldn't have been so deplorable. Jack's handsome face popping into her mind at that exact moment forced her to react.

Yep, Zac had deserved to be slapped!

Whatever game Dr. Zac Danvers was playing, she wasn't interested. She should forget about him. For crying out loud, he lived two hours away and was her best friend's brother! What had she been thinking? She already had her ideal boyfriend—Jack.

Later, while eating her favorite Thanksgiving dessert, Alex stewed silently, avoiding anything Zac-related, such as listening to his deep voice as he conversed with others at the table. The deep breaths she took between bites of pumpkin pie did nothing to help the food as it struggled down her tight throat.

As soon as Jack was finished, she pushed back her chair, then snatched his plate away, and stacked it underneath hers. "Excuse me. I'll be back," she said to no one in particular.

After rinsing the dishes in the kitchen sink, she returned to the dining room. Jack was chatting with Dr. Danvers. The kind one. Not the younger, arrogant, totally hot one.

Alex squeezed her eyes shut and counted to three. "Sorry to interrupt," she said, addressing Zac's dad. She shot Jack a pleading look. "Mind if I have a word with you...alone?"

"Do you mind, Dr. Danvers?" Jack lay a hand on the older man's arm and smiled apologetically. So polite. He would probably ask before kissing someone without warning—unlike a certain other male at the table. Alex clenched her fists, refusing to so much as peep at Zac.

Dumping his napkin on the table, Jack stood. "I'd love to finish this discussion another time."

"Of course." Dr. Danvers winked. "When a woman wants a private word, it usually pays to make it happen sooner rather than later."

Zac cleared his throat loudly, forcing Alex to glance his way. He was annoyed. Why? This was none of his business. Except, what she needed to talk to Jack about did involve Zac. Was it her imagination, or had her face gotten rather warm?

Without waiting, Alex grabbed Jack's hand and led him out of the dining room and down the hall to the mudroom.

Jack checked out the cluttered, narrow space and raised a questioning brow at her.

"I need to talk to you, and I don't want to be interrupted," she explained.

With a mischievous grin, he planted his hands on her hips and nudged her closer. "You sure you just want to talk?"

Needing to get this off her chest before she lost her nerve, she shoved his hands away. "I need to tell you something, and I don't want to be distracted."

"O-kay." He folded his arms across his chest. "Go ahead. I'm listening."

"Were you aware Mel sent Zac to apologize to me?"

Lips in a grim line, Jack nodded.

"Well, Zac found me, and he apologized and..." She swallowed hard, her courage swiftly deserting her. Was this wise? If Jack told her another woman had kissed him, would she be understanding or mad?

"And?" Jack prompted gently.

"Well, he..."

"Alex, what did Zac do? Did he hurt you?" Jack's soft, caring tone convinced her to tell him the truth.

"He kissed me," she said, her voice wobbling a little.

"What? You've got to be kidding! He's been absolutely awful to you all afternoon."

"I know. That's why I slapped him...hard."

"Serves him right," Jack smirked.

They were quiet for a moment, Jack rubbing his thumb and forefinger over his mustache stubble while she tried to guess what was going through his mind.

"Why on earth would Zac kiss you?" he eventually asked, pinning her with an inquiring look.

Offended, she blew out a huff. Why wouldn't someone want to kiss her? So far, Jack had only held her hand, other than that awkward kiss after bowling the other night. Her kiss, meant for his cheek, had landed on his mouth instead, surprising them both. There had been no sparks, and the kiss ended as abruptly as it started.

She shrugged. "I guess he wanted to."

Jack's gaze softened, and his eyes twinkled. "Him and me both."

"You want to kiss me?" She blinked as his eyes darkened, gasping when his strong hands tugged her hips closer. His tongue, flicking over his lower lip, drew her attention to his mouth. What would it be like to kiss him properly? Would it be like Zac's desperate kiss, which had sent electric pulses to every part of her body, making her forget where she was for a second?

"May I, Alex?" Jack's deep, husky voice broke into her musings. She didn't reply, couldn't. Instead, she slipped her hands up over his muscular chest to around his neck while he closed the last millimeter between them.

Warm lips met hers. Slow and deliberate and pleasant.

***

The next morning, Alex awoke with a smile on her lips. Yawning, she stretched, then snuggled back under the covers and continued daydreaming. Piercing blue eyes returned with crystal clear clarity, so did the sensation of liquid warmth spreading through her body as their lips met. The touch of his fingers on her skin—

Enough!

Jumping out of bed, she busied herself with her morning routine. Anything to prevent her from reliving Zac's presumptuous kiss over and over again. She focused on the only relationship in her life with potential—the one with Jack.

Last night, he'd hinted at watching a movie today, and after the kiss they'd shared, being alone in a dimly lit theatre held a certain appeal. Except, when she pictured the scene, the man sitting with her had much darker hair.

Shaking the vision from her head, she scanned the news stories on her iPad and ate her blueberry oatmeal. Halfway through reading an article about a local, fatal traffic accident, her phone buzzed on the counter.

She accepted the call. "I was just thinking about you."

"Good things, I hope?"

"Always," she said, closing the cover of her iPad. "So...what's up, Jack?"

"I was thinking...as much as I love the idea of being in a dark cinema with you, I kind of need exercise. Or I might go stir crazy." Jack's chuckle sounded nervous. "Are you up for racing around on the ice? At the eleven o'clock session?"

"Why not?" Probably for the best. It wouldn't be right to be kissing one man and dreaming of another. She and Jack hadn't dated for long. She needed to give them a fighting chance. Besides, Zac wasn't an option.

When Jack's knock came at ten forty-five, Alex grabbed her coat and purse and yanked open her door.

"Hi," she said, quickly stepping over the threshold and pulling the door closed behind her.

Jack gave her a crooked grin. "You in a hurry or something?"

Shaking her head, she dropped her purse to the ground and shrugged into her coat. He immediately stepped forward to help.

"Thanks." She slung her purse over her shoulder and eyed him. His smile widened as he reached for her hands and closed the distance between them.

"Hi," he murmured, pressing his warm lips to hers for a second. Easing back, he peered at her thoughtfully. She waited for him to say more. Instead, he led her toward the elevators, where he made a show of clearing his throat.

"You okay?" she asked.

"About you and me skating," he said. "It's...we won't be alone."

Cute. Was that really what was worrying him? She stifled a laugh. "I'd hardly expect you to rent out the whole rink just for me, Jack! I'm not even sure that's possible."

His frown remained, making her feel a little apprehensive.

"Actually, Steven invited us ice skating...along with the whole gang."

Was that all? Relief flooded her. Surely he didn't think she'd mind having their friends with them? It would be fun. And there were typically lots of other skaters on the ice anyway, so it's not like they'd ever be alone. She sent him a reassuring smile. "I assume 'the gang' means Steven, Melanie, Sophie, and Julie, right?"

"Right."

"I'll survive." She winked to lighten the mood.

Jack's jaw twitched, his facial muscles remaining tight. Seriously, what was up with him?

"Jack, it honestly doesn't matter if our date's being crashed," she said, trying to get him to loosen up. "We can go skating alone another time."

As long as Zac didn't turn up.

All at once, her stomach tied itself in knots. Of course, he'd be there! No wonder Jack was acting peculiar. Clearly, Zac's unpredictable behavior was a cause for concern. She pursed her lips. Great, now she was worried too.

Fifteen minutes later, they entered the facility hand in hand, and Alex's nerves intensified. Steven was leaning against a pillar in the lobby, a pinched expression marking his usually relaxed features. They had barely finished greeting him when the rest of the group arrived, and Alex couldn't help seeking out Zac.

Her pulse raced at the sight of him in his perfectly fitted blue jeans, paired with a maroon bomber jacket over a white henley shirt—one of her favorite outfits on a man. Not wanting to be caught staring, she looked away to see Steven scoop Sophie into his arms and spin her around. High-pitched peals of laughter echoed in the vast entryway.

Smiling, Alex's attention switched to the others, and she waved in their direction. Melanie smiled tightly before slipping away to where her daughter was with Steven. Julie seemed guarded, while Zac's gaze was fixed on Jack as if Alex didn't exist.

Fine.

He was probably regretting the kiss, embarrassed even. He should be.

"Do you get to skate a lot, Jack?" Zac asked casually, though an undertone of tension showed in his eyes.

Alex stiffened, her hand gripping Jack's tighter. Was Zac going to make this into another competition?

"On occasion," Jack replied, his eyes narrowing, possibly in suspicion. "I'm not a pro, but I can hold my own."

"Good." Zac sounded pleased. "I'm on call. If I have to leave, can I rely on you to take care of Julie? Apparently, she's not the strongest skater."

Really? Alex had an immature desire to stamp her foot. She huffed instead. Was she invisible? How did Zac know she didn't need Jack to take care of *her*?

Julie glared at Zac, her cheeks a healthy shade of pink. "You don't need to worry about me. I'll be fine. "

"Hey there, everyone," Steven said, interrupting the otherwise awkward moment. "Can I please have your attention?"

They all turned to face him.

"Here are your tickets," he said, handing them out.

Over at the skate rental counter, Alex bent to remove her shoes.

"Do you know your size?" Jack asked her while untying his laces.

She lifted her fur-lined boots onto the wooden surface at the same time Zac's musky scent reached her nostrils. Something brushed against her arm, and her heart raced. She peeked at Zac's profile to see a tick in his jaw and held her breath, half expecting him to make some kind of derogatory comment. But he didn't.

"Alex?"

"Yep?" She snapped her attention back to Jack. "Oh, my size...it's nine." She shifted closer to Jack, feeling a sudden coolness where Zac's arm had been.

Once her skating boots were securely fitted, she tucked her hand firmly in Jack's, and they made their way to the rink's entrance. There they watched Zac patiently escort a stumbling Julie onto the ice. Alex stifled a giggle at the comical scene. The poor woman was obviously a beginner, but judging from Zac's smooth strokes on the slick ice, he knew what he was doing. Good thing, too, otherwise Julie would've landed flat on her face.

When did Zac get time to practice? Melanie often joked that her brother worked twenty-four seven.

"Shall we?" Jack's voice drew Alex away from her thoughts.

"Yes, please."

They warmed up with a few fast laps, then Jack slowed and moved to the side.

"What's up?" she asked, following him.

He motioned toward Melanie, skating alone. "Do you mind if I go talk to Mel? Find out what's bothering her?"

"Of course not. Go."

Jack skated off, and guilt tugged at Alex. She should be checking up on her best friend. But Melanie hadn't taken her advice about Steven, so most likely, she wouldn't want it now either.

The handsome doctor and his incompetent partner passed by her at that point. Deciding it was time to skate again, Alex pushed off, leaving a comfortable distance between them. Not close enough to hear their conversation, but near enough that she could watch their interaction.

Soon after, Zac came to an abrupt stop, and Alex had to grab the side to avoid a collision.

"No problem," she overheard him saying on his phone, his tone professional. "Give me a minute. I need to find someplace more private. I'll call you right back."

He turned to Julie. "It's work. Sorry."

"You did warn me. It's fine, go."

Luckily, Alex managed to duck her head at the last second, pretending to check her laces as Zac glanced around before leading Julie to the side railing. "You'll be fine here," he said. "Try to get Jack's attention, okay?"

Julie nodded, although she didn't look too happy about being left stranded.

Why was Zac so insistent on Jack being the one to rescue Julie? Before she had a chance to contemplate the question, she spotted Steven heading toward Julie. Grateful Jack was clearly off the hook, Alex skated away.

Where was her boyfriend anyway?

Scanning the ice, she discovered him still chatting with Melanie. The conversation appeared intense, so Alex continued gliding over the smooth surface, happy to give Jack more time. When a small hand slipped into hers a moment later, her heart skipped a beat. "Sophie!" she exclaimed. "You're lucky you didn't give me a fright."

"I knew you wouldn't fall, Miss Alex." Sophie grinned. "You're way too good a skater."

"Thanks." Smiling, she squeezed her goddaughter's hand. "You having fun?"

"Tons. It's so cool having so many people to skate with." She peered around at the crowds on the ice. "I wanted to skate with Uncle Zac, but he's disappeared."

"Sorry, he had a work emergency and had to get off the ice."

She shrugged. "It's okay. At least Uncle Zac's here. He hardly ever comes to visit us. He's always working," she whined. A split second later, her tone brightened, and she raised her twinkling blue eyes. "Let's go faster, Miss Alex."

"Sure."

They sped up, mindful of the slower skaters in their path. Sophie easily kept up with her, but the longer they skated, the warmer Alex became.

About to suggest a break, she turned to Sophie as a flash of red passed by. Sophie's arms spun like a helicopter before she fell and landed hard on her back just as another skater sped by. When Alex dropped to her knees, Sophie's eyes were closed, and blood was squirting from her neck.

As Alex struggled to breathe, her gaze shot around the rink. "Help, please!" she shouted, pressing Sophie's limp hand against her tight chest. Where were the staff? What should she do? Frankly, the first aid training she'd had at school was useless in this situation!

A man wearing the staff uniform crouched next to her and immediately placed his hands on Sophie's neck, stemming the flow of blood. Another uniformed person arrived and gently prodded Sophie's little limbs while speaking soothing words to her. A crowd gathered around them, but there was no sign of Melanie and Steven. Where were they?

Alex's heart started beating wildly.

"I can't leave my goddaughter alone," she said, beginning to feel a little hysterical. "I need to get word to her mother. Is she going to be okay? Why won't she open her eyes?"

"We've called 911," one of the men said, giving her a sympathetic look.

"That's my daughter!" Melanie's strangled cry came from out of nowhere as she rushed over toward them.

Alex's vision clouded. *Finally.*

"What happened, Alex?" her friend asked in a wobbly voice, tears streaming down her face.

"I don't know." She shook her head and swallowed back a gulp. "One minute, Sophie was alongside me, then she was on the ground. It all happened so fast." She stretched to touch Melanie's arm. "I'm so sorry, Mel."

Everything happened in a blur after that until a frazzled-looking Melanie unexpectedly snagged her wrist. "Find Zac and tell him what's going on, please, Alex," she urged.

"I will."

How inconvenient.

Drawing in a deep, calming breath, she squared her shoulders. She'd do this for Melanie because no matter how hard she willed it, she'd never be able to avoid her best friend's brother.

Chapter Four

With the emergency call from work over, Zac headed back toward the rink entrance. The session wasn't due to end for another half-hour, and he was keen to continue skating since he didn't often get the chance. Not that he could consider it exercise, really.

He didn't mind babysitting Julie on the ice, but it would've been fun whizzing around like his niece.

Or with Alex.

As if thinking about her conjured up her presence, she strode toward him. A smile crept onto his face, and his heart jumped in excitement. She'd come to find him! Had their kiss been playing over and over in her mind like it had in his?

Minus the slap, of course.

She neared, and he immediately noticed she was wringing her hands, not smiling. His first thought was, what had he done? His earlier attempts at ignoring her had barely worked. On too many occasions, his gaze had strayed in her direction. Had it bothered her to the point that she'd come to chew him out?

It hadn't been easy watching her comfortable manner with Jack, nor their little intimate glances.

More annoying had been Jack's possessive hold on her when they'd first arrived. He found it interesting that Jack felt the need to clarify his position as the man in Alex's life. Was his presence that much of a threat to Jack?

The closer Alex came, the easier it was to see the fear in her eyes. Zac narrowed the distance between them, his pulse accelerating.

"What's wrong?"

"Sophie's hurt." Her voice was full of emotion, and from the red rim around her eyes, he could tell she'd been crying.

He sucked in a breath as tightness gripped his chest. "What happened? Where is she?"

"S-she was knocked over on the ice," Alex said, her tears leaking. "They took her in an ambulance."

Without second-guessing how Alex might feel about it, Zac wrapped her in his arms. Her body went rigid for a second, shuddering briefly before she hugged him back. Inhaling her sweet scent, he let her cry while savoring the experience of having her in his arms. The circumstances weren't brilliant, but nevertheless, he was grateful for the opportunity to console her.

After too short a time, Alex hauled in a deep breath and physically retreated from him, swiping at her eyes as she did so. "It's my fault," she said in between sniffs.

Her scrunched-up brow spoke to his heart. Clearly, she cared deeply for Sophie.

Their eyes met, and guilt flickered across Alex's beautiful face.

"I-I was skating with Sophie," she said, her unsteady voice gaining strength as she carried on. "I should've reacted faster, pulled her up the second she fell down, then the second skater wouldn't have hurt her."

He grasped her upper arms, disregarding the sudden sparks of electricity, and looked her directly in the eye. "It's *not* your fault, Alex. It was an accident. You're *not* responsible for another skater's actions."

She shook her head. "You didn't see—there was so much blood, Zac!"

Alarm shot through him at her words. Still, he forced a neutral expression. "You did nothing wrong," he said firmly. "You *have* to believe that."

She gave a reluctant nod, and he finally released her.

"I better get to the hospital." Melanie would be wondering where he was, and with Dad in surgery all day, Zac was the only doctor in the family who could be there for support and guidance. "Will you be alright, Alex?"

"Jack—"

How could he forget?

"Of course," Zac said abruptly. With one last look at her gorgeous face, he turned and marched in the direction of the exit.

Not too long after leaving Alex, Zac skidded into a 'doctor's only' parking bay outside the Emergency Room. Cutting the engine, he raced up the stairs to the hospital entrance, slowing down as he arrived in reception.

He scanned the area for Melanie and quickly located her. Again he schooled his expression into a practiced, neutral one, then dashed over to where she sat next to Steven.

"I'm so sorry, Mel," he said, hugging his sister tightly. "I'll see what I can find out." Easing away from her, he peered into her tear-filled eyes. "Is there anything you need?"

She glanced back at Steven and shook her head.

"Just make sure Sophie's okay, please."

It didn't take him long to get information about Sophie's condition—a perk of being in the medical profession and being a reputable doctor. When he walked back into the waiting room, his sister rushed toward him.

"How is she? Did you see her?"

"I did."

Steven joined them, slipping his arm around Melanie's waist.

"It appears that another skater's blade must've accidentally clipped Sophie's neck while she lay concussed on the ground. The blade sliced her external carotid artery," Zac said, grimacing. "I bet a trail of blood sprayed onto the ice."

No wonder Alex had been so freaked out. The shock must've been terrible, worse considering it involved her goddaughter. The first aid training teachers were typically given wouldn't have prepared Alex for that kind of situation.

Conscious Jack was the one currently comforting Alex, Zac's temperature rose. He wished he could've stayed with her instead, but his sister and niece needed him too.

"There *was* an awful lot of red ice," Melanie agreed, rubbing her temple and pulling him out of his selfish thoughts.

"Well, they need to repair the artery, so Sophie's being prepped for surgery. She also needs a blood transfusion because she lost a lot of blood—four units, to be precise. There's an issue though, she's AB negative, and they don't have sufficient reserves." He turned to Steven. "You're a match. Are you willing to donate your blood?"

Shock registered on Steven's face. Clearly, the man was completely unaware of the implications. Zac needed to have a word with his sister...later.

"Will you, Steven?" Melanie asked, a touch of desperation in her voice.

"Of course, whatever she needs."

"Fantastic," Zac said, pleased for the easy solution. His respect for his sister's boyfriend grew. "If you come with me, Steven, we'll get you sorted and ensure the blood's ready the minute the surgeon requests it."

Later that afternoon, Zac joined the group gathered in the waiting room. He tried not to search out Alex but failed. No evidence remained of her previous tears, yet her arms were wrapped around her body protectively, or was it defensively? She also wasn't making eye contact with anyone while she nervously chewed on her lip. Seemed she was still dealing with guilt.

A strong urge hit him to pull her aside and further ease her conscience. Except, they had an audience. More importantly, Jack's arm was around her shoulders as he held her close to his side. Again the man was staking his territory–Zac couldn't blame him. If Alex was his girlfriend, he'd do the same.

Averting his gaze, he focused on Sophie's doctor. Hopefully, his news would relieve some of Alex's and Melanie's worry.

"The operation was a success," the doctor said. "Sophie's been transferred to the ICU and is in a stable condition. Though, at the moment, I'm afraid only family members may see the patient."

Melanie dragged Steven by the arm, following the doctor to the ICU.

"Hey!" Jack muttered. "Steven's not family. So how come he's going?"

An interesting question, but Zac wouldn't get involved. It wasn't his place. Shrugging at the others, he trailed his sister.

***

Alex stared at Zac's back as he disappeared toward the private wing of the hospital. The man was undoubtedly in his element here. A minute ago, he had oozed confidence while standing beside Sophie's doctor. Even when Alex had broken down earlier, Zac had taken it all in his stride, holding her securely in his strong, comforting arms. Never mind his insistence that none of Sophie's accident was Alex's fault.

Recalling the earlier incident at the ice rink, she sighed.

Jack squeezed her shoulder. "Everything alright?"

"Better, now I know Sophie's going to be okay."

"The doctors here are more than competent." His lips pursed as an unidentifiable emotion flashed through his eyes. "Besides, I'm sure Dr. Danvers will be on their case if not."

She frowned. "What's bothering you, Jack?"

His gaze swung away for a second, then returned. "I don't like the way Zac tracks your every move."

"W-what? He doesn't," she said, shaking her head.

His arm slid from her shoulders as he spun to face her. "You'd tell me if Zac was acting inappropriately, wouldn't you?"

The vulnerability in his gaze cut to her heart, and she swallowed. "What do you mean?"

"Like, if he tried to kiss you again?"

Her heart stuttered. Did she want Zac to kiss her again? And, if he did, would it be different because it wouldn't be such a surprise? With a concerted effort, she put a stop to her wayward thinking.

"I don't think you need to worry about Zac repeating his mistake," she said. "Not when he knows how I'll react."

"Good." Looking relieved, Jack peered over at the doors on the far side of the massive waiting room. "What do you say we get out of here? Mel will let us know if there's any further news about Sophie and, I don't know about you, but right now I could do with a king-sized burger or two, with fries."

Gripping his muscled forearm, Alex laughed. "I guess it takes a lot of nourishment to stay this fit. I'm just glad it's not *me* paying the check."

Jack smirked, his hand covering hers. "Is that your way of saying you like how I look?"

"Nope. It's my way of saying I'll gladly join you for a burger and fries since you're paying." She winked, adding, "But if you have to know, yes, I like how ripped you are, Jack. Not to mention, handsome."

Pleasure seeped across his features, and she could've sworn his cheeks went a little pink. It was nice to know she could affect him. Unfortunately, the only man who seemed to do the same for her was presently visiting with his niece. And the chances of her seeing him again soon were basically none—he was returning to New York tonight.

If she was lucky, she'd see him at Christmas.

Chapter Five

Zac slung his arm around Julie's shoulders and examined Steven's kitchen. Not too shabby for a rental apartment. The black granite countertops, combined with glossy white cupboard doors and stainless steel appliances, worked. A red espresso machine added a splash of color. The room wasn't massive, but it didn't feel like they were in the way at all.

On the other side of the small island, Melanie looked a little flushed while sorting out tumblers for the eggnog and avoiding eye contact with Steven. She wasn't acting herself, and Zac wondered if he should be worried.

He glanced over at Steven, who was tracking Melanie's every movement, and frowned. Why did the guy's lips seem unnaturally red? By arriving earlier than expected, had he and Julie inadvertently interrupted a heavy make-out session? If so, things were getting pretty serious between his sister and her boyfriend.

A loud knock from the front door made Zac's heart thump. "I'll get it," he said, stepping away from Julie.

It had to be Alex...and Jack. They were the only two missing from this cozy pre-Christmas dinner party Steven was throwing.

Though it had been a month since he'd last laid eyes on Alex, Zac could easily conjure up her gorgeous face just before he'd kissed her—that intimate moment was often in his thoughts and perpetually at the back of his mind.

At the door, he took a deep breath, rubbed his hands down his pants, and exhaled slowly. Showtime.

"Jack, Alex, come in," he said, clinging to the door handle. His throat went dry as he peered at Alex. Stunning in a red fitted dress, her blonde curls bounced over her shoulders. Their gazes collided, and for a second, her pretty green eyes lit up. Then her focus swung over his shoulder, and her expression shuttered.

"Is Mel here already?" she asked.

"She's in the kitchen, pouring the eggnog."

"Perfect." Alex brushed past without looking at him, her familiar flowery scent filling the air as she went.

Jack chuckled. "Sounds like just what the doctor ordered."

After Melanie handed out the festive drinks in the kitchen, Steven pinged his glass with a spoon. "First off, thanks for coming tonight. It's great to see you all, especially you, Zac."

Zac acknowledged the comment with a brief nod.

"I'd like to wish you all a Merry Christmas." Steven lifted his glass and smiled. "I look forward to spending more time with you all in the coming year."

"Hear hear," Jack said, his arm moving protectively over Alex's shoulders. When she smiled up at her boyfriend, a sharp pain stabbed Zac's chest.

Unable to watch the happy couple a moment longer, he pecked Julie's cheek, and she turned to face him.

"I'll be back," he said in a low voice. "I need a bit of fresh air, okay?"

"Don't worry about me, I'll be fine," she whispered, touching his arm.

Later, Zac strolled into the living room and surveyed the scene. A crackling fire glowed in the fireplace, gifts were piled under the tree, and the smell of winter berries floated in the air. Festive music played in the background, adding some cheer to the evening. The fresh air hadn't worked for him, but maybe this would.

He joined Julie on the love seat, briefly resting his hand on her thigh as he leaned closer. "I meant to tell you earlier, you look amazing."

"Such a charmer," she said, covering his hand with hers and smiling back. He loved that she never misunderstood his compliments. They had settled quickly into an easy friendship, aware both were pining after someone else. Julie made a charming plus-one whenever he needed a date in New York, and in New Haven, she helped him fit into a group full of couples. They never took each other for granted and never expected more than what had brought them together in the first place. Totally platonic friends, nothing more.

"So, who's doing what over the holidays?" Jack's question broke into their private moment.

Julie was the first to respond. "I'm spending Christmas with Zac's family. My foster parents invited me to join them, but they're taking their four kids across the country to visit their grandparents, and I didn't want to use up all my vacation days." She inclined her head toward him. "Zac didn't want me to be alone for the holiday, so..."

"Makes sense," Jack said, looking anything but happy—as if it had anything to do with the guy!

Confused, Zac's jaw clenched. Julie wasn't *his* girlfriend. Shifting his gaze to Alex, he was surprised by her stony expression. Sure, Alex didn't like Julie, but she'd be spending Christmas with Jack, so why would Julie's plans be any of her concern either?

"You're still coming to us for Christmas, aren't you, Alex?" Melanie asked, and Zac frowned.

Wait. What?

That couldn't be true.

Alex's smile appeared forced. "I am."

A thrill shot through him—he'd see her again in two days! Alone. What he couldn't understand, though, was why hadn't Jack insisted Alex spend Christmas with him? Dare he hope their relationship wasn't as strong as it seemed?

***

The first stab of jealousy had come a few weeks ago when Melanie mentioned Julie's numerous visits to New York. Alex felt it again as she contemplated the couple across the room. It wasn't any of her concern, but at least Zac appeared happier and more relaxed lately. On the outside, he and Julie resembled a good match. So why did Julie keep flirting with other men? Not that it was any of her business. Zac was free to date whoever he wanted. She didn't care.

Yep, she definitely didn't care.

Except, annoyingly, whenever she watched him touch or kiss Julie, a knife twisted into her heart.

"How's the long-distance relationship working for you, Zac?" Jack asked, pulling Alex back to real-time.

"Eighty miles is hardly long-distance." Zac's tone was dismissive. Again, he and Julie exchanged warm smiles.

Alex wanted to throw up, the tightness in her chest returning. Jack hadn't asked if she wanted to join him on Christmas day. He'd just assumed she'd celebrate with the Danvers, like usual. Did he honestly think she wanted to watch Zac and Julie parade their sickeningly perfect relationship in front of her? How she would survive the day, she didn't know, but it wasn't like she had a choice.

Tuning out the conversation, she stared first at the tree's decorations, then the presents under it. Julie regularly got all the attention. If it wasn't Zac fawning over her, it was Jack. He'd never admit it, but she'd caught him checking out Julie on several occasions. Did he have a secret crush on her? His goodnight kisses implied not. One thing was certain, Zac's kisses made her knees go weak.

Jack's didn't.

Alex stole a glance at Jack. As usual, his attention was on Julie. She crossed her arms and huffed. Not that he seemed to notice.

When they moved out to the balcony, Alex settled next to Jack on the rattan furniture. The seating, covered in large cream cushions, was rather cozy. But despite the moderate amount of heat coming from the patio heater, she still felt the need to fasten her coat buttons. Aware of Zac's gaze directly on her, the task took longer than necessary. She blamed it on her icy fingers and refused to make eye contact with the man.

Thankfully, Melanie brought out a huge pot of hot chocolate, and Alex gratefully warmed her fingers on a mug, her gaze lifting to the dark sky punctuated by millions of twinkling lights.

"Can you see Orion?" Steven asked.

"Yes," Jack responded first. "It took me a while to figure out the bow and arrow making up 'The Hunter'."

"The only stars I can ever recognize, besides the Milky Way, are Orion's Belt," Julie said.

Biting back a sarcastic comment, Alex took a sip of her hot drink.

Using Julie's finger as a pointer, Zac guided it from the Belt, down to Sirius. "Can you see the blue-white star?" he asked, his voice confident and deep.

"The brightest one in the sky?" Julie's sugar-sweet voice was beyond irritating.

Not letting it get to her, Alex imagined having Zac's full attention and being the one he held instead.

She shivered.

Jack's arm slipped around her waist, nudging her closer. "You okay?" he murmured.

Nodding, she zoned out Zac's smooth, baritone voice. Then, careful not to spill, she swirled the liquid in her mug.

"Hey!" Julie objected sternly, a short while later, "I don't get to see Zac *that* often, Steven. I'd rather you didn't crash our precious time together."

Overprotective much?

Alex squashed the uncharitable thought. She wasn't jealous, not really. Jack helped his sister Charlotte with her kids in his free time. The rest of the time he was working or otherwise they went out together, in a group. She admired Jack's work ethic, she did. Yet Zac worked just as hard, and *he* made time to see Julie, alone. But what was the point of comparing them? Zac wasn't her boyfriend and never would be.

He lived in New York.

She shuddered at the memories the city invoked. If she had anything to say about it, New York was a place she would never set foot in again.

"I wish my class was here," she said, changing the topic. "I could teach them all about the stars on a clear night like this."

"You must miss them during the holidays." Zac's friendly tone took her by surprise. Before she could get too caught up in his kindness, she looked away.

Jack took her hands in his, cocooning them in his warm ones. "You'll make a great mom one day."

The sincerity in his words nearly choked her up. "Thanks. I've always wanted at least three children, but the older I get, the less chance there is of that happening." She attempted a half-smile. "Unless I want to be pregnant the day I get married."

Beside her, Jack stiffened. She peeked at him and found him staring at the heater. She must've hit a nerve. Which, though? That she wanted children or to get married?

Needing to escape, she jumped up and snatched her empty mug from the table. "I need a mug of hot water," she said.

As she was sliding the balcony door closed behind her, she overheard Zac saying, "I'd better see if she needs help finding the kettle."

Seriously?

***

A few giant strides were all it took for Zac to catch up with Alex. Then, as she was about to pass under the mistletoe, he used his hand as a barrier and glanced upward. She did the same.

"You followed me on purpose!" she said before staring up at the mistletoe again, then dropping her wary gaze to his.

Did she have any idea how cute she was when she was flustered? He couldn't take his eyes off her, and he hoped she couldn't hear his heart beating like a drum on steroids. Heat radiated off her body, and his breath caught in his throat.

Of their own accord, his hands slid either side of her beautiful face, her silky strands tickling his skin. He inched closer until he could feel her warm breath on his lips.

Her eyelids dipped.

Taking that as an invitation, he pressed his lips softly to hers. The kiss started out tentative and undemanding until Alex grabbed his shirt front and kissed him back. Then it escalated, deepening fast. His left hand slipped behind her neck, their bodies molding together in a perfect fit. When he finally broke the kiss, their breaths were coming hard and fast.

He eased away from her, not keen on getting slapped again. Her eyelids fluttered open, revealing dilated pupils. She stared at him, said nothing, did nothing. The last thing he wanted to do was break the magic spell, but they were lucky they hadn't been interrupted already.

"Alex," he said quietly, deliberately removing his hands from her warm body.

"Yes," she said, her voice husky.

"My shirt."

"Oh." She immediately released her hold on it, an adorable pink blush creeping up her neck.

Waving a hand in the direction of the kitchen, he willed his breathing to return to normal. "Shall we continue?" A fleeting look of confusion and something else he couldn't define crossed her face. "You wanted some hot water," he prompted.

"Um, I need the bathroom first."

As he watched her walk away, his heart continued to pound. Good thing she hadn't decked him one. Running his hand over his head, he racked his brains—had he ever been kissed like that before? *No.* Alex was one incredible woman! Except she wasn't his, but he was beginning to think Jack didn't deserve her.

Exhilaration passed through him instead of the guilt he expected. He wasn't wrong. Alex had definitely kissed him back! Shaking his head, he smiled. She'd be heading to the kitchen next, and he'd be right there waiting.

A minute later, Julie sauntered into the kitchen and set a blanket down on a barstool. "Where's Alex?"

"Bathroom," Zac replied, struggling to contain his grin.

She scrutinized him for a second. "Okay, spill."

"Mistletoe."

"You kissed her? Again?"

"Yep." He nodded, slipping his arms around her waist.

Reaching up with both hands, she covered his cheeks. "So no slap?"

"Not this time." He tried not to sound smug.

She clucked her tongue in her teeth. "Maybe you should avoid the mistletoe."

"Why?" he asked, quirking his brow.

"Because I'm concerned—"

"What exactly are you concerned about, Julie?" Jack appeared in the entrance, pot in hand, his brow scrunched up.

"My well-being," Zac answered for her.

"I see." Jack headed over to the kettle and flicked the boil switch before turning back to them. "Don't you think Zac's big enough to look after himself, Julie?"

She shrugged.

"You find that blanket?" Jack's gaze remained fixed on her.

"It's over there." She pointed to the stool. "Are you making more hot chocolate?"

His eyes narrowed. "Yes, why?"

"I'll help...unless you know where Steven hides the tin."

Zac couldn't help chuckling. "Seriously?"

Julie punched him playfully. "Yep. Otherwise, Sophie tries to help herself, and Steven finds brown dust all over his counter. Drives him crazy."

"Control freak." Winking, Zac released her and collected the blanket. "I'll take this out."

With any luck, he'd run into Alex under the mistletoe again.

Chapter Six

A fire crackled under the tinsel-covered mantelpiece. Red and orange flames danced to the beat of a silent tune, wandering free in whichever direction they chose. Alex welcomed the warmth pervading the otherwise empty room. Empty of anyone else except her. Just how long *had* she been hiding out in the Danvers' living room?

Longer than was polite, for sure.

Trying to remove the knots in her neck, she moved it from side to side, then rolled her shoulders. The tension eased a little.

Sighing, she focused on the pine-scented Christmas tree, its white lights flickering on, off. The ornaments were utterly mismatched, but she loved that each one contained a story. Such a wonderful Danvers' tradition. One she hoped to do with her own family one day.

Swallowing the sudden lump in her throat, she battled with rising emotions. She should've been with Jack today, creating their own 'first Christmas together' memories.

If only the Danvers realized the torture she'd endured earlier while the presents were handed out and during Christmas dinner. Torture watching their son with his stunning girlfriend. The man who caused her heart to skip a beat every time he looked at her and made her forget everything with his kisses.

She glanced at her wrist. Time to make a move.

Standing, she smoothed her dress. If she asked nicely, Steven would take her home. A throat cleared, and she spun around.

"Zac!" So much for avoiding the man.

"I was told you needed a lift home."

She shook her head. "Steven—"

"Has left."

"What do you mean? He can't have left," she said indignantly. "He just went for a walk with Melanie."

"His truck pulled out a minute ago. Mom's in the kitchen with Mel. She and Sophie are staying the night."

"Oh, okay." Alex's stomach tightened. What was going on? Steven hadn't even said goodbye.

Minutes later, she was in the back seat of Zac's car and finding it a challenge to get comfortable. She'd rather be anywhere else than with him. Of course, with Julie riding shotgun, they weren't alone. *That* would be awkward.

Had he really kissed her only two short nights ago?

"Best Christmas by far." Julie's cheerful voice cut into Alex's thoughts.

"Yeah. It was pretty good." Zac smiled across at Julie. "Especially when we won the Christmas Carol Dictionary game."

"It's always about winning with you, isn't it, Zac?" Alex blurted out. The second his surprised gaze met hers in the rearview mirror, she was sorry for snapping.

"Sure," he said, yet his tone held no agreement, and a pained look passed over his face.

Turning her head, Alex stared out the passenger window. Brightly lit yards decorated with festive characters were a welcome distraction. Lashing out at Zac was wrong, but she didn't get him. How could he kiss her the way he had, then just walk away and treat her like it didn't mean anything? Like he didn't care?

All she could think about was that kiss.

"So, Alex, if you're back at school on the third, what are your plans for the rest of Christmas break?"

Julie's sincere sounding question made Alex feel worse. She certainly hadn't hidden the fact she wasn't fond of the woman. No wonder Zac was dating her. No matter what lemons life threw at her, Julie still managed to maintain a sweet attitude.

Looking forward again, Alex immediately regretted it. Zac was staring straight at her as if her answer was of great importance. She fixated on a loose thread on her skirt. "No particular plans. Jack and I will probably take long walks in the snow, assuming we get some."

"Sounds perfect." Julie's hand slid onto Zac's thigh. "Pity New York hardly ever gets snow."

"What can I say? I'm not a miracle worker. Not when it comes to the weather, at least." Zac's sardonic comment was so typical of him. If Alex wasn't so mad at him, she'd have laughed at his words.

"I wonder if Jack had a good Christmas?" Julie asked sweetly, looking over her shoulder at Alex. "I bet he missed you tons."

"No doubt," Zac muttered.

Gritting her teeth, Alex smiled tightly at Julie, then dug in her purse for her phone. The last time she'd checked it was before lunch. Afterward, she'd left it on silent. For all she knew, Jack had been desperately trying to get hold of her.

"Mind if I turn on the radio?" Julie's hand hovered over the button.

"Nope," Alex answered quickly. Christmas tunes blaring from the speakers would make small talk impossible. *Perfect.*

Unlocking her phone, she smiled at a text from Jack: ***Missed u. Wished u were here. Kids had a gr8 time. Can't wait 2 c u in the morning xx***

Her fingers flew over the keyboard. ***Me 2. Glad kids had fun. Axx***

Leaning back against the leather seat, she closed her eyes and pictured a different scene. Her and Zac, married, waking up to soft snowfall and squealing children bouncing on their bed. His lazy kiss before they opened gifts from underneath their Christmas tree. The lingering smell of pancakes surrounding them, mixed in with the scent of coffee. Smiles and hugs all around.

The sound of a car door opening jolted her awake. Zac was getting out.

Alex shivered. Was she home?

She peered out the window toward the sidewalk, but nothing was familiar.

The front passenger door swung open. "Enjoy your break, Alex," Julie said before accepting Zac's hand and climbing out.

Alex nodded, not in the mood for false platitudes.

"I'll only be a couple of minutes," Zac said.

"Take your time."

She willed him to go, but the door remained open, allowing cold air inside.

Eventually, she huffed. "You gonna shut that door, Zac?"

"Maybe you could move." He gestured to the front passenger seat. "So I don't look like a taxi driver?"

She swapped places begrudgingly, and he left with Julie.

Waiting for his return, Alex couldn't help imagining the goodnight kiss they were likely sharing. She traced a thumb over her bottom lip, recalling Zac's lips on hers. Her pulse spiked, and it took a few deep breaths to slow it down.

The driver-side door opened, and Zac quickly settled into his seat without a word. Shifting the stick into reverse, he set a hand on the headrest behind her and pumped the gas. Not once did his eyes meet hers. Alex should've been relieved they were on their way again, but her body went onto high alert.

It didn't matter. She'd be home soon.

Determined to keep her eyes off him, despite his musky scent capturing her attention, she concentrated on the view through the side window. Unlike where she lived, this neighborhood was full of apartment buildings, broken only by the occasional open space.

As silence filled the interior, she stole a glance at Zac's profile—clenched jaw and pursed lips. Was playing taxi stressing him?

Too bad.

In no time, he parked in front of her place. Melanie must've given her address because she certainly hadn't.

"Stay there," Zac said, jumping out of the car and rounding the hood to open her door.

When he stuck out a hand to assist her, she faltered. His eyebrows pulled together. "I don't bite," he growled.

Grimacing, she slipped her hand into his and was thrilled by the delightful tingles traveling up her arm.

Once the passenger door was shut, she tried tugging her hand free, but he held on firmly, blatantly ignoring her quizzical look. He dragged her forward instead.

"You don't need to walk me to my door." She huffed. "I'm quite capable, you know."

"Oh, I know."

The whole way to her front door, she worried he could hear her thumping heart. Finally, he released her hand, allowing her to retrieve her key from her purse. She inserted it into the lock and spun it. About to push the handle down and make her escape, he spoke her name so softly she barely heard it.

Turning, she studied him. Was that a hint of mischief she saw?

"What do you want, Zac?"

Pinning her with his intense gaze, he took a step toward her. Instinctively she stepped back, but the hard surface of the door trapped her. His body, mere inches away, leaned in, his hands landing on the wood either side of her head. Manly muskiness invaded her senses, and from his warm breath reaching her lips, she guessed his intentions. She couldn't breathe, and it took all her willpower not to close her eyes.

"Kissing you again is all I've been able to think about the past two days," he said in a low voice.

Before she had time to respond, his lips touched hers, and the magic began. Warmth flooded her body, and when his tongue parted her lips, she didn't stop him from deepening the kiss. His hands brushed her shoulders, dropping inside her coat to encircle her waist. Her own hands fought for release and joined around his neck. She sighed contentedly. She was exactly where she wanted to be.

All too soon, his lips left hers, and she had to force her eyes open. The way he was smiling at her melted her insides.

"You never disappoint, Alex," he said huskily.

She giggled. "Except for the time I left my mark on your cheek."

"Yeah, I'm always a little cautious when your hands are free."

When she casually removed her hands from his neck, he immediately let her go and stepped back.

"You don't trust me," she teased.

He shook his head, still smiling.

"You're the one who shouldn't be trusted, Zac. You just kissed a woman who has a boyfriend, and don't forget Julie." She tried to say it lightly, but it came out sounding accusatory.

"You're right." He frowned, his tone suddenly serious. "I should go. Look after yourself, Alex."

Swinging away from her, he strode to the elevators without a backward glance. As the metal doors opened and he disappeared from view, she felt unexpectedly numb.

Way to go, Alex!

***

The whole way back to his parents' house, Zac chastised himself. What was he doing kissing Alex, even if she rocked his world every time?

Because she was totally right. She had a boyfriend; a very real one. Jack was a great guy, and he didn't deserve to be cheated on.

He, on the other hand, did *not* have a real girlfriend. Julie was flirty and way more touchy-feely than a regular friend would be, but everyone knew that about her, didn't they?

So what? He couldn't actually ask Alex out. She wasn't single. Somehow that vital fact slipped his mind whenever he got within two feet of her. She was like platinum, drawing him in like a magnet. Denying either their chemistry or attraction was useless. Even Alex would admit it was mutual. Otherwise, she'd have pushed him away or slapped him again.

Reliving their kiss thrilled him to his toes. So much so he almost forgot to stop at a red light. Slamming on the brakes, he gave himself a mental shake. He needed to stop thinking about the angel who invaded his every thought. She'd be the death of him if he didn't get over her somehow.

If only he knew how.

Chapter Seven

Zac rubbed the scar on his chin as he watched his niece happily racing around Jack's back yard with her party guests. It was hard to believe his last visit to New Haven had been two months ago.

Sophie might only be eight years old today, but before he knew it, he'd be at her sweet sixteen.

Sighing, he took a swig of his beer before meticulously turning each dog on the grill. Next to him, Jack nursed sizzling burgers. The smell of meat on a barbecue, no matter where or when, was always appealing. Even if the meat happened to be hotdogs and not prime steak.

"Did you see? Steven's here." Jack pointed across the pool to the last man Zac expected.

"What the heck?" His blood boiled. Steven had promised Melanie he wouldn't leave New Haven, then he'd gone and done exactly that. If it weren't for the responsibility of not letting the food burn, Zac would be over there decking the man right now.

"Easy, Zac. I invited him."

"You what?" He glared at Jack, the man who was like a brother to Melanie.

"Don't do anything stupid. Give him a chance to explain before you drag him out the front door. I promise you things will work out for the best."

Highly doubtful. Ever since Steven had left on Christmas day, Melanie hadn't been herself. He hadn't worked out precisely who had broken up with whom, but he was pretty sure it was for the best. Steven had moved all the way to Portland, Maine, for goodness sake!

After examining Jack's smug expression, Zac then demanded gruffly, "Tell me what you know."

Jack didn't flinch. "Have a word with Steven. Preferably a quiet one. Find out for yourself what he's doing here."

Once the last dog was off the fire, Zac strode over to where Julie sat talking to the man of the hour. Stopping beside their table, he took great delight in watching Steven visibly squirm in his seat. Then, as Zac stretched his arm across the table, he remembered Jack's words and kept his emotions in check.

"Steven, good of you to come," he said evenly.

"Hello, Zac." Steven rose slowly from his chair, maintaining full eye contact as he gripped Zac's hand.

"Why exactly *did* you come?"

Julie playfully punched his arm. "Zac, be nice!"

"I couldn't miss Sophie's birthday," Steven said, crossing his arms.

Interesting. Why would a man drive over two hundred and fifty miles to attend a child's birthday party? Unless he knew the truth.

"You're right." Zac nodded. "You, of all people, shouldn't miss her birthday." He glanced behind him toward his sister, organizing food for the children, then back at Steven. "By the way, I know."

Julie frowned. "You know, what, Zac?"

Grabbing her hand, he pulled her up into his arms and shot Steven a smile. "Mind if I steal her away?"

"I'm fine. Go." Steven waved them off.

***

Alex's primary objective was to avoid Zac as much as possible. If his heavenly kisses were all she could think about, keeping her distance was imperative. Not the easiest of tasks, given he was the birthday girl's uncle. Over the past hour, she'd found herself all too often in his vicinity, despite Jack's generous-sized back yard filled with party guests and paraphernalia.

With Zac helping Jack at the grill on the far side of the pool, now was the perfect time to speak to Melanie's ex-boyfriend. Last time she checked, Steven—the uninvited guest—had been camped at one of the picnic tables, nursing a beer. She headed in that direction.

Just as the temporary seating came into view, Alex spotted Zac marching toward Steven and Julie from the opposite direction. His determined expression made her wonder if he was also keen to interrogate Steven.

Heart racing, she dived for cover behind a clump of evergreen shrubs. Since she wasn't close enough to hear the conversation—only observe—she had to wait until Steven was alone before she could vacate her hiding spot and talk to him.

By the time Charlotte hollered, "Time for cake!" from the back step of the house, Alex was satisfied the truth was out, and Steven would be making things right with Melanie.

Taking a deep breath, she scanned the ground. Shredded colored paper from the desecrated piñata sparkled in the late afternoon sunshine. It would take Jack and her ages to pick it all up later, but she didn't mind. Her goddaughter was worth it. But right now, a piece of Sophie's rainbow-layered cake would sure go down a treat.

Everyone gathered around while Melanie lit the candles then beckoned to Alex to stand beside her, Steven, and the birthday girl.

"Zac, come stand next to Alex, please," Melanie said, obviously spotting her brother at the back of the crowd. "I want both Sophie's godparents in the family pictures."

Alex stiffened. So much for avoiding him.

As Zac took his place without a sideways glance, his musky scent, the one she associated with him, wafted toward her. If only her heart would stop racing! She threw Jack a 'help me' look, but he showed more interest in the photographer.

"Say cheese," Julie instructed, her camera poised.

Automatically smiling, Alex waited as several pictures were captured in quick succession. She made a mental note to ask for a copy. The hot doctor, his warm arm loosely around her waist for the photoshoot, had nothing to do with it. Sophie was her godchild, after all.

"How about you blow out your candles now, Sophie?" Julie waited in position until all eight tiny flames had been doused with one powerful breath, then went back to work.

A chorus of cheers erupted, and Zac's hand dropped away as someone started singing Happy Birthday. Alex joined in, not daring to look at Zac. His strong baritone voice filled the air, its smoothness reminding her of her first morning coffee—something she couldn't do without.

***

Zac waved as Julie's car disappeared down the road then expelled a long breath. Melanie would definitely need help tidying up Jack's back yard. Time to face the party mess, and Alex. His plan of avoiding her, to keep his hands and lips to himself, had worked until the photos. Resisting the opportunity to touch her was futile. She was his kryptonite.

Out back, the scene wasn't as bad as he'd anticipated. Melanie, Jack, and Alex had clearly been working hard. His gaze landed on the dirty barbecue grills at the opposite end to where Alex was clearing tables. That would work.

A little while later, he nearly jumped out of his skin when a hand touched his shoulder. Turning, he peered straight into Alex's beautiful, serious face.

"Would you mind...helping me with the trash?" She indicated the pile of bags over by the main table. "Jack went in to help Charlotte bath the kids, and Mel left to get ready for her date with Steven."

He looked at her blankly.

"I can't move it on my own."

"Of course. Sure. No problem." He gave the grill one last stroke with the stiff brush and shut the lid.

They worked in silence, Zac feeling strangely tongue-tied now he was alone with Alex.

On their way back to get the last two bags, he suddenly came out of his stupor. "Melanie has a date with Steven?"

Alex's lips lifted into a brief smile. "Yes."

"I'm surprised Mel's talking to him."

"You know he's Sophie's dad, right?"

"I guessed."

"What?" She stopped and stared at him. "When? How?"

"Sophie needed a blood transfusion after her accident. Steven had the same rare blood type, and Mel had noted him as the father on the hospital forms. Those two facts pretty much convinced me I was right."

"So you've known for months and didn't say anything." Alex sounded a little mad.

"It wasn't my place. Besides, Mel begged me not to say a word. I told her I'd tell Steven at Christmas if she didn't do it before then."

"But then he left, and you thought it didn't matter anymore," she said, her voice rising.

Was she judging him? Because this was none of her business! She might be Sophie's godmother, but she wasn't family.

Pushing past her to the side gate, he collected the final two sacks and swung around, almost bumping into her.

"Sorry," he mumbled, marching off to get the rest of the job done. Alex followed him and waited at the gate.

"Thank you," she said.

"You're welcome." The least he could do was be polite, a character trait he usually struggled with when it came to Alex. Easier to protect himself by mistreating her. That way, she wouldn't look at him the way she was right now. Apologetic.

"I'm sorry, Zac. I was judgmental. I had no right." Her genuine remorse made him want to kiss her, but sheer willpower kept him rooted to the spot.

He gave a curt nod instead.

She took a couple of steps closer, narrowing the distance between them. Her flowery scent, the one he'd memorized, filled his nostrils. If she came too close, he wasn't sure he'd be able to keep his promise.

"I knew the truth long before you, Zac, and I said nothing for the same reason. I love Mel, and I didn't want to do anything to jeopardize our friendship."

He tilted his head. "She's lucky to have you as a friend. You're faithful and always putting her first. I know she's grateful for everything you do."

Alex moved forward another step. Clenching his jaw, Zac fisted his hands, his breath catching in his throat. If he reached out, she'd be in his arms in a second.

"I'm confused," she said, her brows drawing together. "What have you done with Zac? You know, the one who's usually running me down and behaving despicably." Her words were tempered with a half-smile, her green eyes appearing lighter and brighter.

She took the final step.

Heart pounding, he shrugged. She couldn't make this any harder for him if she tried. "I'm trying to be a better man. Around you."

Their gazes locked.

Pushing a stray hair behind her ear, his fingers lingered on her smooth skin. She leaned into his touch, and the next moment her warm lips were on his. Initially surprised, he quickly returned her kiss. Wrapping his arms around her, he drew her closer. Her soft fingers brushed through the hair at the back of his neck, and, in no time, their tongues were tangling in an increasingly familiar dance.

He was powerless to stop. This woman softened every hard piece of him. She wormed her way past his defenses by breaking them down with every stroke of her tongue, every touch of her lips. Her hands on his skin sent liquid warmth to his whole body. He needed to pull away soon, or it would be too late to mask his body's responses.

Alex broke the kiss first, loosening her grip on his neck. Opening his eyes, he met her glazed ones.

"Alex?" His voice came out in a croak.

"I know. We shouldn't," she whispered, shaking her head. "I couldn't help myself."

"We can't keep doing this." His thumb skimmed her cheek. "It's not fair to anyone. Least of all us."

Releasing her, he shifted back, putting a safe distance between them.

"You need to decide what, no, who you want, Alex. Then you need to follow through with that decision."

She frowned. "What about you, Zac?"

"Sweetheart, I *know* what and who I want."

Chapter Eight

From her privileged viewpoint at the main table, Alex looked out over the sea of guests enjoying lively conversations at their tables. She twisted slightly to her left, zeroing in on the key members of the wedding party. Melanie, Steven, and Sophie—blushing bride, grinning groom, and their delightful daughter—finally a family.

She sighed. She wanted love like that.

Jack was an incredible guy, and she loved spending time with him, but their relationship was...comfortable. And, if she was completely honest, his kisses left her wanting—not like Zac's.

It was impossible not to remember each and every kiss. Thanksgiving's one had shocked her. Never mind that explosive kiss under the mistletoe six months ago. Fireworks had gone off in her head, and her knees had almost buckled.

The memory had a similar effect.

Grateful she wasn't standing, she stifled a giggle and continued her walk down memory lane. Christmas day had produced a breathtaking, or rather breath-stopping kiss outside her front door. Telling Zac he couldn't be trusted wasn't her finest moment, especially when he could've said the same thing about her!

Their last kiss, at Sophie's party, had been entirely her fault. Afterward, Zac's cryptic words, "I know what and who I want," had bothered her endlessly.

Still did.

During the past three months, Zac hadn't visited New Haven once. So, if he'd meant her, then he hadn't made his intentions clear at all. Instead, Julie was the one spending weekends in New York. Had he been referring to her? And was that what he expected? A long-distance relationship? Because if so, she wasn't interested.

Been there, done that, got burned.

Seemed Zac wasn't her future—not that he'd ever suggested it. Just kissed her.

Was she settling with Jack, though? Because settling was not for her, notwithstanding her ticking biological clock. Stringing him along was wrong; he deserved better. A furtive glance at Jack's handsome profile revealed his clenched jaw. He couldn't possibly have an inkling about her thoughts, could he?

Smoothing a hand over her cotton candy swing dress, she expelled another long breath.

"You okay?" Jack's hand slipped onto hers, his caring tone soothing her frazzled nerves. It also made her feel guilty.

She gripped his hand, sending him a half-smile. "Just wondering when we get to dance."

"Soon." He nodded in the direction of the band, currently shuffling about on the stage. "Steven and Mel will dance first, followed by the maid of honor and best man." He winked at her. "That's us."

Her smile widened. "Haha. Like I didn't know."

A few minutes later, the bridal couple waltzed to "From This Moment On" by Shania Twain. Steven gazed at Melanie throughout the dance as if she was the most precious thing in the world. Alex had never seen a man more in love. Wasn't that what all women wanted? She swiped at her damp cheeks, hoping her waterproof mascara was half as good as its packaging promised.

Loud laughter diverted her attention back to the other couple at their table. Julie's huge smile was directed at Zac, whose back was to Alex. Silently, she begged him to turn around. He did, and their eyes connected for a fleeting moment where his amused expression sobered, intensified. Whenever she snuck a peek and caught him watching her that exact way, she felt annoyingly giddy.

The first dance ended, and Jack stood, so attractive in his black and white penguin suit. Not as swoon-worthy as a certain doctor, but close. "Our turn," he said, his hand extended.

Smiling, she placed her hand in his and rose.

The shiny, wooden floor was perfect for dancing. Leaning her head on Jack's shoulder, she reveled in the safeness of his arms, her heart continuing its steadfast beat.

See? Comfortable. No pulse-racing, temperature-raising chemistry here.

"Okay, folks, time to add some interest to the evening," the DJ announced a few songs later. "I challenge everyone to change partners for the next few songs." He made beady eyes at the bridal couple. "That includes you, Steven. No matter who your beautiful bride dances with, trust me, she's going home with you."

Laughter filled the room as Steven reluctantly released Melanie into her father's arms.

Alex smirked. *Safe choice.* She'd barely finished her thought when Zac materialized in front of her and Jack. Her traitorous heart skipped a beat or three.

"Alex?" Jack raised his brows at her.

She knew she should object, but somehow her mouth wouldn't work.

"Fine. Take your chances." Shaking his head, Jack released her.

Left alone, Zac took a cautious step forward.

"Hi," he said, his gaze roaming the length of her. She gave him a tight smile, ignoring the butterflies bouncing in her stomach. "You're absolutely gorgeous, Alex." His husky voice, inches from her ear, sent tiny thrills throughout her body. Willing herself not to respond as 'drown in me' blue eyes locked onto hers, she tried to look away but couldn't.

Inserting some impatience into her voice, she asked, "Are you going to dance with me or not?"

"I'd love to." His dimple made an appearance, giving her jelly legs. The man truly knew how to charm a woman. Women. In fact, she bet all the females in New York felt just as weak when he dazzled them with that grin.

Zac reached for her hand as the first few notes of "Amazed" by Lonestar began.

Her heart sank. *Seriously! Now the DJ goes back to slow songs?* Her eyes darted to the exit doors. Before she could bolt, Zac slipped an arm around her waist and drew her close. The touch of his hand on the small of her back sent heat surging through her body.

"I've been dreaming about holding you in my arms all day," he said, his voice low.

She glared at him but begrudgingly placed her free hand on his shoulder. His intense gaze dropped momentarily to her lips, returning brightly lit with mischief and desire.

"Don't," she warned.

"What? You're not worried I'm going to kiss you, are you?"

Cheeks heating, her heartbeat marched into double time. The feel of his strong hand in hers was more than she could stand. Taking a deep breath, she tried to control her emotions.

"Don't you think dancing with me looks a little odd, Zac?"

"Why?"

"Because you hate me."

"You know I don't!"

"Everyone else thinks so."

"I don't care what they think," he said grumpily.

Huffing, she fixed her focus over his shoulder and stared into space, trying not to enjoy his warm embrace. At the words, 'I don't know how you do what you do. I'm so in love with you', she cringed. When his thumb gently, and oh so slowly, began to caress hers, she nearly lost all rational thought.

Did the man have no shame?

"Stop that!" she hissed, meeting his way-too-attentive gaze.

"What?" he asked innocently, the hand resting on her back drawing her closer.

"You know exactly what you're doing," she ground out, attempting to drag her eyes away from his but finding it impossible, again.

Lowering his gaze for a second, Zac murmured, "Tell me you don't want me to kiss you right now."

She glanced down at his mouth and chewed on her bottom lip. "I don't."

A smile split his gorgeous face as his eyes searched hers. "Liar."

"No." To reinforce her denial, she shook her head vigorously. But who was she kidding? She desperately wanted him to kiss her. More and more, with each second she remained in his arms.

"You're lucky there's an audience." His warm breath on her skin sent shivers down her spine.

"I can't do this." Tugging her hand free, Alex stalked back to the main table where she grabbed a full glass of white wine and gulped it down. Closing her eyes, she breathed in deeply.

When she set the empty glass back on the table, an arm slid around her waist, causing her to stiffen. Her head whipped around. "I don't—"

Jack looked perplexed.

"Sorry. I thought that..." She wrinkled her nose. "Nothing."

"Dance with me again?"

"Definitely."

Threading their fingers, Jack led them back toward the twirling couples. Since Zac was nowhere in sight, Alex breathed a little easier.

Jack held her close, staring strangely at her. She tossed her head away from his earnest gaze, only to catch Zac's eyes instead.

Oh!

Snatching a breath, she swung her attention back to Jack. Without warning, his mouth dipped to hers in a passionate kiss as if staking his claim.

Why?

Whatever the reason, this was an excellent time to ensure Zac forgot about ever kissing her again. So she kissed Jack back.

Glancing in Zac's direction afterward, she got a taste of her own medicine—Zac and Julie were sharing an equally intense kiss. Tightness gripped her chest. Was he trying to make her jealous? She shouldn't, couldn't have designs on a man who belonged to another woman. She had no right. She wasn't single...yet, and Zac definitely wasn't.

The minute the song was over, she dragged Jack off the dance floor.

"Hey, what's the hurry?" His eyes sparkled with excitement. "Where are we going?"

"Outside."

In a secluded spot, she turned to him.

Jack's smile faltered. "You look awfully serious. Is everything okay?"

"You're an incredible guy."

"Oh, no, I hear a but coming."

"But...I'm not the right person for you, Jack." Pain flickered in his eyes, but she rushed on regardless. "You deserve so much more than me. You deserve someone who turns your world upside down, who makes the world and everyone in it fade away when you kiss them."

"How do you know that's not you?" he asked, sounding petulant.

"It's not. I believe that person is still out there."

"Really?" He dropped her hand, his tone angry as he asked, "And who exactly would that be?"

"You'll figure it out, Jack. Just keep your heart open."

"You know what I think, Alex?"

"N-no," she stuttered, disarmed by his fierce expression. Jack never glowered, ever. If she didn't know better, she'd be worried he might strike her.

"I think that's a cop-out. You've made up this 'perfect' person for me as an excuse to break up with me. Is there someone else?"

"No." Shaking her head, she stepped closer.

His palms went up. "Admit it. The truth is you don't think I'm good enough for you."

"No, that's not true! If anything, you're settling being with me. I want so much more for us *both*. Think about what I'm saying. You'll agree."

He shook his head.

"It's a shock, I know, and I'm sorry, Jack. Once I'd admitted the truth to myself, I knew I had to tell you."

"So when you kissed me so ardently earlier, you didn't mean it?"

"Don't, please."

His voice rose, became insistent. "Are you telling me you didn't feel anything when I kissed you?"

"Of course I did!" she cried out before lowering her voice. "But even you can't tell me fireworks went off, despite the great kiss."

Seconds passed in silence as his tortured gaze remained on her, his lips pursed. She didn't know what else to say. Suddenly, her stomach clenched, and her hand flew to her mouth. "Oh, no! We're supposed to babysit Sophie for the next two weeks while Mel's on honeymoon."

Jack's frown deepened.

"Would you prefer I do it alone?"

She prayed not but couldn't blame him if he did. Perhaps she should've considered her timing a little better before ending their relationship. Taking it back was impossible, so she'd have to live with the consequences.

He scrubbed his hands over his face and sighed

deeply. "I need time to process what just happened, so you take Sophie tonight." He paused. "I'll join you tomorrow afternoon."

The muscles in her stomach loosened. "Thank you, Jack."

Shoulders slumped, he peered toward the doors. "I'm going in. You coming?"

She nodded, hating that she'd hurt him. But it was for the best. Hopefully, she wouldn't regret it and end up old and alone.

Chapter Nine

"So how did it *really* go, playing happy families with Jack?"

While Alex carefully considered Melanie's question regarding the past two weeks, she peered over at the long line of customers waiting to order. This place sure was popular. Convenient, too—Steven had taken Sophie for some quality father/daughter time at the nearby ice rink. Her gaze shifted back to Melanie's face, which had a post-honeymoon glow.

Alex inhaled deeply. "Honestly? Challenging."

"Oh." Melanie frowned. "Why's that?"

"Well..."

Still fresh in her mind was Sophie's constant questioning about Jack's absence the first day. Dare she explain how, by the time he arrived two days later, Sophie was happy with just her godmother's company? How Jack's initial attempts at interaction with Sophie had been ignored? About the tension between them, which Sophie may or may not have picked up on? Whatever the reason, it was only after he'd built a fire and roasted s'mores that Sophie told her, "Uncle Jack's almost as 'cool' as you, Miss Alex."

No, Melanie didn't need to be burdened with all of that.

Buying some time, Alex sipped her iced coffee, eventually blurting out, "Actually, Jack and I broke up."

"What? You're kidding! It was *that* bad?" Melanie's alarmed expression bordered on comical.

"Gosh, no, Mel! Sorry, that came out wrong." Alex gave her a reassuring smile. "Looking after Sophie went great, once Jack and I settled into a routine."

"But when did you break up then, and why? Who broke up with whom? Are you okay? Jack didn't cheat on you, did he? Did you cry?"

"Whoa, so many questions! Let me explain from the beginning."

"Sorry, my lawyer side took over. I'll try not to interrupt." Melanie lifted her green tea and sipped it.

"I broke up with Jack at your wedding because, truthfully, Jack and I had been muddling along for some time. Our relationship wasn't growing. For a while, I suspected he wasn't fully committed to us. When I confronted him, he denied it, but ultimately he agreed."

Melanie sucked her teeth.

"What?" Alex asked, biting her lip.

"I'm concerned, that's all. Jack's like a brother to me, and you're absolutely family, so..."

Leaning across the table, she squeezed Melanie's hand. "You're worried about future get-togethers, aren't you? Don't. Jack and I are still friends. It took two weeks, but he's made his peace, and so have I."

"That's a relief." Melanie smiled. A few seconds passed before she spoke again. "Thanks again for having Sophie. She couldn't stop talking about all the fun things you guys did. You are the 'bestest ever' according to our daughter."

"She's a wonderful child, Mel. I'll miss not seeing her every day."

"About that...Steven and I were talking last night. We wondered if you'd be Sophie's caregiver for the rest of the summer?" Alex opened her mouth to speak, but Melanie raised her hand and continued, "I *was* going to put her in Peterson's childcare program, but she'd definitely prefer it if you looked after her instead."

Stunned, Alex stared at Melanie. If she spent her vacation taking care of Sophie, it would help keep her mind off a particular hot doctor. At least during the day. Her nightly dreams were another matter.

"I know it's a lot to ask, but you wouldn't be required to do it for the whole time. If you changed your mind at any stage or needed a break, Sophie could easily go into childcare. They don't require much notice." Melanie leaned forward, her eyes pleading. "We'll pay you, of course."

"That's not necessary, Mel," she said, shaking her head. "It'd be my pleasure."

"Really? Oh, that's brilliant! Sophie will be ecstatic." Melanie jumped up from her seat and hugged her. "Thank you. I can't tell you what a weight off my mind this is."

As they finished off their drinks, Alex thought about the next couple months. Keeping her goddaughter occupied daily was precisely what she needed to not only keep her mind off her failed relationship with Jack but off Zac too. Although...who was she kidding? Sophie's presence would be a constant reminder of the child's uncle.

Maybe she shouldn't have been so quick to say yes to Melanie's proposal.

***

Zac stared at his reflection in his old bedroom mirror. Outwardly, he was the epitome of success and confidence. On the inside, well, that was another story.

"Zac! Don't you need to leave now?" Mom shouted from the kitchen where she was preparing dinner for her and Dad.

"I'll be down in a second!" he replied. She was right. He needed to go soon if he wanted to be on time.

"People who are reliable earn respect, Zac. Respect builds trust and faith. All important qualities in a relationship." Mom's wise words were permanently ingrained in his memory. She'd said them often enough when he was growing up.

Another memory he couldn't erase was Alex and Jack's passionate kiss, roughly a month ago now. That kiss should've killed any hope he had of being with Alex. Yet, he couldn't deny their chemistry. When Alex had said she didn't want him to kiss her at Melanie's wedding, she'd definitely been lying.

But an occasional kissing partner wasn't what he wanted. He wanted a life partner. Julie was great, but they both knew they weren't soulmates. If Alex knew his relationship with Julie was based solely on friendship and not romance, he might have a chance at convincing her to leave Jack.

Except...he'd made a big mistake kissing Julie at his sister's wedding. A stupid, short-sighted mistake! Suffering from a bruised ego, he'd wanted to make Alex jealous. Instead, he'd created another problem—how to make Alex believe the kiss meant nothing. That would be a struggle.

Breathing deeply, he ran his fingers through his hair. Pointless to dream about something that was never going to happen. Either way, he needed to set the record straight with Julie. Ever since the wedding, she'd made excuses not to visit him in New York. Equally, he'd avoided New Haven, unwilling to risk running into Alex. After he and Julie talked tonight, he could move on, maybe try dating again—in New York.

Eyeing his light blue shirt collar, he frowned. Too stuffy. He undid the top button for the third time, then skimmed his hands over his smooth jaw. Forcing his lips upward evened out the lines scattered on his brow.

Time to face the music.

***

Julie flipped her long auburn hair over her shoulder and glanced around the buzzing restaurant, no doubt noting the fully occupied tables.

Zac took the opportunity to scan his immediate surroundings—the shiny silverware, starched white tablecloths, and floral centerpieces—all at odds with the establishment's casual decor. Somehow, it worked.

"So, Union Café," she said. "How *did* you manage to get a reservation, Zac? I thought this place had a waiting list for months."

He waved his hand dismissively. "Oh, I know a guy who knows a guy."

"Seriously?"

A chuckle escaped his lips as he raised his glass of Merlot. "I called in a favor. A patient of mine knows the owner. They're related or something." At her raised brow, he added, "I saved his life a while back, so I guess he felt he owed me."

"It goes to show; it's all about who you know." She swirled the wine in her glass before taking a sip. "Not that I'm complaining. What woman in her right mind would turn down a dinner invitation to a fine-dining French restaurant?"

An unwelcome thought crossed his mind as he gazed into her pretty green eyes. "Were you going to say no?"

She shook her head, then nodded. "Actually, yes, I was."

"Why?"

Averting her eyes, she stroked her infinity tattoo on her right wrist. She did it whenever she was nervous. Was she hiding something? Not that he could judge, he took the cake when it came to secrets. Alex's stunning face, just before he kissed her, came to mind. He mentally shook it away.

Julie raised her chin and looked at him directly. "Things between us have been different since you kissed me at Steven's wedding."

"They have?"

"Something changed that day, Zac."

"You make it sound like a bad thing."

"Not bad, exactly, just different." Her finger resumed its rubbing of black ink. Circling round and round. "I admit you took me by surprise with that kiss," she said, not meeting his eyes.

What could he say? Alex kissing Jack had maddened him so much he'd used Julie to try to make Alex jealous? Not that it had made any difference.

Julie blew out a breath. "I spent hours trying to work out if your feelings for me had changed or if you were just retaliating because Alex had allowed Jack to publicly stake his claim."

Zac swallowed down a lump of guilt. Using Julie had been so wrong and extremely unfair. "Julie, I—"

Waving her hand, she almost knocked down her wine glass. "It's okay. You don't need to explain. I knew the score when we began spending time with each other. Now...I guess what I'm trying to say is, I've been rethinking our situation, and hopefully, like me, you've come to the same conclusion."

"Your appetizer, ma'am," their smartly dressed, elderly waiter said, interrupting them.

"Wow, this looks great." Julie gave him her most dazzling smile as she touched his arm.

Without flinching, the man turned to Zac. "And for you, sir," he said, serving the second appetizer.

Wow, Zac marveled, a male immune to Julie's charms. That had to be a first.

"Enjoy. I'll be back with your mains in due course," the waiter said before leaving.

"Shall we?" Zac asked, picking up his fork.

Julie gave a firm nod. "Definitely."

They dug in as soft classical music played in the background while other diners' quiet conversations continued around them.

After a while, Zac glanced over at Julie. "How's your food?"

"Interesting. The different flavors of pear, pecan, and Roquefort cheese together are kinda delicious." She lifted her fork to him. "You want a taste?"

"No, thanks." He chuckled. "Apple, walnut, and watercress salad is enough of a change for me."

As he ate, he wondered whether they were on the same page about their relationship. Did Julie want what he wasn't able to give her?

"Listen, Zac," she said, pushing her plate aside.

Hearing the apprehension in Julie's voice, Zac lowered his fork and gave her his full attention.

"It's time we stopped looking like...we're a couple," she began hesitantly before continuing with greater confidence. "You need to give Alex a chance to see what an amazing single guy you are and that you're meant for one another. If she can't figure that out, you need to move on, find a woman you can have a future with instead of wasting time with me."

He blinked.

"Don't you agree?" she asked softly, her warm hand landing on his cheek. Her compassion-filled eyes peered deeply into his.

"You're right." He squeezed her hand. "Except, you mean a lot to me, and I don't want to lose our friendship. Besides, spending time with you is never a waste."

She batted her eyelashes. "You say the most charming things, Dr. Danvers. I care about you too, you know."

He should've known she'd understand.

Once they were done eating, their waiter served Julie's cod and calamari, and his sirloin steak. The beefy meat smell, mingled with garlic's distinctive aroma, presumably from the sauce on Julie's plate, had him salivating.

"The thing is, Zac," Julie said, adding a bit of broccoli to the battered calamari on her fork, "the next few months are going to be hectic." Her brow furrowed. "I won't be able to visit."

"Oh. Why not?"

While he savored every bite of his excellent entree, she shared her surprising news. By the time his meal was finished, part of him was elated at her good fortune, the other part disappointed. She deserved to be successful and happy, but he would really miss her company on the weekends.

Julie's expression became pensive as she stared upward over his shoulder. He figured she was peering at one of the stained glass, semi-circular pictures.

Displayed above the window lintels, each was unique.

Was she searching for a prediction for her future?

Following her lead, he examined the image across from him. An elderly woman—dressed in a black cloak with a white hat and apron—sat on a cliff's edge staring at the turbulent sea below. A chill tore over his skin, and he shivered, refusing to believe it was a sign of what was to come.

Fixing what he prayed was an encouraging smile on his face, he grasped Julie's hand in his and waited until she made eye contact.

"Everything will work out, Julie," he said with a whole lot more confidence than he felt. "Just wait and see."

Chapter Ten

Official status single. Would it make any difference to Alex? Probably not.

She already *had* the perfect boyfriend.

Zac dragged his attention back to his computer screen and the medical diagnosis he was meant to be reviewing. The words remained a jumbled mess, no matter how hard he tried to focus.

He took a deep breath in and let it out slowly. Not that it did any good. Reflecting on his weekend trip to New Haven and the woman who lived there was messing with his concentration levels. He had to face facts. Alex was still front and center of his every thought.

And it had to stop.

Using every ounce of willpower he had, he blocked all else from his mind and scrutinized the details of the email in front of him—for the third time that morning.

Something was missing. The symptoms gave the impression of being unrelated. Maybe—

A sharp knock forced his eyes to the door. Dan Wilson was leaning against the doorjamb with one hand in his trouser pocket and a lop-sided smile on his face.

Zac racked his brain for an explanation as to why his practice partner looked way too relaxed for his liking.

None came to mind.

"Do you have a spare minute to meet Trevor Johnson?"

The name seemed vaguely familiar, but Zac couldn't place it. He frowned at the salt and pepper haired man who reminded him so much of his father.

"The temporary replacement physician?" Dan prompted.

Still none the wiser, Zac stared at him.

"Don't tell me you've forgotten I'm taking my family to Asia in August?"

"What?!"

Dan straightened, his usual earnestness returning as he stepped into the office. "We discussed this months ago. You agreed, Zac," he said, sounding angry and annoyed.

Oh boy. In the dark recesses of his mind, a memory surfaced from two days before Christmas—a Friday, if he remembered correctly.

He'd just switched off his computer and was hastily packing his medical bag when Dan approached, saying, "Before you go, I need to run something by you."

"Can't it wait until after Christmas?" Zac zipped up his bag and scanned his desk to make sure he hadn't forgotten anything. "I was expected in New Haven this morning, and now I'm not even sure I'm gonna make it to an important dinner party."

The emergency patient they had just finished dealing with had thrown a wrench in his plans. If he didn't make it to Steven's place tonight...no, he had to. Missing an opportunity to see Alex again was not an option.

"It really can't wait, Zac. I've decided to take my whole vacation allowance in August."

"What? You can't do that, Dan! What about all your patients?" Zac felt his temperature rising. "I can't possibly handle yours on top of mine for four weeks!"

"You'll be fine. Trust me, I've found an excellent cover physician, Trevor Johnson. You won't even realize I'm gone."

"I take it there's no way you're gonna change your mind about this?"

"Afraid not. With flights organized and hotels booked, my wife'll kill me if I cancel, *and* the kids are so excited about going. Frankly, so am I."

In the end, he *had* reluctantly agreed to the plan.

Zac rolled his office chair backward and rose to his feet. He met his partner's penetrating gaze and said, "I remember now."

"Good." Dan huffed, checking his watch. "I hope Trevor hasn't left already."

Buttoning his jacket, Zac straightened it with a few tugs of the bottom edge. "This had better not take too long—I have a more pressing matter to resolve." Alex's image popped into his head. Squeezing his eyes tight for a few seconds, he did some mental rearranging. As soon as this meeting was over, he needed to get back to solving his problem—the complicated medical issue he'd been emailed late last night. Not his love life.

The men made their way down the corridor toward the front of the practice. Not knowing what to expect as they approached the waiting room, Zac's heart rate quickened. Would Dan have chosen an older, more experienced physician like himself, or someone Zac would feel comfortable leading?

Hopefully, the latter.

From just inside the reception area, a mocha-skinned man in a white coat smiled tentatively at them. Tall, with an athletic build, Zac guessed the guy was in his late twenties, possibly early thirties. The visitor strolled their way, wearing a confident, slightly cocky expression. Expecting the usual hint of arrogance from a fellow physician, Zac was surprised by its absence. Instead, the guy's bluish-green eyes seemed to burn with excitement.

Zac stuck out his hand. "Dr. Johnson, I believe."

"Trevor, please. It's an honor to meet you, Dr. Danvers," he said, his handshake firm. "Not every day one meets a 'Top New York Doctor'." The admiration in Trevor's voice was unmistakable, but the reference to the recent accolade made Zac wince. Anytime someone mentioned his success, he felt the pressure to excel—a pressure his father had instilled in him.

"Okay. Trevor," he said begrudgingly. "And it's Zac. Being called 'Dr. Danvers' by a colleague, albeit a temporary one, would make me feel too much like my dad."

A look of confusion passed over Trevor's face. Apparently, the man hadn't heard of his father. Funny, most doctors had—both young and old—in Zac's experience. He glanced at Dan, who was regarding him closely.

"How about we give Trevor a tour of the practice?"

From the intensity in Dan's eyes, Zac figured he'd better not argue.

"Of course. Follow me, Trevor," he said.

After showing off the premises and wowing Trevor with their state-of-the-art medical equipment, Zac finally returned to his office. A million thoughts rushed through his mind while he held a steaming mug of coffee in his hand. Dr. Johnson came across as self-assured and was pleasant enough. Given his credentials, there was little doubt he was capable of filling in for Dan —at least on paper.

The real question was, would Dan manage to do a proper handover in just two short weeks? Zac barely had enough time to grab a coffee most days, never mind eat lunch. He sure as heck wasn't going to take on any extra patients if this guy couldn't actually cope.

All his negative speculation was interrupted by the flashing green light on his desk phone indicating his next patient had arrived. Any concerns he had would need to take a back seat for now, like everything else in his life.

***

Two weeks later, Zac peered around the Italian restaurant as the throb in his temple slowly dissipated. Families of all sorts and sizes filled every second table. The occasional couples he spotted didn't strike him as being on first, second, or even third dates, but rather in established relationships.

Next time, he'd google the place first.

Honestly, he wouldn't be on a date if it wasn't for Dan. It was the last thing he needed tonight, even if it was Saturday. He should be getting ahead of his caseload at the hospital, freeing up a little extra time in case Trevor needed assistance with any of Dan's patients from Monday onward.

About to fly halfway across the world for a month's vacation, Dan's parting gift as they'd left work yesterday had been to order Zac to wine and dine his friend's daughter, Emma Williams.

"You deserve at least one night off before I leave, Zac," Dan had insisted. "Emma's twenty-five, recently divorced, and has expressed an interest in you." When Zac raised an eyebrow, Dan had quickly added, "If you need her marital status clarified, she caught her husband in a compromising position. More than once."

Yeah, that had been a little too much information, in Zac's opinion. He recalled being briefly introduced to Emma—a petite brunette with chocolate-colored eyes—at an awards ceremony the previous year. In an emerald form-fitting dress, she'd been stunning.

Now the same woman sat in a cream silk shirt, scanning the menu across from him, as striking as he remembered and classy too. Her unique scent was a welcome change from the usual Chanel No.5 he encountered. Sparkling fingers and a diamond necklace resting on her lightly tanned chest screamed 'expensive taste'.

Frowning, he picked up his menu. "I think this was a mistake."

"Oh." Her disappointment clued him in on how his comment must've sounded, and he swiftly softened his expression with a smile.

"I meant this place, Emma," he said, waving the menu around. "Not having dinner with you."

Relief flooded her pretty features before she cast a glance at her surroundings. Would she also notice the lack of starched white tablecloths, the remnants of fallen food hiding under the tables, and the dazzling lights instead of scented candles?

"The atmosphere's cozy. It's fine." Emma's attention turned to the card in her hand for a second before she discarded it. "I'm going with the lasagna and salad," she said, smiling sweetly. "It's been a long time since I had my grandmother's standard Sunday comfort lunch."

"Is she still around?"

Emma's eyes lost their brightness for a second.

Moving her head from side to side, she answered in a strained voice, "She passed away a few years ago. Cancer."

"I'm sorry. It's hard to lose a loved one."

"Thanks." She unfolded and folded the paper napkin into a different shape before asking, "Have you?"

Leaning against the hard wooden chair, he laid his forearms on the table and linked his fingers. "My gran died too, from a heart attack six years ago."

"I'm sorry for your loss, Zac. Were you close?" she asked softly.

"Not in the last few years of her life. I moved to New York to study straight after I graduated high school. Once I qualified as a medical student, I didn't get to visit her very often. A physician's free time is pretty limited."

Sitting up straighter, her expression brightened. "Speaking of which...Dan tells me your practice is doing extremely well."

Here we go, another gold digger.

Zac crossed his arms and fought a sudden feeling of disappointment. Why did everything revolve around one's monetary success? He and Dan worked hard. They deserved every dollar they earned. Being considered a means to financial freedom? Not what he wanted.

Emma wrung her hands together. Of all the conflicting emotions visible on her beautiful face, worry stood out the most. His jaw tightened. Was she concerned he wouldn't be interested in her anymore?

Darn right, he wouldn't!

"I know what you're thinking, Zac, and you're wrong," she said indignantly. "Your bank balance means nothing to me. I might be employed as an interior designer, but I don't need to work. Ever."

The muscles in his shoulders relaxed, as did his jaw.

"My grandmother was extremely wealthy and generous to a fault. She left me a huge trust fund, which will see me through to the end of my life." Emma shrugged. "No matter how lavishly I live or how long."

"Wow." Running a hand through his hair, he contemplated the woman before him. Nice to know she wasn't after his money. Money could buy plenty of things, but not love. "Not what I was expecting to hear."

"If it's alright with you," she said, her voice taking on a hard edge, "I'd rather not be compared to most other women in the city."

"I'm sorry, Emma. I should've given you the benefit of the doubt before jumping to the wrong conclusion. It's just...I've been pursued often for my income potential and hardly ever because of my good looks or excellent bedside manner." He let out an embarrassed chuckle. "Your honesty's refreshing."

Her easy smile returned, and as he peered around the room again, genuine laughter bubbled up inside of him. Releasing it felt terrific.

"What's so funny?"

"This place really isn't a good fit for you, is it?"

"It's perfect, and I'm exactly where I want to be," she said, covering his hand with hers.

When their gazes collided and held, he knew she meant it. Heat rose up his neck. But as he struggled to pull his eyes away from Emma's pretty ones, another set of eyes—Alex's green ones, to be precise—materialized in his mind.

Now all he felt was torn.

Chapter Eleven

Enough was enough—time for action!

Zac marched up to the red brick building and punched the code into the keypad beside the front door. The buzzer sounded, granting him access to the doctor's office, but he paused. Bone weary from working the whole weekend, he had to suppress the urge to head straight home instead. It was hard to believe the past week had all but whizzed by like a lightning bolt.

There were advantages to being swamped. It left no time to think about Alex. To wonder how her summer was going or wonder if he crossed her mind as many times a day as she did his.

With a groan, he redirected his musings. Would Emma still be waiting for his call? Their date last Saturday hadn't started out brilliantly, but it *had* ended on a high note.

"Best night I've had in a long, long time," she'd told him, a smile lighting up her eyes as he dropped her off at her penthouse apartment. Her expression had turned serious. "Will I see you again, Dr. Danvers? Or will you be too busy, especially with Dan away for a month?"

"I'll call. I promise."

That had been over a week ago. He'd be lucky if Emma even wanted to go out with him again. This August was always going to be the longest and possibly busiest month of his life, yet he certainly didn't want or need any added stress from Trevor. The stand-in physician was supposed to make his life easier. Not give him an ulcer!

Breathing in deeply, Zac re-entered the code, pushed open the glass door, and walked inside. Given the office wasn't due to open for a while, he was surprised to discover his temporary colleague already working through the daily case files.

So much for having a bit of time to figure out how to broach his concerns.

He would just have to wing it.

"Everything alright, Trevor?" he asked after rapping on Trevor's open door.

The new doctor glanced up from his seat, his face full of surprise. "Yeah," he replied, swiftly relaxing his features. "Just making sure I'm prepared."

"Listen, about that...would you mind coming into my office for a chat?"

"Not at all. Want me to grab you a coffee first? I just poured myself a fresh one." Trevor pointed at two mugs on his desk—one steaming, the other stone cold. The guy must've arrived at the crack of dawn.

"Sure. That'd be great. No sugar and a splash of milk."

Not long after Zac had finished sorting through some patient files in his office, Trevor entered holding two mugs and took a seat across from him.

Reaching out for the sorely needed caffeine fix, Zac took a sip of the strong coffee. "Thanks, I needed this." Lowering his mug, he smiled briefly. "Honestly, I'm thankful you're covering for Dan. You're doing a fine job, and, according to the ladies in reception, our patients have had nothing but good things to say."

"But?"

"No buts. I really appreciate the dedication and great care you take in dealing with each case."

A genuine smile softened Trevor's otherwise solemn expression. "As I said before, Zac, I'm thrilled to have the opportunity to work with you. I consider it an honor. When Dan mentioned if things went well this could become a permanent position, I was a little surprised. Especially since I'd heard your partnership was solid and greatly admired by your competition."

A tightness developed in Zac's chest. "What—" His voice cracked a little on the word, and he quickly cleared his throat, then tried again. "What do you mean?"

"You know, with Dan wanting to move his family to Virginia, I assumed he meant you'd be needing a new partner. It's one of the reasons I jumped at the offer—a chance to become a part of this practice."

His heart sped up. Why hadn't Dan mentioned he wanted to leave? Was he hoping this would be a good trial run, so when he dropped his bombshell, he'd have a plan in place?

"I'm sorry, Zac," Trevor's voice broke into his swirling thoughts. "I didn't realize Dan hadn't discussed the possibility with you."

Clasping his fingers together, Zac leaned his chin on them and closed his eyes for a second. Then he took a deep breath to calm his racing heart and met Trevor's concerned gaze. "I was completely unaware," he said.

Trevor looked ready to bolt as he pushed back his chair, his fingers spread across the armrests. "Shall I give you some time to process?"

"No need." Worrying about the future would have to wait until later. There was a more pressing issue to discuss. "I wanted to talk to you about something else."

Shifting his chair forward again, Trevor regarded him with curious eyes.

"If the intention is ultimately for you to be my partner, we need to set some ground rules," Zac said. "Firstly, unless it's an emergency, my appointments are not to be interrupted. Secondly, if you need my consult on a patient, email me. I'll find a suitable time in my schedule and let you know when I'm free to discuss the case."

Nodding slowly, Trevor visibly swallowed. "Okay."

"Listen," Zac said, lightening his tone, "in only one week, you've proved you're extremely capable of making decisions for your patients. You've been checking everything with me because you're worried about making a mistake. Am I right?"

Another nod.

"Trust me, you won't, so go with your gut. I have faith in you; you just need to have faith in yourself."

This time, Trevor all but beamed. "Coming from you, that means a lot."

"Also, I have plenty on my plate. Are you willing to take on any new patients?"

"I think I can handle that."

"Fantastic."

***

Zac shoved the remains of yet another microwave dinner across his kitchen island and out of reach. Tossing it into the trash could wait; he wasn't in the mood. At least Trevor's newfound independence had freed Zac up to concentrate on his own cases and jam-packed appointment book.

The result? Another week over. With any luck, the next two weeks would race by too.

After scanning some medical articles on his iPad—the only news he couldn't afford to miss—he pushed the gadget aside and bounced his leg on the barstool's footrest. What next?

His attention strayed to the coffee maker. Bad idea. He'd consumed far too much caffeine recently.

Settling on a beer, he grabbed a bottle from the fridge, headed over to his favorite spot, and sank into the corner sofa's soft seat. He smoothed his hand over the cushion's edge and noticed more blue threads than usual. Not surprising considering it had been the first piece of furniture he'd purchased in New York. Over thirteen years ago.

His gaze roamed the open plan living area of his bachelor apartment. The light gray walls needed a fresh coat of paint; the slated window blinds—originally white—looked cream, and the once bright colors of his coffee table rug had dulled from all the direct sunlight. If Alex were to drop by, how would she view his home? Not that she would ever visit, or stay for that matter.

A man could dream.

Still, the antiquated furniture ought to be replaced and the decor updated. There were a couple of fixed coffee stains on his bedroom carpet, and his ensuite shower door stuck constantly. No point in putting off the inevitable. It wasn't like he'd be moving out or getting married anytime soon. Not when the latter required a girlfriend!

Running his finger around the beer bottle's rim, he decided he'd find a remodeling expert when Dan got back from vacation. Although...wasn't Emma an interior designer?

Rising with a grunt, he snagged his phone off the kitchen counter and returned to his seat to type out a message: ***Hey, Emma, I'm sorry, work's been crazy. Any chance you're free for dinner tomorrow night? I'd love to see you. Zac***

Before he hit send, he lifted his drink to his mouth and paused. He'd promised to call two weeks ago. During their date, he'd gotten the distinct impression she liked him and understood his work commitments.

Would she forgive him for ghosting her? A couple of swigs of cold liquid hardly eased his nerves, but they did give him the courage to push send.

Sighing deeply, he rested his head on the sofa's backrest. The old grandfather clock chimed eight times, making him think of Julie.

"I love your clock. It reminds me of the one my grandmother had when I was little," she'd said the first time she visited.

Julie hadn't been bothered by his dated place. Instead, one of her favorite pastimes had been to chill out in front of his old TV.

"Both HD and non-HD look exactly the same to me," she'd said, smiling contentedly as they watched a recent box office release.

"You're so easy to please," he'd said, laughing.

Julie had always made him feel better after a long week at work. He recalled the time she'd cooked him mashed potatoes and decorated it like a snowman. He'd been tickled pink when she'd used a carrot for the nose, peas for the eyes, and red pepper strips for its lips. With her, there'd never been any pressure to impress. She took what he gave and demanded nothing more.

He fired off a quick text: ***Hey, stranger, how're things going? Miss you. Give me a call. Zac xx***

It would probably be a few days before he heard from her. Knowing he was no longer a priority in her life saddened him.

Without meaning to, his gaze gravitated to the group photograph from Sophie's eighth birthday party, where one face consistently stood out. Blocking it with his hand was useless; his mind conjured up Alex's image anyway. His heart stuttered, thinking about the way her green eyes sparkled whenever she looked at Sophie. How her shining blonde hair fell softly to her shoulders and made him want to run his fingers through it. And when he remembered the way her lips moved perfectly under his, his pulse quickened.

Letting out a guttural sound, he sat up straighter, scrubbed his hands over his face, and stared at his phone. *Emma, reply,* he willed.

A few seconds later, as if in answer to prayer, a message tone sounded. Emma: ***Good 2 hear from u, Zac. Yes, text dinner details.***

Great, I'll pick you up at 7. I promise a more appropriate place this time.

She replied instantly with both a smiling and a laughing emoji.

He opened his phone's browser, and as he scanned the romantic restaurant choices he knew Emma deserved, he felt marginally more cheerful. Maybe he wasn't destined to be alone. Alex had Jack—her choice—and he had the possibility of Emma.

If he ignored the dull ache in his chest, things were definitely looking up.

Chapter Twelve

Alex placed her hands over her bloated stomach and grinned appreciatively at Melanie and Steven. "Best meal I've had since Christmas! Thank you guys so much."

Hopefully, she wouldn't regret her overindulgence. After all, tomorrow *was* her last day off before fall term.

"I'll admit—" Steven tempered his otherwise serious tone with a half-smile. "I was a little disappointed about missing out on tonight's date night until Melanie mentioned she'd be serving a roast dinner with all the trimmings. A*nd* warm chocolate fudge cake for dessert."

Alex laughed. "I imagine that sweetened the deal."

"Absolutely." Steven nodded.

She winked at Melanie. "What a relief."

"After all you did with Sophie over the summer, Alex, a meal was the *least* I could do." Melanie fake glared at Steven, then turned back to her, "Do you know she slept like a log each night?"

"Not surprising."

Keeping Sophie and herself busy every day had been Alex's mission. Easy enough with morning activities such as swimming, ice skating, and dancing, never mind museum visits and playdates. Their afternoons had been spent cooking healthy lunches together, going on long walks, painting, coloring, playing board games, or finishing puzzles. Recalling it all was exhausting!

"It was my absolute pleasure, and you more than compensated me for my time." Alex glanced in the direction of her goddaughter's bedroom. "Besides, having Sophie around made me realize how much I want a family of my own."

"I'm so sorry things didn't work out with Jack." After exchanging a look with her husband, Melanie reached over to give her hand a squeeze. "We were sure an engagement was in the cards."

Ducking her head for a second, Alex took a deep breath. "I've started dating again."

While Steven's gaze was fairly curious, Melanie's brightened. "You have? That's awesome! Anybody you want to see again?"

"Michael Smith."

"Ooh, tell us more." Her excitement was contagious enough to make Alex laugh.

"He's a math teacher at school."

"Really?" Concern dotted Melanie's brow. "Why is this the first I've heard of him?"

Looking amused, Steven stood and began gathering the dirty dishes. "I'm pretty sure you don't know *all* the teachers at Sophie's school, my darling."

"More than you do, sweetheart," Melanie smirked.

This is what she wanted, Alex mused, a man to share the mundane daily things with, as well as all the special times.

"Michael teaches the higher grades," she said as Steven loaded the dishwasher.

"Is he any good?" Melanie asked.

She smiled. "He's amazing, and also, patient, kind, and intelligent. Easily the best-looking guy at work. The kids love him, and so do most of the female staff, unattached or otherwise."

"Sounds like a real catch," Steven said, returning to the table to pick up their empty coffee mugs. "Any refills, ladies?"

They shook their heads.

"Mind if I leave you two? Netflix and I have a date."

Melanie peered adoringly up at her husband. "Of course, sweetheart. I'll be heading to bed shortly anyway."

"Okay." He planted a lingering kiss on her lips.

Feeling a stab of jealousy, Alex looked away. The constant reminder of what she didn't have in her life made her wish her best friend wasn't married and so in love. But then she recalled the years Melanie had spent alone, raising a child. She deserved a love like Steven's. Honest, pure, and perfect.

"Goodnight, Alex," Steven said once he dragged his eyes off Melanie.

"You too. Enjoy your show."

"Thanks, I will."

Steven wandered off toward the living room, and Melanie leaned forward. "So why the sudden interest in Michael?"

"Not sudden. He's asked me out several times, but the timing wasn't right."

"Well, you're single now."

"Exactly."

"I'm happy for you, Alex. Sounds like you're not the only one who's moving on."

For some reason, her breath hitched. "What do you mean?"

"Lately, my brother's been talking about someone called Emma."

"Oh." The punch to her gut took her breath away.

Was Zac two-timing Julie? Anything was possible. The man had shared sensational kisses with her while still seeing Julie. Thank goodness she hadn't ever told Melanie about Zac and his kisses. As far as she knew, Melanie thought she and Zac didn't get along. And that was for the best.

"I think he's keeping it on the down-low. Probably worried we might make too much of a fuss and want to meet her. Anyway, I'll keep you posted."

Alex frowned. Sounded serious if Zac wasn't keen to expose his relationship with another woman. Not that she cared. It was none of her business, yet she had to ask. "What about Julie?"

"I assume they must've called it quits. Zac would never cheat."

"I guess." With her heart suddenly racing, she made a show of checking the time. "I should go, Mel. It's been an amazing evening, but I'm tired, and I'm sure you are too."

Melanie stifled a yawn. "Yep, this pregnant lady needs her beauty sleep. I'll see you at school bright and early on Monday morning."

"Can't wait."

At home, Alex took a cool shower then curled up in bed. Though her heart rate was normal again, the tightness in her chest remained. Was it guilt? Because Melanie was so wrong about her brother. He was a cheater. But so was she.

How was she going to keep from blurting everything out when she saw Melanie again?

Simple. By staying strong.

Five months had already passed, and Zac hadn't kissed her again. Not that she'd exactly seen him since his sister's wedding. Apparently, he'd come to visit Julie six weeks ago, yet he hadn't contacted her. She hadn't expected him to, really. Not when his parting words at Sophie's party implied he was waiting for her to decide.

Well, she certainly wasn't about to travel to New York to see if the attraction she felt could develop into anything. Especially now he had an Emma. So there was nothing to tell. It was over. Not that it had begun. He obviously wasn't interested in her for anything but the occasional passionate kiss.

Maybe Zac and Julie were over, or maybe they were on a break? Either way, it wasn't any of her business, and neither was this Emma. She wouldn't want to date Zac anyway, even if he asked, which he hadn't. And long-distance relationships were out of the question.

Why was she thinking about a man who'd kiss a woman the way Zac had kissed her while dating someone else anyway? The sooner her heart caught on and understood the man was a player, the sooner she'd get over him and move on...with someone like Michael, who ticked all the right boxes.

If that's how she felt, why did the hero of her dreams always have Zac's face? Possibly because he set her heart racing with just a smile or a look, or because he'd made her feel cherished with his earth-shattering kisses.

Every single time.

***

Relaxing his fisted hands, Zac quickened his pace along the gravel path while breathing in the crisp September air. A minute later, he shook his head.

What was he doing navigating Central Park at the crack of dawn?

The whole of last night, he'd tossed and turned, worrying about how he was going to grill Dan today. When he'd woken up, assuming it must be late, he'd been surprised to find the sun still napping. No matter how hard he tried to go back to sleep, it had proved impossible. And so he'd decided on this ridiculously early walk to work. The walk that had become more like a march.

With a concerted effort, he shortened his stride and managed to slow down.

So *what* if Trevor had fitted in effortlessly with their team for the past two weeks? Dan's no-nonsense demeanor was what Zac had missed. Ever since Trevor's revelation, he'd itched to demand an explanation from his partner. But he'd held back, aware of Dan's right to enjoy his well-deserved vacation.

All around him, leaves floated in the light breeze like butterflies. Fall might be on its way, but passing the Shakespeare Garden, he could still smell the licorice scent of the orange daisy-like flowers.

The reddish light of the sun's first rays was peeking through the trees, and although the sunbeams held no warmth yet, by midday, they certainly would—a great start to the Labor Day weekend.

And Zac couldn't wait.

Emma had managed to secure tickets for the tennis open tomorrow, so they'd be watching Nadal playing Mayer in round three of the men's singles.

For after the parade on Monday, she'd promised a barbecue with friends along with an 'unforgettable fireworks display'. The weekend would end with a literal bang—another thing to look forward to, especially as he couldn't go home for the holiday.

Home.

Silly how, after so many years in New York, he still thought of New Haven as home. It made him think of his sister and their FaceTime conversation the previous Sunday.

"Hey, Mel," he'd said when her face appeared on the screen.

"Well, hello, brother dear. Don't you look relaxed, and dare I say, happy?"

Right then, Zac had decided he would stick to a regular phone call next time. That way, she couldn't read too much into his facial expressions.

"Is there something you want to tell me?" she asked, her eyebrows raised.

"How's the pregnancy going?"

"Dad's happy with my progress."

"Good to hear."

"Tell me what you've been up to, Zac."

He shrugged. "The usual—work, a few dinners out. Dan's back next Friday and... oh, I'm going to the tennis open next weekend."

"Dinners? With who?" Her voice rose in excitement, making him groan inwardly for stupidly mentioning anything.

"Really, Mel? Did you not hear the tennis part?"

"I'm sure you'll love the *tennis*, Zac, but are you seeing someone? Or are you doing the usual and dating every hot woman in sight, once and only once?"

"I love you too, Mel. How's my favorite niece?"

"Zachary Danvers, don't change the subject! Besides, I need details before I spill about Sophie."

He remained tight-lipped.

At first, she pouted, then she used her whiny voice—the one she knew he couldn't stand. "Please, Zac. Have some sympathy for a heavily pregnant woman whose husband is perfect, whose daughter is wonderful, and who needs to hear some gossip."

"Okay, but just to be clear? You look amazing, Mel, considering you're due at the end of the month."

"Thanks, but stop delaying."

"You know I plan on being there as soon as my niece or nephew's born, right?"

Melanie let out an exasperated huff. "And you know I'd come to New York and murder you if you weren't gonna be here, but if you don't tell me who you've been eating romantic dinners with, I'm going to find another godfather for this child I'm carrying." Her free hand settled on her adorable baby bump, and an ache had formed in Zac's chest.

"You drive a hard bargain, Mel." Sighing, he counted to three. "Her name's Emma, and it's been two dinners." He refused to count their first one as a date—a family restaurant was no place to enjoy a romantic dinner.

"Finally, a name!" Her grin reminded him of a child in a candy store being told they could choose whatever they desired. "Emma sounds pretty. Is she pretty?"

"You're incorrigible, Mel!"

"Answer the question, Zac!"

"Hey! Don't go all lawyer-like on me."

At that point, his sister turned away from the camera and shouted, "Sophie, come talk to Uncle Zac. I gotta go pee."

The rest of the call knocked him for a six. All Sophie talked about was 'Miss Alex this' and 'Miss Alex that'. The more he heard, the more he admired the woman. Kind, patient, and dedicated—basically a superstar. She'd baked, cooked, skated, swum, danced, drawn and painted pictures, and visited museums and parks with Sophie—the list went on and on.

Alexandra Masters was going to make a fantastic mother and a wonderful wife one day. Sophie even raved about the lunches Alex had cooked for her. Well-balanced meals, if he could believe his niece. Listening patiently to all her news, Zac hoped he responded appropriately, but as soon as he could, he ended the call.

He could only hear so much about the woman of his dreams.

As he waited to cross the street at the corner of fifth and seventy-ninth, his thoughts turned to Alex's boyfriend. Jack was the luckiest guy on the planet. Whenever Zac spoke to Melanie, he dreaded hearing an announcement. No way would he be attending Alex's wedding.

Good thing he lived many miles away because if he *did* live in New Haven, he would ask Alex to marry him instead.

Boyfriend or no boyfriend.

An hour later, Zac was in his office with Dan, who lounged in one of the wingback chairs, his sun-kissed appearance giving off a healthy glow.

"A month was a long time, but vacationing with your family apparently suits you," Zac said.

"It certainly did." Dan's smile split his lightly wrinkled face. "I assume everything went well while I was away."

It wasn't a question, and Dan's smug expression brought back all those unwanted feelings of betrayal and disappointment Zac thought he'd dealt with. "All things considered," he said, his tone colder than intended.

"I knew Trevor would be a good fit, and since neither of you contacted me while I was away, I was obviously right."

Incredibly, Dan seemed oblivious to his indignation.

“Actually, the first two weeks were more stressful than I ever imagined,” Zac said, his anger simmering under the surface. “Honestly, I was ready to tear my hair out, Dan. Your replacement was more of a hindrance than a help.”

Dan’s face fell, and he seemed at a loss for words.

Zac let him stew for a few seconds, then carried on. “Only after I had a serious word with Trevor about trusting his gut did he become a new person. The one time he asked about contacting you, I put the fear of God into him. I said if he so much as texted you, I’d throw him out on his ear and bad mouth his name all over town.”

Dan scowled. “You didn’t.”

“Of course not! I told him your phone wouldn’t work overseas, and he believed me.”

“I owe you, Zac. Time with my family was a real eye-opener; it made me re-think things.”

“Like ditching me and moving to Virginia?”

“You weren’t supposed to know about that.”

“Don’t you think I had a *right* to know?” Zac’s voice rose as his anger got the better of him.

“You did. But I hadn’t decided one way or another before I left for Asia, and I didn’t want to cause you any undue stress.”

“Really, Dan? You must’ve been rather serious since you mentioned it to Trevor; gave him expectations.”

“I’m sorry. I should’ve warned you first. I made a mistake.”

They sat in silence for a few beats before Zac became impatient. “So, *have* you decided now?”

“I’m not moving.”

A whoosh of air he hadn’t realized he was holding in escaped.

"My wife and I talked a lot about leaving New York. The kids too. We all agreed it's not the time to make any big changes. I contemplated Virginia because I felt my family was unhappy here, but I discovered they're not. They only wanted more time with me. So I made a different decision. Before I make it official, I wanted to talk it over with you."

Zac swallowed, rubbing the scar on his chin.

"I thought it would be prudent to make Trevor a permanent partner. It would lighten both our workloads and grant me additional time with my family and you with yours in New Haven." Dan leaned forward, his expression hopeful. "Is this something you could get behind, Zac? I believe your sister's second child is due soon, and I assume you'd want to visit for longer than one day, right?"

"Yep, and I think it's a fantastic plan."

"Phew," Dan said, swiping a hand over his brow.

"I don't know why we haven't considered this before." Zac paused, his excitement growing at the possibilities. "Trevor's taken on a handful of new clients, but I suppose we could hand over a few of our own. Maybe even the more challenging ones?"

At Dan's disapproving frown, he chuckled. "Just kidding!" he said, raising his hands. "He'll also need his own space. How about we clear out that third office we've been using as a glorified filing cabinet?"

"That's a brilliant idea!" Dan's grin was contagious, though Zac couldn't see which of theirs was the widest. "This is the right thing for us, Zac. I feel it in my bones."

He knew it, too. No doubt, Melanie and his parents would be thrilled with the news, *and* he'd finally get to see Alex more.

Suddenly, he had a thought, and his smile faltered.

Could he really handle Jack's girlfriend being present at every turn?

All his recent elation steadily deflated, similar to a balloon receiving a pinprick. Being in the same city, most likely the same venue and even more possibly, the same room as Alex on multiple occasions, was going to test his willpower to the limit.

Maybe having extra time on his hands wasn't the answer.

Chapter Thirteen

Desperate to stop the ringing, Alex batted aimlessly at her nightstand. Still half asleep, she eventually curled her fingers around the offending object and peered bleary-eyed at her phone screen. Five o'clock!

Wincing, she swiped open the message from Steven: ***At hospital. M in labor. Sophie slept over with grandparents. S***

Okay, so, for now, she was off the hook for babysitting duties. As she set her phone down, a sigh of excitement escaped. The baby was finally on its way!

Pulling the comforter right up to her neck, she squeezed her eyes shut and tried to return to a blissful state of unconsciousness.

Not that it worked.

Wide awake, probably two hours before the sun, it seemed pointless trying to get back to sleep. Though it could be hours yet, visions of holding Melanie's baby invaded her thoughts, and she couldn't wait.

No point wasting her day.

She pushed off the covers and slipped her feet into fur-lined slippers. Even if she went for a run, showered, and had a cooked breakfast afterward, she'd likely have enough time to prepare her next week's lesson plans before needing to head over to the hospital.

After finishing her last bit of schoolwork around lunchtime, she grabbed her phone for the hundredth time, jumping when the text tone sounded. She scanned Steven's latest message: ***Baby boy just delivered:) Visiting hours 'til 8. Come when it suits. S***

At long last!

Thirty minutes later, she arrived at New Haven hospital, grateful for the relatively easy parking. Holding a blue gift bag in one hand and a bouquet of yellow, blue, and white flowers in the other, she slammed the door closed with her hip.

She'd just reached the top of a short flight of stairs to the entrance when her name was called. Glancing over her shoulder, she saw Jack bounding up the last few steps. He looked cool and casual in a white v-neck T-shirt paired with a light gray knit sweater, black trousers, and sneakers.

"Alex! I thought it was you." A smile lit his handsome face, and for a nanosecond, the little tug on her heart had her doubting her decision to call it quits.

"You look great, Jack."

"So do you," he said, his gaze skimming over her. "Gorgeous, actually."

She flushed. The long-sleeved red dress, which floated down to her ankles and had a scooped neckline wasn't her usual style, but she'd felt like changing it up. The possibility of running into Zac today hadn't entered her mind at all.

Jack stuck out a hand. "Need some help?"

She eyed the diaper cake he held and laughed. "I'll manage, thanks."

"Suit yourself."

At the main reception, they were given directions to Melanie's private room in the maternity ward on the fourth floor.

After pressing the elevator call button, Alex smiled at Jack. "I've been waiting to hold this baby since Monday—Mel's *actual* due date."

The metal doors slid open, and they stepped inside.

"Be warned," Jack said, sounding ominous. "He'll most likely look like an alien." She arched an eyebrow, and he grinned. "You know—pointy head, puffy eyes, and a flattened nose."

She giggled. "Similar to your nephews when you first saw them, I suppose?"

"Yep. Ugly and beautiful at the same time."

After the short ride, they stepped off the elevator toward yet another light-colored wooden desk. The wall covered in brightly painted pictures of storks and sailboats around a lake assured Alex they were in the right place.

A woman, wearing a floral print shirt, looked up from behind the reception counter. "Can I help you?"

"Which room for Melanie MacAlistar, please?" Jack asked.

"Down the corridor. Last door on your right."

"Thank you."

Inside the doorway, Alex paused, her gaze darting around the smart, modern room. Over on the far side, Steven held a white bundle, his face a picture of tenderness and joy.

A long couch was situated conveniently under a large picture window, and a changing table was positioned opposite the hospital bed. Melanie lay in bed, her hair in a tangled mess on the pillow. Her face was drawn, despite the sparkle in her eyes.

Jack reached her first. "Congratulations, Mel," he said, kissing her on the cheek.

"Thank you, Jack, and thanks for the cake." Melanie waved at his gift.

"You're welcome," he said before moving over to Steven, no doubt to inspect the 'alien'.

Chuckling, Alex off-loaded the flowers, as well as the bag containing a small white teddy bear and a box of Steven's favorite chocolates, onto the nightstand.

"Another miracle, Mel," she said, bending to embrace her friend. "And this time with the father around. I'm so proud of you." She straightened, quickly clasping Melanie's hand in hers when she saw tears threatening to fall.

"I did it the right way this time, didn't I?" Melanie sniffed, peering over at her husband. Steven was doing that you're-the-only-one-in-the-world thing with his eyes as he gazed at his wife.

Alex's stomach tightened.

Banishing the ridiculous feeling of jealousy, she forced herself to focus on the reason for her visit. "I would say fatherhood suits you, Steven," she said warmly, "but we already knew that, so congratulations on the birth of your son. I bet Sophie was thrilled to meet her brother."

"She was, and we took pictures, but I'll show you later." Steven beamed with joy. "I'm a little busy at the moment."

Alex stepped toward the men, her eyes on the baby. "Mind if I hold him? Maybe you and Jack could grab us some coffee?"

Patting Steven's shoulder, Jack grinned. "You look like you could do with some caffeine, man."

"Yeah, probably."

"Hey, my husband is hot!" Melanie exclaimed loudly, then muttered, "Even if he *is* more tired than me."

Steven laughed, carefully placing his child in Alex's outstretched arms, and walked over to his wife.

"Thanks, darling. I love you," he said, bending to kiss her soundly on the lips. He nodded his head toward Alex. "Why don't you rest while Alex is here? I'll be back in a bit."

"Okay," Melanie agreed, her eyelids fluttering closed as if under his spell.

Steven mouthed to Alex, "She's exhausted," then pointed to the beige couch.

Taking the hint, she strode over to the window and sank into the comfortable seat.

Once the men were gone, she happily inhaled the baby's powdered scent while examining the tiny human in her arms—not an alien at all. Gorgeous with dark blue eyes, a sprinkling of fuzz for hair, and not an imperfection in sight.

She so wanted one of her own. Another reason it wouldn't have worked out with Jack. At the mere mention of children, he'd grimaced alarmingly. She suspected he figured his sister's three were plenty.

Did Zac want children?

She had no idea. Not that it had anything to do with her, though maybe she'd ask him sometime, just out of interest.

For that matter—where was Zac? The notion he could appear any second had her heart picking up speed.

***

Steven's text had come in at five a.m, and soon after, Zac had been driving down the I-95 toward New Haven.

At the hospital, he'd found his mom pacing in the waiting room, and he'd offered to grab them some cafeteria coffee. Then, while they'd sat on hard plastic chairs with their drinks, it was the anticipation of the imminent birth that had kept him alert.

Not the fact Alex could've shown up at any time.

Roughly an hour ago, he'd finally gotten to meet his nephew. The experience had been awesome, but now he needed to stretch his legs. So, nursing his third coffee of the day, he ventured out of the building and along sidewalks scattered with red, orange, and bronze leaves. Fresh air, quite different from the hospital's antiseptic-smelling air, filled his lungs while his mind drifted to last night.

After watching the latest Flatliners movie with Emma, they'd enjoyed a lively debate about the similarities and differences between the two versions. It was only when he caught Emma stifling a yawn that he'd noticed it was midnight.

Easy to regret the late night, in hindsight.

The hospital building came back into view, and without warning, Zac's stomach knotted. Alex hadn't arrived...but she would, and he couldn't stay away much longer. It wasn't fair to Steven, who needed a break, too, especially since he was exhausted after not sleeping all night.

Fourteen weeks and six days—that's when he'd last seen Alex. Longer since he'd held her in his arms and felt her lips on his. Yet, their last kiss was still fresh in his mind.

He should be over her by now. Particularly with someone amazing like Emma in his life. Reminding himself Alex wasn't available helped a little, but only in his head.

Mind over matter. It had to be.

Clenching his fists and pursing his lips, he strode back to the maternity ward. As he drew closer to Melanie's room, he heard a soft, familiar voice, and his pulse skyrocketed.

He crept into the doorway and paused. Alex sat on the couch under the window, her entire focus on the child she held. She was absolutely stunning in her red dress.

Smiling, he pulled out his phone—thankfully on silent—and captured the moment. A quick glance toward the bed showed his sister fast asleep. Good. He could send her the photo later.

"Hello, Zac," Alex said, her voice emotionless, her expression guarded.

The cool greeting hurt, but what had he expected? They weren't exactly friends, and it's not like they kept in touch. Faking a smile, he injected nonchalance into his tone as he said, "I see you've met the latest addition to the MacAlistar family."

"He's gorgeous," she murmured, staring down at the baby in her arms.

"He's not the only one." The words flew from his mouth before he could stop them.

Alex's head shot up, her brows pulled together in consternation. "Zac, don't."

A noise behind them had him spinning on his foot.

"Don't what?" Jack stood just inside the room, a cup of steaming liquid in each hand, concern written all over his face. Next to him, Steven appeared equally uneasy.

Zac froze.

"Don't...just stand there," Alex said, recovering quickly. Pushing to her feet, she moved toward him. "Please, take this precious child. I have to leave."

Was she leaving because his presence made her uncomfortable or because Jack had brought their coffee? How long had she been here anyway? He must've just missed her.

As Alex passed the blanketed baby over to him, her hand brushed against his, sending tiny sparks up his arm. He had to resist the urge to rub the affected area.

"See you around, Zac." Alex didn't quite meet his eyes and sounded decidedly frosty.

"I wouldn't count on it," he responded tersely, willing her to look at him. When she did, the hurt he detected hit him unexpectedly. Still, he couldn't help trying to protect himself. "I'm heading back to the city in the morning. There are important things I need to get back to."

Not true, Dan had told him to take as long as he needed, but Alex didn't need to know how seeing her with Jack affected him. Nor about the building desire he had to take her in his arms and kiss her. It was better if she thought she didn't matter to him.

"Oh, okay." Surprise crossed her face and possibly disappointment. But maybe he just saw what he wanted to see.

Alex headed over to Jack, her smile affectionate as he handed her one of the coffees. "Thanks, you're a lifesaver," she said warmly.

An ache formed in Zac's chest. How he longed for her to smile at him that way. Like he was important to her. Because she meant the world to him.

"I'll walk out with you," Jack said to Alex, then turned to Zac. "Glad you made it. It's been a while since we saw you. Take care, Zac."

With his throat closed tight, all he could manage was a short nod.

Jack shook Steven's hand. "Congrats again, man. I'll be in touch."

"Thanks for coming and for the gifts." Steven brushed his hand over Alex's elbow. "See you soon?"

She nodded, and the couple left.

Steven glared at Zac. "You said you'd be staying for a few days."

"I was. But something's come up, and I need to be back in New York tomorrow." He hated lying, but he couldn't stay here in this city knowing Alex was so close by, yet so far away.

Unnerved by his brother-in-law's silence, Zac broke eye contact and searched for another topic. "Why don't you have a rest?" A perfectly reasonable suggestion considering the black rings under Steven's eyes. "I've got your son."

Thankfully, Steven didn't argue with him. Instead, he wandered straight over to the couch.

Zac followed him to where the generous picture window overlooked the hospital parking lot. It was easy to spot Alex in her red dress, conversing with Jack in front of her car. Unable to hear their words or read their expressions, Zac held his breath while his gaze remained glued to the scene playing out four floors below.

After a long embrace, the couple shared a brief kiss. It was torture to witness, but he hoped the reality of the situation would freeze his heart once and for all.

A man could only hope.

Chapter Fourteen

The next morning, Zac rubbed his eyes then peered at the clock on the nightstand—09:59! Why hadn't Mom woken him up?

He listened carefully, but the house was utterly silent. Visiting hours began at ten, so he assumed his parents had taken Sophie to the hospital.

Yawning, he stretched out his arms and twisted his neck from side to side. If he was quick, he could probably shower, grab some breakfast, and be at the hospital within the hour. He'd already made plans to take Emma out to dinner tonight, so he didn't have a choice in sticking around too long after lunch. Anyway, the sooner he left, the better—less chance he'd bump into Alex again.

Zac entered Melanie's hospital room just before eleven and found her rubbing circles on her son's back. Despite the eight-year age gap between her children, his sister already appeared to be an expert at caring for a newborn.

"Hi, Mom," he teased.

Melanie pursed her lips. "It's weird hearing you call me that."

"Sorry, I couldn't resist. Where's Steven?"

"I sent him home to rest." At his raised eyebrows, she grinned cheekily. "Poor man slept there overnight." She pointed to the sofa under the window and grimaced. "I thought it looked comfortable enough, except he woke up complaining of backache. I should've realized it was a bad idea, what with him tossing and turning all night."

"I won't complain about the twelve hours solid sleep I had then."

Chuckling, she shook her head. "Best you don't."

She repositioned her son so that Zac was able to stare into his cute little face. As it reddened, Melanie's nose wrinkled.

"Guess his diaper needs changing," she said.

Zac took a step closer. "Let me."

"You sure?"

"Hey, I may not have been around much when Sophie was little, but I do remember watching you change a diaper. Besides, I'll need the practice if I plan on being a hands-on dad one day."

"Be my guest then." She handed over her stinky son with a grin.

After a lot of instruction, the little guy smelled all powdery and adorable again. Warmth filled Zac's heart as he gazed at the baby's sweetest face. How long would he have to wait for one of his own? A vision of Alex holding this same child yesterday came to mind. She'd painted the perfect picture of mother and child, and a longing to complete that scene someday made his chest ache.

"All done," he said, smiling tightly and lowering the precious child back into his mother's arms. Balling his hands into fists, he swung away from them and headed to the window.

"You know, you'll make a fantastic father someday, right?" Melanie said brightly.

He shrugged, looking through the dirty glass and expecting to see storm clouds to match his sudden mood. Instead, the sky was blemish-free.

"Is it something you and Emma have discussed?"

Turning slowly, he jammed his hands into the pockets of his denim trousers. "Emma's much younger than me, Mel. She isn't exactly in a rush to tie the knot again, and even if she remarries, she'd want to wait a few years."

"I see."

Her disappointment hurt. She probably expected him to marry Emma in the next six months and get her pregnant within the year so the cousins would be of similar ages. Then, no doubt, he'd be encouraged to move back home so his child could grow up with family.

Yeah, that wasn't likely to happen.

Firstly, if he did marry Emma, and honestly, he wasn't even thinking that way, he'd respect her wishes and wait until she was ready to have a child. Secondly, Emma wouldn't wish to live in New Haven when all her family was in New York.

Besides, what would Dad think if he up and left his New York practice? He had a duty to both Dad and himself to stick to what he'd started.

No, his home and future were in New York, no matter what.

Later, when Zac left the hospital, he spotted a pretty face outside the main entrance. Dressed in a red silk shirt and short tan skirt, she strolled right toward him.

"Hey, Zac."

"Hey, Julie," he said, automatically gathering her in his arms and breathing in her familiar strawberry scent.

When they broke apart, her eyes were sparkling, and for what felt like ages, her gaze roamed over his features. With any luck, she wouldn't spot any telltale strain and drill him accordingly.

"It's so good to see you," she said.

He smiled. "You too. You look amazing! Definitely killing the on-your-way-to-being-famous look."

Blushing, she beamed at him. "Charming as ever, Dr. Danvers."

"It's only the truth." He touched her arm. "You on your way to see my nephew?"

She nodded. "I was stuck at work all day yesterday. But I had some time today, so I figured, why not? I bet he's the cutest, right?"

"Yep." He chuckled. "I *may* be a tiny bit biased."

She glanced over his shoulder to the doors. "Listen, are you in a rush? I'd love to catch up over lunch...if you have time?"

"I do." He wouldn't get another opportunity to spend time with her like this, not in the foreseeable future anyway.

While Julie visited with his sister and family, Zac bought a coffee in the cafeteria and waited. By the time she sat down at his table, he'd waded through a bunch of work emails.

"Thanks for waiting, Zac."

"Of course."

He pocketed his phone and briefly studied the large room with its rectangular wooden tables and large open windows letting in the light.

"Not the fanciest of settings, and I doubt they have table service, but if you're happy to stand in line with me, I'm sure they'll have something to curb our appetites."

"It's fine," she said, without looking around. "I'm just glad I bumped into you."

Trust her to make him feel better.

Not long after they had ordered, collected, and eaten their food, their plates were clear. Julie had devoured a whole roasted vegetable pizza while he'd polished off a pepperoni one.

She wiped her mouth and smiled. "That was actually delicious."

"I hope I find space for dinner tonight," he said, patting his full stomach.

Julie lifted a brow.

"I promised Emma dinner."

"Emma?" She tapped her lip. "I don't recall you mentioning her."

For a moment, he'd forgotten he hadn't told Julie about Emma in the few messages they'd exchanged since July. Zac had worried she'd be disappointed, thinking he was settling, so he'd kept quiet.

Swallowing, he looked Julie in the eye. "We've been on a few dates."

"Uh-huh. So I take it you've decided to give up on Alex." Her eyes narrowed. "Is Emma your future then, Zac?"

"I'm not sure."

Relaxing back against her chair, Julie crossed her arms and scrutinized him. "I guess I overestimated your feelings for Alex. I really thought you'd stake your claim, given she's single."

What? His heart skipped a beat. She couldn't be serious!

"What are you talking about? Alex was here with Jack yesterday. I saw them hug and kiss in the car park afterward."

Confusion and hurt crossed Julie's face, but she recovered quickly. "You must've misread the situation, Zac. They broke up at Melanie's wedding. I don't think Jack's seen Alex since they watched Sophie during Melanie's honeymoon."

His jaw went slack, and the blood pumping in his heart made a thumping sound in his ears. Struggling to breathe, he fought for control of his emotions. Taking a deep breath, he closed his mouth and his eyes.

Three months! Alex had been single for three months, and he hadn't known. Melanie hadn't said a word. Did his sister assume he knew or think he wasn't interested in her best friend's love life? Probably the latter. Served him right for never admitting his feelings.

Why hadn't Alex let him know?

Yeah, right, she'd spent all of three minutes in his presence yesterday before she'd pretty much dropped his nephew in his arms and high-tailed it out of the hospital room. Her cold response should put him in his place.

She'd made her decision, just like he'd told her to after Sophie's party. He wasn't what she wanted, even when there was nothing left standing in her way.

Why did knowing that hurt so much?

***

"Benjamin James MacAlistar," Alex repeated as she smiled briefly at the sleeping child wrapped up tight in his blue fleece blanket. Her gaze lifted to his mom. "I love it, Mel. A strong name's important, it gives a child confidence, and I love that you can shorten it to Benji."

Melanie scowled. "Please don't call him that! Benji sounds like a dog!"

"Okay, okay." Chuckling, she held up a hand. "I promise. How about Ben?"

"Ben's perfect. Though, I can easily imagine using his full name when I'm mad with him."

Alex fake gasped. "I hope it'll be a few years before that happens!"

"Obviously," Melanie said with a humorous glint in her eye. Then she sobered. "Sophie's already discovered having a newborn in the house means her mother's not always on top of everything. Suddenly, my daughter's 'forgetting' to put her clothes in the laundry basket, leaving half-empty cups lying around, and taking longer in the bath."

Having a newborn—less than a week old—and an active eight-year-old couldn't be easy, even with Steven, an awesome husband and father, in the mix.

"It sounds like my goddaughter's feeling a little put out by all the attention on Ben," she said, giving Melanie a sympathetic look. "Don't worry, I've planned a special surprise for her at our sleepover tonight."

When Alex had dropped Sophie off two days ago, she'd mentioned to Melanie the possibility of Sophie staying over at hers.

"Oh, Alex, she'd love that!" Melanie had said enthusiastically before her smile waned. "My hands are full with Ben, and, although Steven's been a gem, leaving work early to take Sophie to her swimming lesson and to the playground, he can't do it every day."

"Why don't you let me babysit Ben after school for an hour or so? You can spend time helping Sophie with homework or do a girly activity with her."

"Are you sure?"

Alex had bobbed her head to show she meant it.

"You're a true friend and an ideal godmother," Melanie had said, hugging her tightly. "I can't tell how much I appreciate you."

"Well, one day, hopefully before I'm old and gray, you'll be returning the favor." She had tried not to sound rueful, but it was hard considering the state of her dating life.

"Don't be silly! I predict you'll be engaged if not married by this time next year." Melanie's confidence had been quite touching, albeit misguided.

The rush of emotion brought on by remembering that recent conversation caught Alex by surprise. She swallowed hard and turned away for a moment to take a deep breath.

"So when are you planning to see Michael again?"

Alex ran her hands down her jeans and picked at a raised white spot. Thankfully, just toothpaste, not the glue she'd used on her classroom artwork earlier.

"He wanted to see me tonight, but I told him I had a very important date."

"Alex!"

"Relax, Mel," she said, smirking at her friend's exasperated tone. "He's taking me out to dinner tomorrow night instead. He won't tell me where, just to dress comfortably and make sure I'm warm."

"Sounds intriguing. I want to hear all about it." Melanie glanced down at her son. "He'll be happy for a while yet. Why don't we go grab a snack or coffee? There's something else I want to talk to you about."

On their way out of the nursery, Alex admired the light blue walls and the mid-height border filled with pictures of various vehicles. Steven had won the battle, it seemed—his wife had wanted sea creatures.

In the large, modern kitchen, she got comfortable on a leather barstool and watched Melanie's slow, precise movements from across the granite island. While the coffee maker sputtered out its brew, the only other sound came from a lawn being mowed outside. Melanie turned, looking uneasy as she leaned against the far counter.

Alex frowned. "Should I be worried, Mel?"

"No. It's only...Steven and I decided we want Ben christened the way I did for Sophie."

"Oh." She laughed, the action loosening her stomach muscles. "A little early to worry about it now, don't you think? If I remember correctly, Sophie was six years old then, not seven days old," she teased.

"You're funny," Mel said. "We were thinking of Thanksgiving weekend as Zac's likely to be here then."

Alex's stomach muscles tightened all over again.

"He'll be Ben's godfather, obviously, and we'd love it if you'd be his godmother. I know you two are often at odds, but I'm not expecting you to get married or anything. Definitely not." Melanie shook her head as if to reiterate her statement. "But we *would* like our children to have the same godparents, at least."

"I understand," Alex said, smiling weakly. "It makes complete sense." Attempting to control her emotions, she squeezed her eyes tight for a second. "I'd be honored, Mel."

That evening, once the sun had set and the temperature had dipped, Alex brought an excited Sophie back to her apartment. After putting Sophie's overnight bag in the spare room, she handed her goddaughter a gift wrapped in sparkly pink paper.

Beaming as she hurriedly tore off the wrapper, Sophie dragged out the fifteen-inch baby doll and immediately hugged it to her chest. "Now I have my *own* baby to look after. Same as my mom." Sophie planted a kiss on its head, then snaked an arm around Alex's waist and squeezed. "Thanks, Miss Alex."

"My pleasure, sweetheart." Full of love for this precious little girl, Alex pressed her lips to the child's warm forehead while unexpected tears welled up. How much more would she love a child of her own? Banishing the thought, she focused on her overnight guest instead.

Unsurprisingly, Sophie insisted on carrying her gift everywhere. The doll was placed next to them as they colored pictures of princesses and castles, then lay alongside Sophie on the sofa as they played the Game of Life. It was the cutest thing, hearing Sophie imitating her parent's cooing. Clearly a hit, the doll was treated as well as the real thing, if not better.

For their dinner, they had Sophie's favorite meal—homemade burgers with all the fixings, as well as potato fries with the skins on. They rounded off their feast with ice cream and hot chocolate sauce, eaten in front of Sophie's favorite TV show.

Halfway through the second episode, Sophie raised her hand to cover her wide-open mouth. "It's time to put my baby to bed," she said.

"An excellent idea. Does your baby have a name yet?"

"Jamie."

"I like it. How about you get cleaned up with Jamie? Afterward, you can lay next to him while he goes to sleep, or else he might be a little unsettled sleeping in a new bed in a strange place. Don't you think?"

"Good idea, Miss Alex," Sophie agreed, taking their bowls to the kitchen sink, then picking up her doll and cradling it sweetly.

Later, while reading her baby a short bedtime story, Sophie crashed. Evidently, playing at being a mom was exhausting for her, but that didn't put Alex off at all.

She touched her lips to Sophie's temple and peered into her peaceful face. "Sweet dreams, Sophie," she whispered.

Traipsing back to the kitchen, she made herself a decaf hazelnut coffee—she needed to think, not stay up all night. Savoring the slightly sweet hot drink, she replayed Melanie's words over in her head. "I'm not expecting you to get married. Definitely not."

What exactly did *that* mean?

Wasn't she good enough for Zac, or did Melanie not want her for a sister-in-law? Or did Melanie have that opinion because she thought they hated each other?

What did it matter? The likelihood of her daydreams coming to pass was slim anyway.

Lately, all Melanie spoke of was Zac and Emma—the happy couple. Alex had learned to tune out any news of them.

Except, keeping out of Zac's way wasn't going to work as easily for her, especially as his sister's best friend. And not to mention as Zac's niece and nephew's godmother.

If there was any chance of having a family of her own, she needed to make a concerted effort to forget about Dr. Zac Danvers.

As if she hadn't already tried.

Chapter Fifteen

"Why on earth are you back at work, Zac?" Dan looked puzzled. "I thought you'd be with your family for at *least* a week."

"Nope." Zac tried to step past Dan, but a firm hand on his lower arm halted his progress.

"Were you worried Trevor and I wouldn't be able to cope without you?"

"Of course not!" Zac shook his head. "I trust you and Trevor." No way was he explaining why he'd returned to New York after fleeing New Haven prematurely. After hearing about Alex's relationship status, he definitely couldn't stay. And laying low in his apartment, just to save face, wasn't an option either.

Pushing Dan's hand away, Zac continued in the direction of his office. "I'll talk to you later," he said over his shoulder.

During the week, Zac took on additional cases at the hospital. No matter how much he immersed himself in work, though, his predicament was never far from his thoughts. It wasn't a solution, but the hard work made him feel numb and worn out. As a result, he fell straight into bed every night.

On Friday afternoon, knee-deep in a report for one of his patients, his office phone rang.

"Yes?" he answered, still reading his computer screen.

"Dr. Danvers, a new patient, Miss Anderson, is on the other line. She needs a consult. Can I put her through?"

"Transfer her to Dr. Johnson. New patients are his job," he growled.

"Um, she insisted on having you as her doctor."

"Fine." Sighing deeply, he dragged his gaze from his computer. "Maybe I'll have better luck doing *your* job."

"Thank you, Dr. Danvers," the receptionist said with kindness he didn't deserve.

He mentally counted to ten.

"Miss Anderson," he said evenly, tamping down his irritation, "I'm sorry, but I'm not taking on any new patients. I'll put you through to Dr. Johnson. He's an excellent doctor."

About to transfer the call, a familiar voice exclaimed, "Zac, don't hang up on me!"

"Emma?"

"Hi, Zac."

"I could've sworn my receptionist said Anderson, not Williams."

"Anderson's my maiden name. I was worried you wouldn't take my call."

"Why wouldn't I—?" he started, then broke off.

That's precisely what he'd been doing the whole week. Ignoring her texts too. He couldn't blame her for the underhanded tactic. Guilt kicked in.

"I'm sorry, Emma. I should've contacted you. It's just...I'm going through some stuff...nothing to do with you, I promise. I'm just not in a good place right now."

His attempt at a laugh came out sounding cynical. "Frankly, I'd be terrible company. Ask my colleagues."

"It's okay, Zac. I'm your friend." Surprisingly, she didn't sound angry or disappointed, just concerned. "I'll be here for you if or when you want to see me. All you have to do is call or text. Will you do that?"

"I will." He slumped back in his chair. "Thanks for understanding, Emma."

That weekend, Melanie called, and after exchanging pleasantries, she got right to the point. "Ben's being christened during the Thanksgiving holiday, and Steven and I need you to be there."

Was she kidding! He had no intention of stepping foot in New Haven. Not until he could feel emotionless when he looked at Alex.

He shoved a hand through his hair, grateful she couldn't see his frustration. "I'll try, Mel," he said, hoping to humor her.

"Zachary Danvers! You better more than *try* to be here for your nephew's special occasion. We can't have the service if one godparent is missing. You need to promise to come."

If she wasn't his sister, he'd be scared into submission by the fierceness in her voice alone.

"I didn't want to say anything, Zac, but it hurt when you only stuck around for one night after Ben's birth. I barely saw you. I thought Dan agreed to let you take as long as you needed. I know New Haven isn't New York City, but you have a family here who loves and misses you." He heard the break in her voice and hoped she wasn't crying.

"I know," he managed to say before she carried on.

"You know—" She sniffed, cleared her throat, then took an audible breath. "I'm beginning to suspect this has to do with Alex. Steven noticed your change in demeanor after you saw her at the hospital. You need to get over your problem with my best friend because she isn't going anywhere!"

He didn't know what to say.

"And she's going to be Ben's godmother."

Guessing *that* was easy.

The ache in his chest and the awful feeling in the pit of his stomach grew. Melanie was half right—he was avoiding New Haven because of Alex. Only her reasoning was flawed. It hurt knowing Alex was available but not interested. He kept thinking time away from her would help. Yet, he was stuck between a rock and a hard place.

"I'm sorry I didn't visit for longer when Ben was born," he admitted. "I really wanted to, but I just couldn't. I'll try to make it up to you, I promise. I'll come for Thanksgiving, and I'll be there for the ceremony, okay?"

"Thanks," she murmured. When she spoke again, she sounded a little more upbeat. "I know, why don't you bring Emma? I'd love to meet her, and I'm sure Mom and Dad would too."

"Why on earth would I do that? They'd have Emma and I married off before the end of the weekend."

"I thought..."

"You thought wrong. Emma and I are just friends. She may be interested in more, but she knows I'm not ready for a relationship. My heart belongs to another, sadly unrequited, but until I'm able to let go, there'll be nothing serious between Emma and me, or anyone else for that matter."

"I had no idea." After a few beats of silence, she asked, "Who is she?"

Zac sighed. Pointless worrying his sister with his love life. It wasn't like she could fix it or anything. "I can't have this conversation right now, Mel," he said hurriedly. "There's someone at the door. I need to go."

***

Three weeks later, Zac stuffed his hands into his pockets and stared at the carpet as he left Dan's office.

'A friendly chat'—yeah, right! His partner didn't miss a thing. He should've realized his foul mood wouldn't go unnoticed or unchallenged. Dan's concern was touching, but now it meant he would *have* to get his act together. Pretend, if need be. Either way, he had a professional duty to his patients, and he couldn't let them down. Or Dan.

In a few minutes, the office would be closed for Halloween, so at least he wouldn't be required to face another patient tonight. Tomorrow he'd be acting his heart out, convincing everyone he hadn't a care in the world.

As he entered his office, a light flashed on his desk. He picked up his cellphone and opened the message from Emma: ***Can't wait to go Trick or Treating with you! Don't be late.***

A chuckle escaped his lips. She was such a big kid!

He glanced up, spotted the time on his red, retro wall clock, and groaned. He needed to go.

Grabbing the black cape from his chair and the fake fangs from his desk drawer, he rushed out to hail a cab. Thank goodness he'd had the foresight to wear a black suit and white shirt today. With any luck, he'd make it to Emma's with minutes to spare.

An hour later, Emma was laughing with him and clutching the plastic jack-o'-lantern to her chest. "That was so much fun!"

"I hope they don't send the cops after us." Zac peeped around a corner of the building, fully expecting to see their victims in hot pursuit. Plenty of costumed people roamed the street, but no one appeared to be chasing them. He turned to Emma. "You could've warned me you were harboring a weapon."

"What?" She grinned cheekily, her chocolate-colored eyes sparkling. "And miss the look on your face when I squirted the water?" She shook her head. "No way."

"Fine," he said gruffly, "but it's my turn next."

By the time their lantern was half full of candy, they were exhausted from escaping shocked homeowners. Apparently, no one expected adults to be doing tricks.

Passing by a coffee shop, he grasped Emma's hand. "I could kill for a drink. How about you?"

"Do you need this?" She pulled out her water gun, giggling.

"Ha ha," he said, hiding the toy back in her lantern. "I'm serious."

"I'd love a coffee."

Armed with pumpkin-spiced lattes, they found a couple spare cushioned chairs inside the shop, where they could watch the other Halloween revelers outside.

Zac fixed his gaze on Emma, a genuine smile lifting his lips. "I haven't had this much fun in ages. It's been a blast, all because of you."

"My pleasure. You needed to get out of your funk."

"What?" He pretended to be offended. "Me in a funk, never!"

They both laughed.

Her delight softened his heart. How could anyone not like her? She was fun, patient, and beautiful. He'd been keeping things casual up until now, but maybe he needed to take the plunge, see where this went.

Their gazes collided, and his heartbeat accelerated a notch. He leaned in, covering her hand with his. "You're a good influence on me, Emma," he said earnestly.

When she attempted to pull her hand away, he panicked and tightened his grip.

"I want to see more of you," he clarified, in case she'd misunderstood. He hoped he wasn't making the wrong move. Stroking his thumb over her knuckles, he observed her closely. Tiny wrinkles appeared around her eyes as her easy smile returned, and her hand relaxed beneath his.

"Really?"

He nodded.

"I'd like that too."

Long after their seasonal lattes were finished, their conversation continued to flow. They covered a myriad of topics, from family vacations to dreams for the future.

"I love New York," she said, her lips curving up as a light danced in her eyes. "I see myself getting married here, living in an apartment overlooking Central Park, and running after my children while they enjoy the fresh air and nature, right on their doorstep."

"Your family's all here, aren't they?"

"Yes. I don't know how women have kids and bring them up without the help of parents and siblings." She shook her head. "I just couldn't."

"I know what you mean. My sister, Mel, would've struggled if she hadn't had first my grandma, then my parents to help with Sophie when she was little. Of course, Alex is a great help too."

Now, why had he gone and brought her up?

Emma quirked an eyebrow. "Alex?"

"My sister's best friend and my niece Sophie's godmother."

His jaw clenched. This conversation needed a re-direct, fast. Talking about Alex was out of the question. Bad enough, he was going to have to face her sooner than he'd hoped. Thanksgiving and Ben's christening were only three weeks away!

"It's late," he said, pushing to his feet after making a show of checking his watch. He scooped up their cups. "I'd better get you home."

Outside Emma's front door, Zac let go of her hand and waited for her to find her key. Once she found it, she gave him a wobbly smile.

He took a step closer, sliding his hands onto her hips, his eyes locked on hers. "Tonight's been amazing, Emma. You're amazing."

"So, hopefully, a Halloween to remember." She giggled, her gaze lowering to his lips.

Taking that as a sign, Zac dipped his head and kissed her.

Chapter Sixteen

Alex pulled into Melanie's driveway, killed the engine, and tensed. When had she last seen her best friend's brother? Eight weeks ago? Thanksgiving was the day after tomorrow, and Zac would be here.

Her traitorous heart skipped a beat as she glanced at her passenger in the rearview mirror. "Sophie, you're home," she said.

Engrossed in a book, Sophie didn't even lift her eyes. Not even when a notification pinged on Alex's phone—an animal video from Michael—no doubt one she'd be laughing at later.

Alex recalled their recent second date. Michael had been attentive and charming, as well as humorous. After driving her home, he insisted on opening the passenger door for her. Then, clasping her hand in his, he'd walked her to her front door.

"You're a true gentleman, Michael, thank you."

"My mother would kill me if she discovered otherwise." A broad smile had settled on his handsome face, his gaze drifting to her lips. When he moved into her personal space, she'd planted a restraining hand on his solid chest and felt his rapid heartbeat.

Hers had picked up pace too. “Michael, trust me, I want to kiss you,” she’d said softly. “It’s... I’m just not ready.”

With an unsure half-smile, he’d backed away. “I understand. We can hang out as friends until you are. I can do that.” He’d nodded slowly. “Because you’re worth it.”

Did Zac think Emma was worth it? She must be someone special since he hadn’t made any effort to visit New Haven after Ben’s birth. These were exciting times. His godchildren were growing and changing daily, and he was missing out. Or maybe he was just more interested in developing his relationship with Emma.

Out of the corner of her eye, Alex saw Melanie rushing toward the car. Sophie must’ve too because she released her seat belt and shouted “Mommy!” before hopping out.

Lowering her window, Alex watched as two of her favorite people hugged like they hadn’t seen each other for a week. She sighed. Mother and daughter—such a special bond. Would she ever have that?

“Please, can I watch some TV, Mommy?” Sophie asked, stepping out of her mother’s embrace. “I have the *whole* weekend to do my homework.”

Alex chuckled. *Smart girl.*

“Only for an hour, Sophie-girl.”

“Thanks!” The child scuttled into the house, her backpack bouncing as she disappeared through the open door.

Melanie rounded the trunk to the driver’s side. “Hey, Alex, would you like to come in? We’re ordering pizza later, and you’re welcome to stay. The next few days will be busy, and I’d love the chance to catch up before Zac arrives. After that...” Melanie trailed off.

It would be better if you stayed out of the way. Alex mentally finished the sentence as a sharp pain stabbed her chest.

Well, that suited her fine. Just fine. The closer Thanksgiving got, the more she tried not to think about Zac. At times, she felt desperate enough to concoct plans to be alone with him. Girlfriend or not. At other times, she knew his girlfriend was precisely why she needed to stay away from him. She'd made the mistake of kissing him when he was with Julie. It was wrong, and Alex knew she was a terrible person.

This Emma was an unknown entity. With her joining Zac on his visits home, it meant Thanksgiving, Christmas, and birthdays were going to be challenging occasions. If Emma was the one Zac was destined to be with, then Alex shouldn't interfere.

"Sure. Sounds great, Mel. Let me grab my purse."

They first went to check on Ben, who was fast asleep in his crib. Peering down at his adorable face, Alex couldn't help the tug on her heart. His little lips moved like he was sucking something, and he made the cutest little noises. Resisting the urge to cuddle him, she crept away and waited for Melanie to adjust his covers.

In the kitchen, Alex was handed a frothy hot drink. Cradling it in her hands, she inhaled the spicy aroma of the coffee. "Thanks, Mel."

"No problem." Melanie picked up her mug of herbal tea and blew over the top. "Can you believe this holiday's come around again so quickly?"

"I remember it like it was yesterday," she said, inspecting her hands. "The wonderful meal we had at your parents, the ping-pong match—"

"My brother having to apologize to you for his awful behavior."

"Mmm." She closed her eyes for a moment. That was the first time Zac had kissed her, and she'd slapped him. Sure, he shouldn't have kissed her, but she'd kissed him back too. Feeling her cheeks heat, she lifted her mug to her lips to hide them. "That too."

"I hope he behaves this year. Steven's planning to have words with him the minute he arrives."

"He doesn't need to do that on my account, Mel. I can defend myself."

"I'm sure you can, but I have a feeling this year could be worse."

"I don't understand. Why?" she asked, trying not to sound too curious.

"Zac's been behaving rather strangely lately, and I'm a little concerned. Whenever I speak to him, I get the feeling he's hiding something."

Anxious to steer this conversation in a different direction, Alex said the first thing she could think of– "You must be looking forward to meeting Emma."

Now, why had she gone and brought *her* up?

"Oh, I forgot to tell you, she's not coming."

"What? Why not?"

"The last time I talked to Zac, he made it perfectly clear they were just friends."

"Oh."

"I think he's in love with someone else." Melanie's face took on a faraway look as she sipped her drink. "Actually, his words were–" She tapped her lips with her index finger. "'My heart belongs to someone else, but she doesn't feel the same'. I've no idea who he might be referring to, do you?"

She shook her head. Then, processing Melanie's words and their possible meaning, she drew in a sharp breath.

Had Zac been talking about her? Those incredible kisses had to mean something, right?

Hope bubbled up, and the edges of her mouth tugged upward until she noticed Melanie's troubled expression.

"I love my brother dearly, but I feel sorry for this woman," she said. "He's so dedicated to his job it's a wonder he's found time to like anyone, let alone fall in love. Only a New Yorker could understand him, and it's one of the reasons Emma sounded perfect to me."

Alex pressed her lips together while Melanie tucked a hair behind her ears. She gave Alex a lopsided smile. "It's a good thing there's never been anything between the two of you. I couldn't bear it."

***

Two days later, during her drive to the Danvers' house for Thanksgiving lunch, Alex's thoughts tumbled around like clothes in a dryer. The main attraction? Their son, Zac, of course.

So what if his kisses had been absolutely mind-blowing? He'd never indicated any desire to see her outside of organized family events. He'd never even asked her out!

To be fair, she *had* been dating for most of the time, but she'd broken up with Jack five months ago!

Crazy to even think Zac was in love with her. Besides, Melanie was right. It had to be someone else—a New Yorker—someone who understood his need to work hard, who understood his love of the city. Not a New Haven teacher who couldn't possibly measure up to the fabulous women surrounding him in New York City. Curious, she'd googled some of his events. Photo after photo had shown stunning women wearing exquisite evening gowns.

A bitter laugh escaped. Who was she kidding? She'd never fit in, even if—and that was a huge if—she was the love of Zac's life. And, along with her already conflicted feelings about him, she couldn't ignore Melanie's negative vibes either.

A sedan with New York plates was the first thing Alex noticed when she turned into the Danvers' driveway. The knots in her stomach intensified.

Maybe this wasn't such a great idea.

Before she could shift into reverse, a pickup truck—Melanie and Steven's—pulled in behind her, blocking her escape route.

She smacked the dash a couple of times, then switched off her car and climbed out. Keeping a tight hold on her homemade pumpkin pie, she waited on the path for the MacAlistars to join her. The chilly November breeze blew over her, and she shivered.

"Miss Alex!" Sophie said brightly. "You look so pretty in your purple dress."

She smiled. "Thanks. You look real pretty too."

Beaming, Sophie twirled to show off her red lace skater dress.

"Sophie's right, Alex. You *do* look beautiful, and I bet Michael would agree," Melanie said with a cheeky grin."

"Thanks." Smoothing her hand over the velvet fabric, she remembered the way the full skirt had swirled around her knees when she'd checked in the mirror earlier. One man had crossed her mind when she'd picked out the dress, and it hadn't been Michael.

Steven, carrying Ben's car seat, stopped alongside her. "Good to see you, Alex. Happy Thanksgiving."

"You too, Steven." She peeked at his precious cargo. "I swear your son sleeps more than he's awake."

"I say we enjoy it while it lasts." He chuckled, winking at his wife, who blew him a kiss in return.

Inside the house, Steven took his children to visit their granddad, who was rearranging furniture in the basement. Melanie opted to help her mom in the kitchen with the final food prep, and Alex followed suit.

When smells of roast turkey, sweet potatoes, and cranberry sauce filled the air, Mrs. Danvers smiled gratefully at them. "We're done here, ladies. Alex, would you mind finding Zac? Last time I looked, he was in the living room, sulking." She frowned. "I'm hoping he'll be in a better mood when he sees you."

Better mood? Had they argued? What about? Alex started to shake her head, but Mrs. Danvers' pleading expression made her capitulate. "Of course."

She spotted Zac from the living room entrance, slouching in front of the fireplace with his back to her. An empty whiskey glass was balanced precariously in his right hand, and apparently, he found the unlit firewood fascinating. Her pulse raced as she dragged her hands down the sides of her dress. She couldn't do this.

With a deep sigh, she turned away.

"Alex?" Zac's low, smooth voice touched her like a caress, creating mush of her insides.

Twisting, she gasped. Thick stubble covered his usually smooth jawline while his bloodshot eyes regarded her strangely. With his unruly dark brown hair, he was more madman than GQ model.

"I should've guessed Mom would send you." His unfriendly tone acted like a physical punch to her gut.

She stepped back. "You look terrible."

"Thanks, sweetheart. I hadn't a clue." Sarcasm dripped from his voice, while his clenched jaw made him seem fiercer.

"I don't need this," she said, raising her hands.

Swinging around, she navigated the long hall toward the kitchen on wobbly legs. Tears threatened to fall, so she detoured to the bathroom. Leaning on the sink for support, she realized one thing from that awful encounter—she was absolutely *not* the person Zac was pining over.

***

"There you are!" Mom exclaimed as Zac entered the dining room. She glanced sideways over his shoulder. "Where's Alex? You didn't chase her away with that bird's nest on your face, did you?"

He scowled. "Probably." Though, in all likelihood, his scruffy face wasn't the only thing to blame.

Seeing Alex was hard, just as he'd imagined. Preparing to be indifferent at the sight of her hadn't worked; in fact, he'd been completely thrown. She'd taken his breath away, and his disobedient heart had hammered in his chest. At that moment, all logical thought had fled, his appearance wholly forgotten. Ashamed, he'd reacted terribly to her comment.

Such an idiot! Why didn't he learn? Just because he was hurting didn't mean he had to hurt her too.

Kissing Emma hadn't produced the spark he'd anticipated, so he'd thrown himself into his work again, using this upcoming vacation as an excuse. Not shaving, missing his regular hair appointments, and barely sleeping—those had been the consequences.

As Thanksgiving approached, he'd dreaded this trip more and more. His plan of being in a committed relationship with Emma and treating Alex nonchalantly had been smashed to pieces. Instead, his escalating desire for her betrayed him. Clearly, there was no other woman for him. He'd tried.

"Uncle Zac!" Sophie jumped out of her chair and flung her arms around him. "You look like Santa, but with the wrong colored beard." Her eyebrows knitted together as she stared at him. "I don't think I like it."

Everyone laughed except him.

Taking his seat, Zac glanced at the empty chair and frowned. He really hoped Alex was coming back. One grilling about his appearance and attitude from his dad was plenty. He didn't need another confrontation because he'd scared off their guest.

"I'll say grace." Dad bowed his head, and everyone closed their eyes.

Weren't they going to wait for Alex?

"Father God, thank you for your goodness..."

Apparently not.

Seconds later, a sweet scent tickled Zac's nostrils, and his heart pounded. He immediately shut his eyes as Alex dropped into the chair beside him.

When the prayer was over, he peeked at Alex, shocked by the forlorn expression on her face.

Guilt assuaged him—this couldn't go on. He needed to tell her how he felt. That way, if she verbally rejected him, maybe he'd finally be able to move on.

Once everyone finished eating, Alex began stacking the dishes. "Let me clean up, Mrs. Danvers," she said. "It's the least I can do."

Melanie opened her mouth, but Zac spoke first. "I'll help."

"Thanks, but no need. I can manage," Alex insisted, continuing to clear the plates without looking at him.

"Alex, let him help you," Mom said, using her no-nonsense tone. "He hasn't lifted a finger since he showed up at seven this morning. It's the *least* he can do."

Trust Mom to make him feel better. He glared at her. "I love you too, Mom."

Patting him on the back, she smiled. "You're a good man, Zac. One who needs a decent shave and haircut, but a good man nonetheless."

Melanie snickered while Dad and Steven coughed discreetly.

In the kitchen, Alex remained tight-lipped and aloof, concentrating solely on the business of dishwashing. Zac dried the freshly cleaned bowls and glasses while she stood stiff and unyielding like a cell tower beside him. The whole operation didn't take long. Clearly, she was in a rush to be rid of his company.

The realization hurt.

"Thanks for your help," she said, keeping her back to him, her voice emotionless.

"You're welcome." He ran his fingers over his scratchy chin. "Alex?"

Slowly, her wary gaze met his.

"Can we talk?"

Her brow wrinkled. "Go ahead."

"Somewhere private?" He glanced over his shoulder. "I'd prefer not to be interrupted."

Fidgeting with the edge of her sleeve, she lifted her chin. "If you want to apologize, save it, Zac. I'm used to you by now."

She took a step to pass him, but he stopped her with his hand. Where it touched her skin, his fingers tingled. Their gazes collided, held. He didn't want to beg, but he was desperate. "Please?"

For a long moment, she studied him, then her eyes dipped. "Fine. Two minutes. The porch," she said.

She waltzed out the room while he followed, praying for the right words.

Outside, she rubbed her hands together briskly and stamped her boots. "One minute out here is long enough."

"I'll be quick." Swallowing hard, he pondered where to start but then just went with the truth. "Ever since we met, you've driven me crazy."

Lips twisting, her eyes went a darker shade of green. "No kidding."

He groaned. "I haven't been able to stop thinking about you, and trust me, I've tried." Her disbelieving look gave him pause.

"Carry on," she said, waving a hand. "You *did* hear me say you only have one minute, didn't you?"

Wiping his brow, he nodded. "The thing is—" This was harder than he'd thought. All in or bust, he supposed. "I'm in love with you."

"Oh." She said it like he'd simply told her the sun would rise again in the morning.

"Seriously?" Lightly gripping her upper arms, he peered deep into her eyes. "That's all you've got? Oh?"

She pushed his arms away and crossed her own. "Forgive me if I don't believe you, Zac," she said fiercely. "You haven't exactly acted like a man in love. If this is some kind of ploy to get me to kiss you, it isn't going to work this time."

Clenching his jaw, he fisted his hands and stared at her. "Last time I saw you, *Alex*, you were with Jack. I hadn't gotten the memo you'd broken up with him...*at my sister's wedding*."

"But I imagine you knew before lunch, yet you still behaved badly."

She was right. "I'm sorry," he said, gentling his tone.

Losing himself in her wounded eyes, his heart raced. She deserved more than an overused platitude.

“Will you please forgive me, Alex? It’s just...you threw me earlier with your shocked expression, and once again, my protective instinct kicked in. I didn’t mean to hurt you.”

“That’s no—”

“No excuse for my deplorable behavior, I know. It doesn’t change how I feel about you, though. I love you.” This time he spoke with greater conviction and was rewarded by her countenance gradually brightening. Still, he waited, scared to ruin the moment, knowing his minute was up.

She shuffled closer, placing her hands on his shoulders and peering straight at him. “So, you think you love me, do you?” Her flirty-sounding voice did nothing to help lessen his runaway pulse.

He smiled tentatively. “I do.” Covering her hands with his, his eyes darted to her lips, then rose again. “Desperately, without reservation, and to my detriment, I’m sure.”

Without warning, she closed the distance between them, her lips joining his effortlessly, bringing the spark he’d missed when kissing Emma.

Dropping his arms, Zac slipped his hands under Alex’s coat to her waist. She, in return, looped her arms around his neck. He pulled her against him then, the heat from their bodies temporarily warding off the cold.

As he deepened the kiss, Alex moaned softly, sending his pulse skyrocketing. Glorious seconds passed before he drew back for a beat. Then, after sucking in some vital air, he dived in again for another slow, breathtaking kiss. When she shivered against him, he begrudgingly broke contact.

“Wow,” he breathed. They’d shared amazing kisses before, but somehow this time was different, better.

"That was incredible."

He grinned. It seemed Alex felt the same way he did.

"But honestly, Zac, it's freezing out." A smile hovered on her swollen lips. "Can we *please* go inside now?"

"You took the words right out of my mouth, sweetheart."

"I like it when you say sweetheart like that," she whispered in his ear, giving him goosebumps that had nothing to do with the cold.

Chapter Seventeen

The next day, when Alex arrived at the bowling alley entrance, Jack was leaning against the wall.

"You know you didn't have to wait for me, right?" she teased.

He scratched his ear. "Uh, actually, I promised Charlotte I'd meet her and Mark here."

"I was kidding, Jack!" She laughed. "How're you doing?"

"Good." The worry lines disappeared from his brow as he smiled. After giving her a brief hug, he moved back, keeping one hand on her waist, right as Zac showed up.

Her heart skipped a beat, drinking in the sight of him. He looked mighty handsome—clean-shaven once more and displaying his perfectly toned muscles in a black long-sleeved henley shirt.

Their gazes tangled, and Zac's smile matched hers until his eyes dropped to where Jack still held her. Then his lips morphed into a straight line.

Jack stuck out his hand, his arm finally dropping from around her waist. "Hey, Zac," he said warmly. "Happy Thanksgiving."

"To you too." Zac gave his hand a firm shake before his probing gaze shifted back to her. "Hello, Alex," he said, his tone bordering on frosty.

Her smile fled. "Hello, Zac," she said politely.

What had happened?! The man's attitude was so changeable she never knew what to expect next.

Wringing her hands, she focused on the group fast approaching rather than the confusing man standing in front of her. Thankfully, Melanie and Steven's timely appearance, along with Jack's sister and her husband, broke the tension.

Greetings were exchanged, then Jack spoke up. "Julie's already inside, so that's everyone, Mel."

"Great. I guess we can go in then."

A short while later, Alex stared at the shocking pink ball in her hands.

Fact: Zac didn't like to lose. If she pretended to throw the game, Melanie would be suspicious. So why had her friend suggested this 'friendly' bowling game in the first place?

Tightening her hold on the ball, she positioned herself with her eye on the goal and swung her arm.

Seconds later, Melanie shouted, "Strike!" and their teammates, Julie and Charlotte, cheered.

Yep, just like riding a bicycle!

Alex suppressed a grin, spun on her heel, and strode to her seat. On the way, she purposefully avoided Zac's gaze, as well as Jack, Steven, and Mark's. They would just have to suck it up. Melanie had decided on the male versus female competition, not her.

Jack took his turn for the men's team and flattened all the pins, making Alex smile. He'd always been good at bowling—one of the things that had impressed her when they'd dated.

Julie and Charlotte managed a few pins each, but Melanie's first shot knocked down all the pins, except for one. Her next ball went straight for the single.

Alex grinned. "That's fantastic, Mel!"

Frowning, Melanie peeked over at their competition. "I just hope I can do it again. The guys already have three strikes for their first round."

"Don't worry, I won't let our team down," Alex said.

She was right too. Muscle memory helped her find her rhythm, and her second and third strikes followed. Taking a break in between turns, she figured she could relax enough to spy on the other team.

First up was Jack, who knocked down nine pins then narrowly missed the single. Zac then stepped forward to line up his shot, and she couldn't peel her eyes away. His position was marginally off, and she longed to stand behind him and move his shoulders slightly.

Except, she couldn't. They weren't on the same team, and Melanie would question the move.

Sighing, she kept her itchy hands to herself.

Zac's ball veered right and managed to hit four pins, just as Alex had expected. It was hard to miss his disappointment as he collected his second ball from the ball return area. She shot him a sympathetic look, which he ignored, making her stomach churn.

Had she dreamt his declaration?

If only she could find a minute alone with him. Then they could talk about this thing between them since it hadn't been possible last night.

By halftime, the computerized scoreboard showed their team trailing the men by a narrow margin. Which meant even after they ate, the pressure would remain on her to maintain a perfect record.

She sighed.

Melanie and Steven were called first to the food collection counter, followed by Charlotte and Mark. While they waited, Jack and Julie chatted, and Alex snuck a peek at Zac. Catching him glaring at her, she frowned.

"What?" she snapped.

"Steven mentioned that you used to bowl semi-professionally."

"Uh, I did. Why?"

"Might've been nice to know beforehand, don't you think? You probably should've had a handicap."

"Hey, my score of forty gave our team more than enough of a handicap!" Julie gave a self-deprecating laugh, then eyed Zac. "So don't give Alex a hard time."

Alex sent Julie a grateful look, but Jack continued to scowl.

"Yeah, give her a break, Zac," he said, slinging an arm over Alex's shoulders protectively. "It's just a friendly game."

"So it is." Shaking his head, Zac shoved his hands into his pockets and stalked off.

Feeling attacked, not to mention confused, Alex stared at his retreating back. "What's his problem?" she muttered under her breath. Apparently, things between them had reverted back to where they were before their 'little chat' yesterday.

She turned to Jack. "Would you two mind getting our food when it's ready, please?"

"No problem." He exchanged a glance with Julie, then asked, "You're not going to talk to him, are you, Alex? Because I don't know why you bother."

"Something's eating at him. I want to find out what."

"It's pretty obvious to me," he said.

She froze. "What do you mean?"

"Simple—Zac has feelings for you but doesn't know how to handle them, so he acts out."

"Funny, I didn't realize you'd become a psychologist overnight, Jack."

***

Zac wandered around the noisy arcade, well away from the bowling lanes. He needed to clear his head. Returning to his old ways with Alex wasn't the way forward, but he couldn't help himself. Other than sharing phenomenal kisses, they hadn't yet talked about their relationship. Even after expressing his feelings clearly last night, he still had no idea where they stood.

Loud shouts coming from two men racing on opposing motorbikes made him stop. They were pretty competitive, a trait he could identify with. As he watched the arcade game, the scent of magnolia invaded his nostrils, and a warm hand landed briefly on his arm. He peered sideways into familiar green eyes.

"What's up?" Alex asked.

"Jack."

"Why?"

"He's acting all possessive."

"We're still friends, Zac."

"Sure."

Her gaze narrowed. "Two people *can* be friends after they break up. Or don't you believe that?"

He shook his head. Personally, it hadn't ever happened to him. Wait, did Julie count? Debatable.

He'd never been in love with her.

Facing Alex completely, he crossed his arms. "If you say so."

"I do." She glowered at him. "Why are you worrying about Jack, anyway? I broke up with him, not the other way around."

News to him.

"You want to know why?" Her stern voice reflected the fire in her eyes.

"Why?"

"Because of you."

His brows rose. "Me? How?"

"Your kisses."

"What about them?" he barked, though a flicker of delight moved through him at her admission, and his heart rate kicked up a notch.

"They had spark."

"Is that right?" he asked gruffly, stepping closer.

Alex's expression softened as her fingers reached up to caress his cheek. Enjoying the feel of her smooth skin on his, he waited for her to speak.

"As much as you rocked the homeless look, I prefer this one."

Her head tilted as she scrutinized him a little more before her eyes descended to his lips, then shot back up.

"Although, I do quite like a little stubble on a man," she said, her fingers gliding along his jawline.

Their gazes met and clung, and as Alex's emerald eyes darkened to seaweed, Zac's mouth went dry. His heart began beating in triple time. When he spoke, he kept his tone light. "My kisses *had* spark? I'm not sure I like your use of the past tense."

Her soft giggle sent a thrill of anticipation through his veins. Easing his hands around to the curve of her back, he dipped his head close enough to hers to feel her warm breath on his lips.

"Are you going to kiss me, Zac?" she asked in a husky voice. "Or did I come find you for nothing?"

"Sweetheart, I thought you'd never ask."

***

After yet another earth-shattering kiss, Alex watched Zac check his phone. How could he possibly switch modes so effortlessly when her lips were still tingling? Perhaps he just wasn't as affected by her as she was by him.

"It was Julie," Zac said, pocketing his phone. "Our food's ready." He offered her his hand, his expression unreadable. "Shall we?"

"Sure." Alex took a deep breath, allowing him to curl his warm fingers over hers.

As they made their way back toward the lanes, her heart rate quickened while dancing butterflies took up permanent residence in her stomach. They really needed to talk! Catching his eye, she opened her mouth to speak, but he beat her to it.

"We need to talk," he said.

"I know. But Mel's..." Painfully aware that they were running out of time, her attention took in their surroundings. Too soon, they'd lose their privacy.

"Mel's what?" Zac asked, quirking his brow.

"Nothing."

They rounded the last corner and a strong smell of beef and fried potatoes hung in the air.

She was right; it was too late. Their teams were seated on two side-by-side benches, and Jack's curious gaze was directed at her and Zac.

Wincing, she withdrew her hand from Zac's and marched up to Jack and Julie's bench. She slipped into the seat opposite, where her food waited.

"It smells good," she said, her stomach rumbling. She smiled nervously as Zac, and his totally distracting scent, settled in beside her, his arm accidentally nudging hers as he shifted to get comfortable.

"Sorry," he murmured.

The light touch of his hand on her thigh made her breath hitch, and her whole body tensed. Noting his raised eyebrow, she shook her head slightly and glanced over at the other table before taking a long drink from her soda cup. Did Zac know how Melanie felt about them being in a relationship? Not that they were in a relationship. Unless a declaration and a few hot kisses meant they were involved?

She wished she knew.

"So, Julie, Jack, how are things going?" Zac asked, sparking a conversation between the three involving a topic Alex knew little about.

Rather than participate, Alex dug into her burger and fries meal, acutely aware of Zac's arms and legs pressed against hers. As a result, she occasionally felt the need to peek over at Melanie. Thankfully, her friend's attention was invariably elsewhere.

Alex was just popping her last fry into her mouth while sneaking one last glance at the other table when Zac's warm hand covered hers. Jerking her hand away, she accidentally splashed her soft drink over the table and onto her lap, as well as Zac's.

She rose abruptly. "I'm so sorry!"

"It's fine." A smile tugged at Zac's lips as he snagged a pile of napkins and handed her some.

Dabbing at the dampness on her jeans, she scolded herself for her stupid reaction. Zac could've been touching her hand for any number of innocent reasons.

She scooped up their trash and stepped out over the edge of the bench seat. "I'm going to sort this out," she said, pointing at the conspicuous wet patch on her jeans.

Zac's hand settled on her wrist. "Don't take too long; we'll be starting soon."

Her faced burned. "I'll be quick."

Pulling her hand away, Alex all but stumbled in her rush to leave.

When she rejoined her team, she was up first. Conscious of Zac's eyes on her, she collected her ball and strode up to the line. Aiming, she took a deep breath and fired, then turned to give Melanie space.

The crashing of ten pins filled the bowling alley.

Throughout the remainder of the game, Alex stole glances at Zac. Maybe he was just keeping tabs on their score, but his constant perusal made it hard not to blush. She also struggled to concentrate, not that it mattered. In the end, the men's team won by twenty points.

"At least it wasn't a walkover," Melanie commented to Steven as the group milled about handing out congratulatory hugs.

Steven eyeballed Alex. "You were lucky you had a professional on your team."

"Hey!" Melanie smacked him on the arm.

Grabbing her free hand, Steven drew his wife into his arms and planted a long kiss on her lips. Alex looked away quickly and came face to face with Zac. Her pulse galloped. Was he going to hug her too?

Closing the distance between them, Zac's strong arms encircled her, his muscled body molding perfectly against hers.

"Congrats," he whispered into her ear, sending delicious goosebumps all over her skin. "Next time, you can show me how to bowl like a pro."

Ignoring her heated cheeks, she eased her head back and peered into his twinkling eyes. "Play your cards right, Dr. Danvers," she murmured, "and you might just get your wish." She stepped out of his embrace and made a beeline for Melanie.

The group moved to stand inside the shopping center's covered entrance, and Alex marveled at how easily Zac needled his way in between her and Melanie.

At one stage, his fingers brushed hers, and her breath caught in her throat. As much as she wanted to hold his hand, she wasn't sure she was ready for any probing looks. When his hand moved to warm her lower back, she didn't object.

"So, Zac, will you be back with your family for Christmas?" Mark asked, his expression shrewd.

"Absolutely." He tossed Alex a wide smile.

Giddiness swept over her. Zac considered her 'part of the family'—maybe not quite the way she ultimately longed for, but still. After his admission of love, her dream of being with him now seemed possible, notwithstanding Melanie's feelings on the subject. In time, Alex felt confident whatever her friend's issue was, they'd work it out. Their friendship had survived other disagreements.

"Are you planning on moving back home to New Haven any time soon?" Mark asked. The man was on a roll. Alex couldn't have prepped him better herself.

"No, not the plan. My work and life, they're in New York. People rely on me in the city, and considering my commitments there, I can't leave."

"I see." Mark shot Alex a sympathetic look before focusing on Zac again, hopefully without noticing her alarm. "Pity, 'cause we could do with your bowling skills on a more permanent basis."

Zac chuckled. "Thanks, I appreciate the sentiment," he said, shaking Mark's outstretched hand.

With her head spinning, Alex couldn't stay a minute longer. "Great bowling, everyone," she said. "Thanks for organizing this, Mel. I guess I'll see you all on Sunday."

A chorus of goodbyes came, but not from Zac. She skimmed his taut features, her heart heavy.

What else could she say? If she didn't leave now, she'd cave in and do everything she could to make him smile again.

As she turned to leave, he grabbed her lower arm. "If you're leaving, let me walk you to your car."

"No, thanks. I'll be fine." Snatching her arm away, she dashed out the building, all the while blinking back tears. Repeating past mistakes was something she'd vowed would never happen. How would she ever learn from them otherwise?

Chapter Eighteen

It was the strangest feeling, being in the same church where Sophie had been baptized and where he'd first laid eyes on Alex.

Zac could still recall the moment he'd come face to face with her—his angel—like it was yesterday, and not over two and a half years ago.

Only Alex hadn't worn a halo, nor had she been smiling. But she had been a vision of beauty in her flowing white dress. Slightly curly, shoulder-length blonde hair had swung against her perfect porcelain face, and he remembered his breath catching when deep green eyes had pierced his soul.

Storing those memories, Zac focused on the present. He wasn't sure what had happened after the bowling a couple days ago. Why had Alex rushed off without giving him a chance to speak to her?

He'd wanted to see if she was free to hang out, go for a walk, have a light lunch, or kiss. But her hasty exit left no way of contacting her without asking his sister, and *that* hadn't been an option.

If he'd read Alex's odd behavior correctly, it pointed to her being worried about how Melanie would feel about them being in a relationship. As far as he was concerned, his sister would be thrilled. Who wouldn't want her best friend as a potential sister-in-law?

Was he seriously thinking of marriage?

His stomach suddenly filled with uncertainty. Alex wasn't dating anyone, was she? Because they hardly ever spoke. They shared incredible kisses, but he knew very little about her life in New Haven in real terms.

It wasn't like he could ask Melanie one hundred and one questions about Alex either. The little he did know, he'd gleaned from chats with his sister or from what Julie had told him, and lately, that hadn't been much.

The sooner he got Alex's number, the better. He needed to make his intentions crystal clear. The minute he left New Haven, he had to be certain they were in a relationship. Hopefully, a serious one.

It was a pity he had to return home straight after the christening today; otherwise, they could've gone out for coffee and talked about all these issues. But he'd promised a patient an after-hours consult in person, so he couldn't stick around.

Yesterday had been enjoyable: ice skating, followed by marshmallow hot chocolate, then a movie with sweet and salted popcorn, and drinking soda. But something, no, someone had been missing—Alex.

"Uncle Zac!" Sophie called, skipping up to him and wrapping her arms around his waist.

Dropping a kiss on her strawberry-scented head, he hugged her back. "Hey, Sophie-girl," he said, easing her away from him and smiling. "You look so pretty in your red dress. Is that velvet?"

She nodded, grinning. "Mommy said I could buy it because this is a special occasion."

"It sure is."

A flash of silver in Zac's peripheral vision turned out to be Alex. The sight of her—gorgeous in a shiny gray dress clinging to her slim figure—had his blood flowing faster. Not to mention the coy smile gracing her lips.

"Hey, Alex," he said, pleased he could sound calm with his heart beating erratically in his chest.

"Hi, Zac."

He smiled at her, then leaned down to Sophie. "Why don't you go find your dad in the kitchen? He's pulling out the baked goods, and he might like your help."

"Sure thing, Uncle Zac. See you later, Miss Alex." Sophie gave a brief wave of her hand and left.

Closing the distance between them, Zac reached out to touch one of Alex's soft curls, but it sprang away from him. Instead, he stroked her cheek as he stared at her. "You look incredible, sweetheart," he murmured. She smelled terrific, too, like fresh magnolias.

"Thanks. You do too." Her quiet voice trembled somewhat, though she didn't look away from him.

Pulling his phone from his jacket pocket, he frowned. "I wanted to call you yesterday, but I don't have your number."

For a long moment, she peered at his hand.

"If you'd rather not, that's alright." He started to put the phone away, but her hand shot out and stopped him.

"It's just..." She angled her head, giving him a quizzical look. "Why didn't you ask Mel?"

"Funny." He snickered. "I thought you'd be livid if I did. I'd have asked her ages ago otherwise."

Her slow, seductive smile did strange things to his insides.

"Hand me your phone," she said bossily, not that it bothered him. All he could think while she punched in her details was *mission accomplished.*

Right after that, Melanie showed, and it was all go, go, go.

As soon as the service was over, Zac turned to talk to Alex, but Steven approached them, a determined look on his face.

"Alex, would you mind helping me organize the refreshments? Melanie's deserted me to feed Ben, and Sophie's gone with her."

She glanced at Zac as if asking for his permission.

He shrugged his shoulders. "I was going to find Julie anyway."

After Alex left with Steven, Zac rubbed the nape of his neck. Was he ever going to get a chance to talk to her alone for more than a couple minutes?

He huffed out a frustrated breath, then scanned the room for a familiar face. Jack was over on the far side of the room, talking to his sister, Charlotte, while her husband, Mark, was trying to control the game of tag their three children were playing.

Not wanting to get involved, Zac continued his search, keeping one eye on Alex, who was serving drinks close by. Chatting with everyone, she wore a perpetual smile.

A couple of good-looking men, who stopped at her table, stayed far longer than he deemed necessary. Yet, he couldn't say a thing. It wasn't his place, at least not until they had a talk about where they were headed.

A touch on his arm had him spinning around.

"Julie! Just the person I wanted to see." He wrapped her in a tight embrace, and she laughed.

"It's great to see you, too, Zac."

As they drew apart, Jack stepped forward and shook his hand. "Congrats on making godfather again."

"Thanks. Mel didn't really have a choice."

"I won't take offense then." Jack stepped back, his hands raised.

"I didn't mean..."

Both Jack and Julie laughed.

"Chill," she said, patting his arm. "Jack's just teasing."

Eventually, people started leaving, and the room cleared, except for the family members, and Alex. After cleaning up and packing everything away, they all congregated outside the church's front entrance to say goodbye.

Melanie hugged Zac tightly. "Thanks again for being here. It means so much that you made an effort."

"I'm really glad I did, Mel."

Steven gripped his hand. "Drive safe and keep in touch."

Zac nodded, his attention straying to Alex standing quietly on the sidelines. He gravitated in her direction.

"Walk with me to my car?"

"I thought you were in a rush to get back to New York?"

"I have a few minutes, and I wanted to talk to you." He briefly regarded his sister several yards away before adding, "Alone."

"Okay."

Less than a minute later, Zac leaned back against the cold, hard metal of his driver's door and admired the woman in front of him. His heart thundered in his chest. Alex was so beautiful. The way her blonde hair tipped up on her shoulders, the way her lips parted when she was about to speak.

Extending his hands to her, he smiled when her hands clasped his without hesitation. He tugged until she fit snuggly between his legs.

"Sweetheart," he said softly, his gaze searching hers but finding no answers. "You've been distracted today. Like you were with us in person, but not in spirit."

She blinked, her lips twisting.

"Alex?"

"I've had a lot on my mind," she said, looping her arms around his neck. Her fingers threaded through his hair, giving him goosebumps—the good kind—while the intensity in her eyes mesmerized him to the point where he struggled to think straight.

"Is that so?" he managed to say.

Sliding his hands to the small of her back, he drew her closer still. When her tongue darted out to lick her lower lip, his gaze immediately fell to her mouth. A second later, his resistance crumbled, and his mouth eagerly sought hers. Their kiss was deep and passionate but contained a strange feeling of desperation and longing.

It took his breath away.

Every time he kissed her, he thought he knew what to expect, and every time she surprised him all over again. She was generous and attentive, demanding and exhausting at the same time.

Willing himself to stop before things went too far, he dragged his mouth off hers and rested his forehead on hers. A couple of deep breaths later, his pulse slowed down, and he lifted his head.

"I can't stop thinking about you, sweetheart," he said. "You're all I've had on my mind."

An emotion he could've sworn was sadness—not what he expected—filled her eyes.

"I want to see you again soon; take you out to dinner. Just you and me."

Alex said nothing.

He scrutinized her, trying to work out what she was thinking. “Can I call you when I’m back in New York?”

Various emotions flittered across her face—none he could pinpoint.

“No,” was her unexpected reply.

She shrugged out of his arms and took a step backward. “Look, Zac, I’m sorry.” Her voice wobbled as she spoke. “But this thing between you and me? Stolen moments like this?” She pointed between them. “This is all it can ever be.”

Dumbstruck was the only way Zac could explain how he felt. He absolutely did not want an occasional ‘stolen moment’ every three months or whenever he could get back to New Haven. He wanted to see Alex daily.

Obviously, that wasn’t possible right now, so until he could make things more permanent between them, they needed to spend time together without others around. A relationship had to be built on more than just attraction and some serious chemistry.

While he stood frozen, these thoughts flashed through his mind. By the time he woke from his stupor, Alex was halfway across the parking lot and opening her car door. She’d given him no explanation for her rejection and no chance to say anything to change her mind either.

He should’ve shouted. He should’ve run and caught up with her, even stood in front of her car as she drove out the exit. Instead, he went numb.

***

After scrubbing his hands over his face the next day, Zac lounged against his leather office chair and stretched his legs out. If Alex wouldn’t go out with him, what was the point of it all?

Why work so hard if he couldn't have a family with her one day? Either he was totally misreading her, or there was something else going on, something else stopping her from wanting the same as him.

What if he told Melanie how he felt? Maybe she'd be able to explain Alex's complete about-turn.

Or he could just ask Alex. Thank goodness he'd gotten her number before he left this time. He'd start with a text: ***No more stolen moments, Alex. I want the real thing.***

When she didn't respond immediately, his gaze drifted to the window and the pitch blackness outside. A glance back at his wall clock told him it was only four-thirty. The sun set so early nowadays, she'd probably still be in her classroom preparing lessons.

He sighed. For all he knew, she'd completely ignore him anyway.

At home later, he'd just finished dishing spicy chicken and egg fried rice for supper when he heard the bell text tone he'd carefully chosen.

Wiping his hand down his trouser leg, he lifted his phone off the kitchen counter.

Alex: ***I want gets nothing.***

Seriously?

He stuck his phone in his back pocket, snatched up his bowl, and stomped over to the living room to pick up his TV remote. He jabbed the ON switch and flopped onto the sofa, nearly spilling food in the process. As the screen came to life, two actors appeared in a lip-lock. Quicker than a heartbeat, he changed the channel to one showing dolphins being trained.

Much better.

A hard object dug into his back. Remembering the phone in his back trouser pocket, he swiftly retrieved it.

Then, ignoring the rumbling in his stomach, he typed out another message: ***I love you, Alex. Don't you feel anything for me?***

You know that's not true.

What did *that* mean? Urgh! This woman, still such an enigma!

Shoving his phone out of sight, he picked up his bowl again. How could he get through to her? Make her talk? If only they could do this in person.

He mulled over the possibilities as he finished off his meal, barely noticing the taste of the food or the pictures flittering across the screen in front of him.

He sent another text: ***Dinner doesn't have to be in NYC. I'll drive to NH.***

An hour later, he sent another: ***I want to see you. I miss you already.***

And another: ***Why won't you respond? I know it's the right number!***

A bell sound made his heart leap until he read the words: ***Give it a rest, Zac. You're wasting your time. It's not happening.***

***

Tears poured down Alex's cheeks as she typed her last message to Zac. She'd done the right thing, regardless of the bullet-to-her-chest feeling she was currently experiencing. It was the only way to stop giving him false hope.

From now on, she wasn't going to open his texts either. It was too painful.

She knew she should've been elated that he'd declared his love for her again and wanted to drive all the way to New Haven to take her out to dinner. But what was the point? She was never going to leave here, and he was never going to leave New York.

Stalemate.

The next day, during her mid-morning break in the staffroom, Michael handed her a mug of coffee.

"Thanks." She gifted him with her widest smile and took a sip. "Mmm, exactly the way I like it."

"Anytime, beautiful," he said, gazing at her intently.

Flushing, she ducked her head. Then, after taking a few seconds to compose herself, she boldly admired his chiseled jawline and classic good looks. Definitely easy on the eye. Not in the same league as Zac, but she had to get on with the rest of her life.

"Michael? You know you mentioned wanting to visit the Fantasy of Lights sometime?"

His blue-gray eyes lit up as he gave her his killer smile. "I did."

Her knees should've gone weak, but—

"I thought we could maybe do it together," he said, sounding hopeful.

"I'd love to."

"You mean you're finally going to let me take you on another date?"

She took a deep breath. "I am."

Chapter Nineteen

Close to a week later, Zac was going crazy. Especially since he hadn't had any of his usual Saturday afternoon hospital surgeries. He should count it as a blessing, but all it did was give him time to think about Alex.

At a loss as to what to do about her, he paced his living room, typing out messages and erasing them, bringing up her number to call her, then changing his mind. Eventually he pressed Melanie's speed dial, praying she'd be free to talk.

"Zac, what a surprise! Please, tell me nothing's wrong? You were here less than a week ago, and already I'm hearing from you. Not that I'm complaining, of course. But—"

"Will you let me get a word in edgewise, woman?" he interrupted, chuckling. Maybe if he called regularly, she wouldn't rattle on like it was a rare occasion.

"Sorry, you talk."

"How's everyone?"

"Good. Ben's sucking on his fingers lately."

"Cute. And Sophie?"

"She gave that up years ago," Melanie said in an ultra-serious voice.

"Ha ha. You know what I meant."

She giggled. "Well, Sophie just had test week. Obviously, she aced them."

"Obviously."

"What about you? Busy week?"

"Yeah. Listen, Mel," he said, rubbing the scar on his chin, "I called to talk about Alex."

"O-kay." She hesitated, then asked, "Why?"

"Have you seen her since the weekend?"

She laughed. "Of course!"

"Was she behaving normally?"

"Why, what did you say to her after we left?" Melanie asked, suspicion clear in her tone. "I know she walked you to your car."

"Relax! I didn't do or say anything I need to apologize for."

He hoped.

She huffed out what sounded like a relieved breath. "I'm constantly worried leaving the two of you alone. Every time you visit, she seems to get upset."

"And this time?"

"What's going on, Zac? Why the interest in Alex?"

Taking a deep breath, he exhaled slowly. "Don't freak out, Mel, but I'm in love with her."

"What? You've got to be kidding me! No way!"

Was it really that unbelievable? He bit his tongue.

"You're serious," she said, sounding earnest. "Oh, no."

"What?" His heart raced, waiting for her reply.

"I get it now. Alex is your unrequited love."

She remained silent for a few seconds, and he wondered whether she'd elaborate or not.

"You know I'd support a relationship between you and Alex in a heartbeat," she said, then paused again.

"Especially if it meant you'd move back home. Come on, it's every sister's dream for her brother and best friend to get together," she said, ending with a chuckle.

"Useful to know, but I don't plan on moving back. I live in New York. If anything serious were to happen between us, Alex would need to move here."

The line was quiet for way too long. He checked his phone's signal—full strength.

"What's wrong, Mel?"

"I assume you haven't told Alex how you feel. Or about your expectations if you were to date seriously."

"She knows how I feel. The thing is, she won't even agree to have dinner with me. According to her, I shouldn't waste my time."

"I love you, Zac, but Alex would know how she feels. If that's what she told you, then I'm not sure why you're talking to me about it."

His voice rose as frustration bubbled inside of him. "Because she won't talk to me!" Softening his tone, he added more quietly, "And I just don't know what to do anymore."

"You should know—right about now, Alex is out on a date. Michael's great, and I really like him. He's taking her to see the Fantasy of Lights. Very romantic, in case you weren't aware."

What?

"I think if Alex was interested in dating you or returned your feelings even a little, she wouldn't be out with someone else." She paused. "Do you?"

***

Alex stared at Michael as he climbed into the fancy sports coupé and lowered the driver's door into position. No doubt, her expression was one of amazement as she asked, "Have I just gotten into a car with a drug dealer?"

He grinned. "You're funny."

Giggling, she ran her hands over the heated leather seat. So soft and smooth. The vibrant red color was gorgeous too.

The engine came to life along with a screen the size of an iPad. Michael shifted the vehicle into reverse, and they glided backward, the camera on the dash detailing everything behind them.

She waited until the car was pointed in the direction of the highway before asking, "How exactly does a Math teacher afford such an expensive car?"

"I haven't always been a teacher."

"Oh? I'd never have guessed. Not when all the kids and parents rave about your fantastic teaching style."

He looked over at her with a delighted smile. "Nice to know."

Since Michael needed to concentrate on driving and didn't volunteer anything extra, Alex peered out the window at the quickly fading light. Weird to think it was only four o'clock, but then again, they needed the sun to set for where they were headed.

"What did you do before?" she asked after a bit.

"I used to manage a hedge fund."

"Is that some sort of gardening-type job?"

Shooting her a funny look, he laughed. "No, not at all. I basically managed wealthy individuals' money, invested it in various assets, and took huge risks to maximize their profits."

"I guess those risks paid off?"

He nodded, glancing in the rearview mirror before flicking on his turn signal.

"New Haven's not exactly somewhere I picture a high-powered man like you working. Have you always lived here?"

"I used to live in New York City."

Great. She crossed her arms, the fast-approaching darkness matching her sudden frame of mind. What *was* it about that city and the men in it?

"You're frowning. I take it you're not a fan of the Big Apple?"

"Not particularly." Squeezing her eyes shut, she tried hard to push away the memories from five years ago.

"Why?" A light touch on her arm drew her to his concerned gaze. "What happened? If you don't mind me asking?"

The hurt she'd buried a long time ago returned, reminding her of the day she'd discovered her fiancé's indiscretion. Willing the moisture clogging up her eyes to stay put, she took a fortifying breath.

"I was involved with a man who lived there. We were pretty serious. I found out he cheated on me, and it ended badly."

"What a jerk! He obviously didn't deserve someone as amazing as you."

Her cheeks heated. "Thanks, Michael."

Soft classical music played through the car's speakers, and Alex found it rather soothing. She ignored the emotions trying to get the better of her and plastered on a bright smile.

"I'd love a brief synopsis of your history," she said, injecting enthusiasm into her voice. "It'll tell me what molded you into the man you are today."

"A bit deep for a third date." A cheeky smile grew on his handsome face. "But, I'll go with it."

Changing lanes to pass a slow truck, his fingers drummed on the steering wheel.

"So, I was born in Manhattan, where I went to school and college. While studying finance, I dated a great girl named Sarah and had a terrible crush on her younger sister, Emma. After an apprenticeship in a London bank, I went out on my own. Now I teach."

"Wow, that *was* brief!" She laughed. "So, why didn't you date Emma instead if you liked her so much?"

A muscle in his jaw twitched. "She was five years younger and a senior in school."

"I see. What happened with Sarah?"

"We broke up," he said in a detached voice. Then, as if anticipating her next question, he added, "On my return to New York from London, I found out she'd gotten engaged." His hand lifted to hold the back of his neck. "Establishing my own fund was time-consuming, and I didn't have time to date anyway."

"Emma would've been out of school by then. Did you ever see her again?"

"No."

"Think you'd still have a crush on her if you did?"

He gave her an amused look. "Are you seriously asking me that while you and I are on a date?"

She lifted one shoulder in a shrug.

"It was just a crush. Besides, last time I heard, she was married."

Laying a hand on his arm, she winked at him. "I'm sorry your dream was crushed."

His hand covered his heart. "Don't joke. I was completely heartbroken."

They shared a laugh that wrapped around them like a light blanket before settling into a comfortable silence.

"I visited the Fantasy of Lights years ago," she eventually said. "All the money they raise supports programs which enhance employment as well as education, social, and recreational opportunities for people with disabilities."

"We're supporting a worthy cause then." Michael sounded genuinely pleased.

"I also read an article recently about a new sponsor. Apparently, a family wanted to dedicate one of the displays to the memory of their grandmother, so they donated six hundred dollars."

A smile touched his lips. "That's a wonderful idea."

He made a right turn into the park and pulled up behind a row of parked vehicles.

"You know what?" he said, shifting in his seat to look directly at her. "We should choose the Christmas light display we admire most, so I can make a donation on our behalf. Frankly, with all the good work those programs obviously do, I don't feel our ten-dollar entrance fee is adequate."

"Do you have a figure in mind?"

For the longest time, he held her gaze until she dropped hers.

"You don't have to tell me. It's your hard-earned cash, after all."

"Fifty," he said, sounding sheepish.

She gave an encouraging smile. "Fifty dollars is a wonderful contribution. Every little bit counts."

He looked uncomfortable. "Uh, I meant fifty thousand."

What? Who had that kind of money to splash around?

Blinking, she swallowed down her shock. "You're an extremely generous man, Michael. I-I'm honored to be your friend."

"Thanks, Alex. I think... I'm not sure about the friend part, though."

She pursed her lips, afraid of admitting anything. Luckily, the vehicle ahead moved forward, and Michael focused on following it through the blue-lit tunnel and on to the main attraction.

After a mile-long drive of spectacular winter-wonderland light displays, they reached a restaurant parking area where he parked and cut the engine.

"Wow, that was incredible!" she said, still feeling awestruck. "Thanks for bringing me."

"It was my pleasure." He took her hand in his and caressed her thumb, pinning her with his sparkling gaze. "So, which was your favorite?"

"The woman trying to put the star on top of the Christmas tree."

"Yeah, that was great." He chuckled. "Mine was the man standing on those wobbly presents while holding the woman. Definitely, an accident looking for a place to happen."

Giggling, Alex nodded. "You're so right."

Once they'd sorted out Michael's donation in the temporary event office, they grabbed a quick bite to eat, then climbed back into the warm car to head home.

Christmas carols played quietly on the radio, and with Michael seemingly lost in thought, Alex's thoughts turned to Zac. Was he also out on a date tonight? With the perfect Emma?

Or was he at home pining over her and wondering what to text next?

Tempted to check her phone, her hand dipped into her purse.

"Everything alright?"

Pulling her hand back, she peered at Michael. "Of course."

The street lights whizzed by as the powerful engine ate up the miles, and suddenly, Alex wanted to, no, needed to know more about the man she was out with.

"Tell me, why did a successful hedge fund manager decide to leave the city and become a teacher, here of all places?"

"Well," he said, "I made my first million at thirty but spent the next two years making heaps more, to the detriment of my health and my family life."

"So, you left it all and came here?" She struggled to keep the surprise out of her voice.

"Yep. I decided a change of career, lifestyle, and environment would be beneficial."

He sighed deeply, and for a long while, he kept quiet, his fingers gripping the steering wheel tightly. She refused to push, figuring he'd say more in his own time. What she didn't expect was the bitterness and hurt she heard when he did speak.

"I haven't seen or spoken to my parents since I moved here. They don't believe I made the right decision. Even after all I achieved, they expected me to continue with the long hours and stress. Continue wreaking havoc on my body. To them, I had started something, and I should see it through to the end. Probably the end of my life."

He gave a humorless laugh.

"That's awful!" she said, laying a hand on his leg, which he immediately covered with his own. "I'm sorry. They sound despicable, Michael."

"They're my parents, and I know I'm supposed to love them, but I definitely don't have to like them."

"At least you have parents," she said wistfully.

He sent her a questioning look.

"My mother died giving birth to me. I never knew my father, and I'm not even sure my mother knew who he was."

"That's sad."

Her lips curled slightly. “Fortunately, a wonderful couple adopted me when I was a few months old. They couldn’t have children, so I was their miracle, and they loved me as their own.”

“What happened to them?”

“Five years ago, they chartered a private plane to fly over the Grand Canyon.”

She pressed her eyes with her knuckles and blew out through her mouth as a wave of emotion washed over her.

“It’s okay, Alex. I can guess the rest,” he said kindly. “Now I’m sorry.”

“Anyway, it was my parents who encouraged me to teach.” She sniffed. “They knew I loved children and thought it would be a good fit. They were right. I met Melanie Danvers when her daughter, Sophie, was in my Kindergarten class, and we hit it off. Before long, Mel’s parents had adopted me into their family, you know, especially for family events.”

“They sound like an amazing family.”

She nodded.

“Doesn’t Melanie have a brother in New York? A doctor?”

All Alex could do was nod again and pray Michael wouldn’t hear her heart thumping in her chest suddenly.

“Dr. Danvers has quite a reputation.”

“What do you mean?”

“For being an outstanding doctor,” Michael said, giving her a sideways glance. “He’s always going above and beyond. On-call twenty-four-seven, if I’ve heard correctly. He’s also loved by his patients, especially the female ones.”

Was she jealous?

Definitely not.

"Can I assume this information comes from your friends in New York?" she asked.

"Yes." Stopping at a red traffic light, he cocked his head to one side. "Apparently, all the eligible young women think he's the one to catch."

Sucking in a breath, she schooled her features into a blank expression.

Please don't ask, please don't ask.

"He must visit his family often. You've never been tempted to go out with him?"

Heck, yes, every single time.

"No, why would I?"

"Mmm. Not sure I believe you." The lights turned green, and his focus went back to the road.

"Well, you should," she said, gazing out the passenger window. "Until recently, he had a girlfriend, and besides, we would never work."

"How so?"

"I seem to rub him the wrong way. Bring out the worst in him."

"Right." Judging by his frown, he wasn't convinced.

Thankfully, her apartment building came into view at that exact moment. "Look at that! Home sweet home," she said, forcing cheer into her voice.

Later, curled up in bed, she recalled Michael's chaste kiss outside her front door. She'd wanted him to take things slow, and he'd honored her decision. The man was a gem and a catch.

It still shocked her how much money he had, but at least it hadn't made him bigheaded or entitled. He could've done anything he wanted, gone anywhere in the world, yet he chose to live and teach kids here. And, as far as dating went, he could choose anyone he liked, but he'd chosen her.

So why wasn't she ecstatic and falling in love already?

Alex blamed Zac. His gorgeous face overrode all rational thought, and she couldn't help comparing Michael to him. In no way did Michael come up short. But the reality was when she looked at Michael or thought about him, her heart didn't race. At all.

Chapter Twenty

Crossing her arms, Alex stared at the massive pile of laundry on the kitchen floor. Sunday was meant to be a day of rest. If only she could have a rest from the intrusive thoughts plaguing her every activity. Rest from thinking about Zac's chiseled features, his warm lips moving over hers, his electrifying touch.

Bad enough her dreams were full of his gorgeous face, the splattering of freckles across his nose, the scar on his chin he rubbed whenever he was nervous or pensive. Oh, and that dimple which only came out when he smiled broadly.

She sighed—the clothes weren't going to wash themselves.

Opening the music app on her phone, she chose a Carrie Underwood album, hit 'shuffle', and upped the volume. A few songs in, she paused her music.

Was that the doorbell? She listened again. Yep. Strange, she wasn't expecting anyone.

A delivery man, holding a huge bunch of mixed flowers in a stunning crystal vase, greeted her by the front door. "Alexandra Masters?"

"Yes, that's me."

He handed over the arrangement.

"Wow, it's heavy," she said, misjudging the weight and almost dropping the whole thing.

She flashed him a smile, which he didn't return. Instead, he held out a handset. "I need your signature."

Despite his stiff posture and unfriendly expression, she readily obliged. Then, after he left, she took a moment to admire the beautiful flowers. Michael had gone all out; apparently, having money had its perks.

She inhaled the sweet scent of the petals before removing the florist's card.

TO ALEX, A WOMAN MORE BEAUTIFUL THAN FLOWERS. LOVE ZAC

Warmth filled her heart while her hand flew up to cover her mouth. Zac wasn't going to give it a rest!

Depositing the stunning arrangement in the center of her dining table, she retrieved her phone and messaged him: ***Thx 4 gorgeous flowers.***

I didn't know your favorites, Zac replied.

Pink & white carnations.

Now, why had she gone and told him that?!

After forcing herself to finish her chores and weekly lesson plans, she decided on a Netflix movie. She'd been dying to watch *Christmas Inheritance*, so she made it her reward.

An occasional peek at the generous floral display had her smiling. Clever Zac, ensuring she'd think of him often—like every time she smelled their wonderful fragrance. Her eyes darted to the group photo beside her TV, honing in on his smug face.

Why didn't he just give up? Hadn't she been clear enough?

That same night her dreams were filled with Zac personally delivering the flowers. The dreams all ended the same way, with her pulling him inside her apartment and insisting he never leave again.

The next morning, a man in a brown delivery uniform knocked on her classroom door during second period. Setting aside the book she'd been reading to her pupils, she stood.

"Alexandra Masters?"

She nodded.

"These are for you." He carried the round glass bowl filled with pink and white carnations to her desk, then left.

Annie beamed. "Pretty flowers, Miss Alex."

Johnny, wearing a cute frown, asked, "Is it your birthday, Miss Alex?"

"No, Johnny, it's not."

"Someone must really like you, Miss Alex," Susie commented, to which Katie responded, "It's from your boyfriend, isn't it, Miss Alex?"

Chuckling at their assumptions, Alex spoke firmly, "Settle down, everyone. I don't know who they're from."

"Read the card, Miss Alex, 'cause if it's from your boyfriend, you have to say thank you," Katie instructed.

The kid sure was tenacious, usually a quality Alex loved. Today though, she'd rather enjoy her gift without children's prying eyes.

She glanced at the clock—not too long to recess. "Let's finish this story first, so we know if the prince rescues the princess or not, okay, Katie?"

Thankfully that did the trick, and the bell rang within minutes. Once she'd dismissed the children to the playground supervisor, Alex quickly returned to her classroom and the flowers.

Her heart sped up as she picked up the card and read.

I COULDN'T RESIST; SAME WAY I CAN'T RESIST YOU.
LOVE ZAC

Hearing a soft knock on her door, she shoved the card into her jacket pocket and swung around, hoping her cheeks wouldn't betray her.

"Hey, Alex."

"Michael, hi. What's up?"

"I had an idea," he said. "Rather than sit in the stuffy teachers' lounge later, you want to grab lunch out?"

"I'd like that."

His gaze dropped to her desk, then lifted, full of curiosity. "Nice flowers. Your birthday?"

"No. I'm a summer baby."

"So, they're from a friend?"

"Yes, a friend." That's what Zac was, right? No matter how she felt about him, that's all they could be.

"I wish I'd thought of sending you flowers," Michael said wistfully. He gave her an endearing lopsided smile.

"I won't hold it against you...this time," she teased.

"Good to know."

The second Michael left, she texted Zac: ***Stunning flowers, thx. Not necessary tho, yesterday's were perfect.***

His response was immediate: ***My pleasure. Do you like nuts?***

She scratched her head. What did *that* have to do with the flowers? She scanned the whole arrangement—no nuts.

Yes, with chocolate mostly. Why?

He didn't answer, and soon it was time to bring her class in from recess.

The day flew by, and with the parent-teacher evening straight after school, she barely had time to think, let alone ponder Zac's question. When she finally trudged up the sidewalk to her apartment building and keyed in her code, it was close to eight o'clock. All she wanted was a quick dinner, a shower, and to crash.

Outside her apartment door, her next-door neighbor called out, "Yoo-hoo! Alex, dear?"

Suppressing a groan, she turned. "Hello, Mrs. Lewis. How are you?"

The sweet old lady smiled, thankfully with all her teeth in. "Oh, you know, the usual aches and pains, but otherwise, I'm good. Thanks for asking."

While the woman hovered in her doorway, half in, half out like a coin spinning on its side, her gray-eyed gaze remained fixed on Alex.

"Was there something you wanted, Mrs. Lewis?"

"Oh, yes. Sorry, dear. You weren't in earlier, so the delivery man left your package with me." Mrs. Lewis disappeared for a moment, returning with a thin box the size of an A3 sheet of paper.

Alex surveyed the package's shiny cream wrapping paper. Affixed on one side was a giant gold bow, and on the other, her name and address.

"Thank you for keeping it for me," she said, patting Mrs. Lewis's wrinkled arm covered in age spots. "And let me know if there's anything I can do for you."

"Thanks for the offer, dear. I know how busy you are growing the minds of those little children, so keep up the good work. Although...you might want to find a good man to settle down with and have a family of your own." Winking, she retreated into her apartment.

Alex pressed her lips together. As if she didn't feel enough pressure, what with her best friend already married with two kids!

Entering her apartment, she let the front door slam behind her, then cringed.

A minute later, her irritation was forgotten as she perched on a kitchen barstool holding her gift. Excitement skittered through her as she tore the paper off then read the enclosed message:

I HOPE YOU ENJOY THESE AS MUCH AS I ENJOYED CHOOSING THEM FOR YOU. LOVE ZAC

Wow! Did he think sending flowers and chocolates was going to make her change her mind about going out with him? Not that she was complaining about the extravagant gifts, but they hardly made up for his absence.

And therein lay the real issue.

Proper food should've come first, but the temptation was too great once she inhaled the contents' rich cocoa aroma. Closing her eyes, she chose a chocolate and lifted it to her mouth. Smooth and creamy, it melted deliciously and contained a fresh and crunchy almond in the middle.

She fired away a couple messages to Zac: ***These r way too delicious! Thank u.***

And: ***What r u doing?***

Unlike before, there was no instant reply.

After a reenergizing shower, she climbed into bed and read the next chapter in her romance novel. Lost in the drama of two characters who couldn't see they were perfect together, she jumped when her phone pinged with a notification from Zac: ***Getting to know you.***

Her fingers flew over the screen: ***Don't waste your money.***

You're worth every cent. It makes you communicate with me.

Sneaky, but true. She'd been brought up to say please and thank you. It would be rude not to. But, Michael would start asking awkward questions very soon, and he wouldn't be the only one.

OK. Fine. But please stop sending me gifts. Ask me what u want 2 know.

What's your favorite thing to do on a Saturday night?

Curl up on the sofa with a movie & pizza.

Romance?

U got it in 1.

Which pizza?

Marco Polo's Sicilian.

Alex yawned and looked at the clock—ten o'clock. *Goodness!* She'd better switch off her light, or she'd be a zombie tomorrow, and as much as the kids might enjoy that, she would not. She wanted to keep talking to Zac, ask him the same questions, but she wouldn't. It would give him hope.

Goodnight, Zac.

Before she powered off her phone, a ping sounded.

Sleep well, ttyl.

Ttyl? Oh, right, talk to you later.

For a man who didn't do text speak, Alex was impressed. With a smile playing on her lips, she closed her eyes and went to sleep.

***

The next day, Zac's first thought was of Alex, so he sent her a text: ***Morning, beautiful. Anything exciting planned for today?***

Instead of waiting for a reply, he padded to the kitchen for a much-needed caffeine fix. After he'd taken a couple sips, a message arrived: ***Teaching my 6 yr olds how 2 make Xmas decs.***

He grinned. *Cute.*

Alex: ***What about u?***

Wow, now *she* was asking questions! Maybe his plan would work after all.

I have hospital rounds until lunch & patient appointments booked, lunch through to 7pm.

Another long day then?

Yes.

Admittedly, there was no need for the long days, but historically he'd chosen to take on the evening patients because Dan had a family. That hadn't changed, but Trevor—also single—was leaving at five, sometimes earlier, while Zac continued to slog away.

Time to make some changes.

As Zac grabbed his bag and coat and headed out the door, he checked his phone one last time.

Nothing.

Being a hard worker was a good quality, but it probably wouldn't win him any brownie points with Alex.

Dan had told him once, right in the beginning of their partnership, "The secret to a happy marriage is to be home in time to help with either supper or bathing the kids. I promise you, Zac, it makes all the difference."

Well, he didn't have any of those blessings yet, but he sure as heck wanted them.

With Alex.

Conveniently, the next staff practice meeting was due the following morning. So, sparing a few minutes that afternoon, Zac worked on a proposal.

Afterward, back-to-back patients meant he barely had time to think, let alone grab a coffee, until Trevor knocked on his door at four-thirty, a steaming mug—with a Z on it—in his hand.

Zac took the proffered drink, had a sip, then cradled the mug like it contained liquid gold. "You don't know how much I needed this."

"I figured you hadn't stopped. You're always on the go." Trevor kicked his foot against the laminate flooring.

"What's on your mind? I have two minutes. Talk."

"I know it's not my place, but you work way harder than the rest of us, Zac. I get that Dan has a family, and you don't, but it doesn't seem fair. I wondered..."

When apprehension filled Trevor's gaze, Zac offered a brief smile and motioned for him to continue.

"Would you be agreeable to me working longer hours, or at least halving the extra hours with you? It'd be a win-win situation. You'd get to date again—assuming you wanted to—and I'd earn some extra cash."

"Believe it or not, Trevor, I was thinking something similar."

"Yes!" He pumped his fist. "Then whatever you decide, Zac, you'll have my support."

***

The final bell rang, and Alex sighed in relief. She couldn't wait to get home and for the rest of the day to be over. No matter how often she'd checked her phone, Zac hadn't texted once since yesterday morning. When she exited her classroom carrying two large bags, Michael was striding toward her. He peered down at her hands. "Need any help?"

"Thanks. I'm headed to Sophie's classroom." Smiling gratefully, she offered him one bag, but he took both and fell in step beside her.

A few steps on, she noticed him dragging his feet and slowed to match his pace.

"What's up?" she asked.

For a long moment, he studied her, but she couldn't work out what was on his mind. He cleared his throat. "I was wondering...are you free tonight?"

She gave a slight shake of her head. "I'm babysitting Ben."

His eyes flicked briefly to hers, then away again. "And Saturday night?"

"Sorry. More babysitting."

Clenching his jaw, Michael stared straight ahead. "I should've asked earlier." He sounded annoyed. Did he think she was putting him off?

She touched his arm gently, and he looked at her. "I'm free the following weekend. If that's any good?"

"Believe it or not," he said ruefully, "I'm going skiing with an old buddy from New York."

"Sounds like fun." She tilted her head. "Maybe we should talk in the new year?"

His eyebrows shot up. "You're not serious?"

"No, of course not!" She giggled.

They stopped in front of Sophie's classroom, and she angled her body toward him, an idea forming.

"I don't suppose you're free on Friday, the twenty-second?"

His eyes lit up. "I am."

"Would you be my date for Steven and Mel's pre-Christmas party?"

"I'd love that!" Smiling widely, he handed back her bags. "See you tomorrow?"

"Definitely."

"Great." He dropped a quick kiss on her cheek and left.

A thought crossed her mind, and she suddenly felt sick. How could she have forgotten Zac would most likely be at the party? Now, with Michael there, too, the evening could be super awkward. Should she tell Zac?

No, she owed him nothing, really. Just because they were 'communicating' and he was 'getting to know her' didn't mean he had any claim on her. He certainly had no right to dictate who she dated.

She'd made her position crystal clear—stolen moments, nothing else. And, if that meant they 'accidentally' ended up under the mistletoe, well then, who could blame them if they kissed?

***

Zac's stomach felt unsettled first thing Thursday morning. Searching for a reason, it dawned on him that a whole day had passed without any contact with Alex. He couldn't have her thinking he'd lost interest.

Snatching his phone from his nightstand, he typed furiously: ***Forgive me, sweetheart. Yesterday was crazy but good. How are you?***

An hour later, during his stroll to the office, he felt able to breathe properly again when she replied: ***Fine. Tired. Why crazy good?***

Sorted work stuff out. Why tired?

Babysat Ben 'til 9, then chatted with Mel 'til 10.

Steven not there?

Work dinner. Mel took Sophie 2 ballet.

Bet she loved it.

Yes. Gotta go. Ttyl.

That made him smile. She wasn't saying goodbye; she was giving him hope.

Before she went radio silent, though, he quickly asked one more thing: ***Any plans for the weekend?***

Why?

Just curious.

Babysitting Ben & Sophie Sat.

Okay, have fun.

Around mid-morning, a patient canceled, giving Zac the perfect opportunity to call his sister.

"Wow! I've heard from you twice in less than a week," Melanie said. "To what do I owe this pleasure?"

He chuckled. "Can't I just be calling to check up on my little sister?"

"Sure, but given you usually only call about twice a year—for my birthday, and when you decide to visit Sophie—I have to admit I'm a little suspicious."

He groaned. "You're right. I'm a terrible brother."

"No, you're not! You're just totally dedicated to your work, and I admire you because of it." The tenderness in her voice made him feel marginally better. "But seriously, what's up?"

"Alex."

"I thought we'd been through this. I don't think she's interested."

"Let me be the judge of that."

"Why?" She snickered. "Don't tell me something's happened in all of five days to change her mind?"

"Actually, we've been in touch, and let's just say I'm hopeful."

"Idiot is what I'd call you, brother, hoping for something with Alex. I've seen the way you two are with each other, and let me tell you, it isn't pretty. More like awkward and cringe-worthy."

"Thanks, *sis*, for the vote of confidence."

Seriously? Melanie knew nothing of their private, or as Alex called them, 'stolen' moments. And he wasn't about to spill either.

"I'm sure you have patients waiting, and I need to get to a meeting. So why are you really calling, Zac?"

"Can I spend Saturday night at your place?" He hoped she wouldn't ask any hard questions, considering he typically stayed with their parents.

"Uh, sure. Except Alex is supposed to be babysitting. I don't know how she'd feel about you being there."

"I don't think–"

"Actually," she said, "why don't *you* babysit the kids? Sophie would be thrilled to see her uncle, and I'll tell Alex not to worry. She had to turn down a date with Michael, so now she can go out with him instead."

"No!" The denial came out harsher than intended, and his heart raced. "Better not risk disappointing the kids if I can't make it," he added, more softly. "Alex is the safer choice."

"Oh, okay."

"Also, I'd prefer you don't mention my visit to Alex. No need to worry her unnecessarily, especially if I don't end up coming. Okay?"

"Sure. I'll keep it between Steven and me."

"Thanks, Mel."

While messaging Alex through Saturday morning, Zac managed to keep his schemes to himself. And, by the time his hospital shift was nearly over, he had started praying no emergencies would crop up before he left New York.

His reasoning–he had plans for later that day and absolutely no intention of changing them.

Chapter Twenty-One

On Saturday night, at precisely seven o'clock, Zac pulled up outside his sister's house. His stomach churned as he took a moment to spray fresh mint into his mouth and run fingers through his hair.

He inhaled deeply. If he'd gotten this wrong, and Alex didn't want to see him, things could get awkward. Fast.

One thing was certain, Sophie would be excited, so the trip wouldn't be a complete waste. But he was hoping for so much more.

Slipping on his coat, he collected his gift and climbed out the warm car.

A biting wind whipped around his neck as he headed to Melanie's front door, and he had to grit his teeth. He knocked lightly, barely waiting more than a few seconds before Sophie swung the door wide open.

"Uncle Zac!" She launched herself at his legs and hugged him tightly. "I told Miss Alex it was you, but she said it couldn't be."

Laughing at her exuberance, he slung his free arm around her. "Hello, Sophie-girl. It's good to see you too."

She let go abruptly. “I’m going to tell Miss Alex it *is* you. She’s feeding Ben in the living room.” Sophie’s sharp gaze went to his hand. “Those are pretty flowers. Mommy’ll love them.”

He opened his mouth to correct her, but she rushed off.

Oh, well, it didn’t matter.

Following more sedately, his heart thumped in anticipation of seeing the person he’d missed the most.

When he entered the living room, his breath caught in his throat; Alex’s pretty green eyes were trained on him while she sat on the sofa with Ben in her arms. Sophie knelt at the glass coffee table nearby, happily coloring.

“Funny, Zac,” Alex said, her tone anything but humorous, “Mel never said a word.” Narrowing her gaze, she lowered her voice as he approached. “You could’ve warned me, don’t you think?”

“And spoil the surprise? No way.” He flashed her a smile, offering her the bouquet of red roses he held.

Her eyes brightened, but she made no move to take them from him. “They’re gorgeous.”

“Mmm...you know what I would say to that if I could,” he said quietly, tilting his head in Sophie’s direction.

Alex looked down at Ben, her cheeks taking on a lovely rosy hue. “I’m a little busy at the moment,” she said in a tight voice. “You can put the flowers on the kitchen island.”

Already on tenterhooks at her less than welcoming attitude, Zac chose not to argue.

When he returned to the living room, Alex was standing burping his nephew. She didn’t spare him a glance, so he headed over to Sophie.

"Think I could help you finish this picture?" he asked, sinking down onto the fluffy carpet.

"That would be awesome, Uncle Zac." She handed him a few colored pencils.

While Alex rubbed circles on Ben's tiny back, Zac's eyes roamed over her. She wore blue skinny jeans with a loose-hanging pink T-shirt and looked beautiful. Their gazes collided, and he automatically tipped his head to continue coloring Sophie's castle.

A few minutes later, Alex told Sophie it was time for a bath. Without any fuss, his niece cleared up her belongings, saying, "Thanks for helping, Uncle Zac."

"My pleasure, Sophie-girl." He pushed to his feet and found Alex staring at him.

Was she mad? He couldn't tell. She wasn't happy, that much he could tell.

"Would you like to hold Ben while I get Sophie ready for bed?"

"Definitely." Crossing the carpet, he accepted the contented child, ignoring the spark of electricity as Alex's hand touched his.

Zac wandered into Sophie's room and sank into the comfortable armchair while Ben gurgled and sucked his fingers, gazing up at him with blue eyes. Breathing in the fresh powdery smell, Zac felt a slight wave of envy—Melanie was truly blessed.

Even with the splashing sounds coming from Sophie's en-suite, Ben's eyelids fluttered closed. Zac savored the relative peace until Sophie entered her bedroom in pj's and made a beeline for him.

"Will you read me a bedtime story, please, Uncle Zac?"

Alex appeared, frowning. "Uh, teeth first, Sophie."

"Okay."

His niece skipped back into her bathroom while Alex regarded him warily until a foul smell permeated the air. She reached for Ben. “He needs a diaper change.”

“I can do it,” Zac said, rising.

He started off toward the nursery, but her hand stopped him. “Do you even know *how* to change a diaper?”

“Believe it or not, this isn’t my first time around.”

“I know, but—”

“Trust me, I know what I’m doing,” he snapped.

Ignoring her hurt look, he left the room.

As he sorted out Ben, regret filled him. There was no excuse for his sharp response, but not knowing how Alex felt about his presence had put him on edge.

When he ventured back to Sophie’s room, Alex jumped to her feet, her expression hard.

“I’ll take Ben.”

He handed over the precious bundle, glancing over at Sophie, who was collecting a book from her bookcase. “I’m sorry,” he whispered to Alex.

She dismissed him with a single nod of her head.

“What have you got there, Sophie-girl?” he asked.

“One of my favorite stories. I hope you like it too, Uncle Zac.”

He scanned the book cover—*Matilda* by Roald Dahl. “Good choice.”

While Zac read, he was constantly aware of the woman across the room and totally distracted by her floral scent. He couldn’t wait for them to be alone.

Occasionally, he glanced up and caught her staring intently at him, or was it glaring? He couldn’t decide.

By the end of the first chapter, Sophie’s lids grew heavy. “I think that’s enough for tonight,” he said quietly to her.

"One more chapter, please?"

"I would, but Ben needs to go to bed too, and I'm starving."

"Okay." Sophie flung her arms around his neck and kissed him soundly on the cheek. "Go eat. I don't want you to faint."

Chuckling at her dramatics, he gave Alex space to say goodnight too.

As they were leaving the room, Sophie called out, "Thanks for reading to me, Uncle Zac, and for coming to visit. I can't wait to go ice skating with you tomorrow."

Turning around, he smiled. "Me too." He didn't dare look at Alex. They needed to talk about other things first, before ice skating trips.

"Sleep tight, Sophie," Alex said from behind him, then promptly switched off the light.

***

Unbelievable! Alex huffed. Had Melanie known her brother was coming tonight?

Surely not.

If only she'd been out with Michael, avoiding this stress and these unwanted desires.

Lowering Ben into his crib, she took a deep breath. Then, after pressing a kiss to his forehead, she fiddled with his blanket and moved aside.

When Zac leaned over the crib to stroke Ben's cheek, the tender act melted her insides. The man would make an excellent father one day. With a start, she clenched her fists.

None of this was helpful. She was trying to get him out of her mind. Not fill it with hope!

Slapping on the night light before crossing to the doorway, she stopped long enough to witness the magical starry night appearing on the walls and ceiling.

Zac caught her eye, smiling so intimately her pulse raced. Why was he here?

Letting him 'get to know her' via text was one thing. Having him here and needing to protect herself from inevitable heartbreak was another.

With her mind spinning, she left for the kitchen. In front of the fridge, she took another deep breath. Behind her, Zac cleared his throat, and she turned. "Um...I was going to heat up some leftovers for myself, but..." She trailed off.

Unnerved by his unreadable expression and piercing gaze, warmth flooded her.

"What are you doing here, Zac?"

First, he gave his watch a cursory glance, then he dragged her into his arms. His familiar musky scent enveloped her, accelerating her heartbeat.

"You smell amazing," he murmured.

"Zac," she said, pushing against his muscular chest. He didn't budge. "Y-you said you were hungry. I can't fix you anything if you're holding me."

"You don't need to feed me," he whispered huskily, his gaze smoldering.

What? Hadn't he said he was hungry?

Slowly, his head dipped, and her eyelids instinctively fluttered closed. But, before his lips could meet hers, the doorbell rang, and her eyes flew open.

Who on earth—?

"Perfect," he said, releasing her and striding toward the front door.

"What's perfect? Are you expecting someone?"

He didn't answer, but a short while later, he returned, bringing the delicious smell of pizza with him.

"You ordered Sicilian from Marco Polo's?" she asked, amazed.

"Yep. I'm ready to eat. Are you?"

Her stomach grumbled, and she nodded.

Fine. If Zac thought kissing could wait, then so be it.

While they shared the gigantic pizza, they watched *Pride & Prejudice*—Zac's choice.

Alex should've been irritated. Here he was crashing her night, ordering her food, and choosing her entertainment. How had he known it was one of her favorite films anyway? Unless...he'd planned it and asked his sister. An unbidden smile crept onto her face.

"What are you thinking about?"

"Nothing. It's just that..." She waved her hand between the TV and the take-out. "This is actually nice."

His eyes traveled to her lips. "I told you we could do this." She held her breath as he wiped some sauce from the corner of her mouth but then shifted away to focus on the TV screen.

Disappointment took root. Again.

What was he up to?

She'd said stolen moments were all they could have, but here he was behaving like they were on a date. Perhaps he was trying to prove something—coming all the way here to spend an evening together doing her favorite things.

Could it possibly work?

Suppressing a sigh, she peeked at his handsome profile. What would he do if she touched the small scar on the bottom of his chin? If she leaned up and kissed him? He laughed unexpectedly, and she lost her nerve, quickly transferring her attention to the images on the screen.

By the time they were halfway through the movie, she was snuggled against his side, his arm slung comfortably over her shoulders, their fingers entwined.

Imagine, this could easily be my life.

If only.

When the credits ran up the screen, Alex tilted her head and stared straight into Zac's blazing eyes. "I love that movie," she said. "I haven't seen it in a while...in fact, I think it's been about—"

His face inched closer. Stopped.

The desire in his eyes had her heart galloping. She swallowed hard and continued, "About three yea—"

The rest of her words were silenced as Zac's mouth covered hers hungrily, his lips tasting and teasing. She drew him closer by curling her hand around his waist. This was what she'd been waiting for all night.

Running his tongue along the crease in her mouth, he parted her lips. She let out a soft moan, allowing him to deepen the kiss. As a warm, liquid feeling seeped throughout her body, she sank into him.

When he pulled away abruptly, she stifled a groan. He stood then, bringing her with him, and before she could utter an objection, he was kissing her again. Oh, so slowly.

If he kept it up, she'd be in a puddle at his feet. Not that she minded. But, honestly, being held in his arms and kissed like this? She could stay this way forever.

Eventually, he broke the kiss and let out a long breath. He peered toward the kitchen. "Coffee?"

She could only nod.

Minutes later, they lingered at the corner of the island with their lattes, the air between them charged.

Needing a distraction, Alex's gaze shot briefly to the stunning red roses. The man sure knew how to spoil a woman with gifts, but she wanted so much more.

"Zac? Why did you come this weekend?"

"To see you."

"I get that, but why?"

"It's been fun texting, but I figured we could do with some alone time, just you and me. I wanted to show you this can work."

She ran her finger around the rim of her mug. "So you plan on coming to New Haven every weekend?"

"Yes."

"You don't expect me to travel to New York?"

"No."

She bit her lip. "How long do you think you'll be able to keep it up...the two-hour trip each way?"

One side of his mouth hitched upward. "Remember I told you I'd sorted out something good at work?"

She nodded, sipping her coffee.

"Well, from next Friday, I'll finish at one every week, and I won't be expected back until ten on Monday mornings."

"Wow...that's good, I guess."

"You guess?"

With a determined look, Zac put both their mugs down.

"Alexandra Masters," he said, cradling her cheeks, "I think I fell in love with you the second I laid eyes on you, the day Sophie was baptized."

Her heart started a stampede she couldn't control, and her throat tightened.

"I think I did too," she whispered, shocked when the words came out. Despite her doubts and the stumbling blocks in their relationship, she knew it was true. Admitting it was a huge step.

Zac eased back, his loving gaze locking onto hers, taking her breath away.

"Are you saying you love me, Alex?"

"Yes."

This time, when his lips touched hers, they seemed different, more confident. He made her feel treasured, wanted, and loved as if she was the only woman in the world. His lips melted hers, savored hers. His tongue worked its magic, sending divine tingles to every part of her body.

The experience was life-changing, making her yearn for more. Their bodies edged together until there were no gaps. She slipped her arms around his neck, her fingers diving into the hair at his nape. It felt so right.

All too soon, it ended with Zac's intense gaze holding hers captive afterward.

"You're amazing and beautiful, sweetheart." His voice was raw and husky when he spoke. "And kissing you is so dangerous." He caressed her cheek, his thumb traveling to trace her bottom lip. His touch was electric.

Thinking straight was impossible with his hands holding her like delicate glass and his body pressed up against hers. She pushed him away, and with a few backward steps, put enough distance between them, so no part of their bodies touched.

Concern etched his features.

"We need to finish our conversation," she said.

Arching a brow, he took a step toward her.

She held up her hands. "Answer this question. How long do you think you'll keep up the weekly travel before you decide you need a break? Or an awards ceremony, or an important birthday party, or a medical emergency comes up, and you just can't pass it up?"

"I promise you, sweetheart—I want you in my future. And not just as my niece and nephew's godmother. I want to date you, and I'm committed to commuting until you and I are ready to take the next step."

"The next step?"

He gave a firm nod. "Yes, you know, getting engaged...then...married."

A thrill went through her at his words. He'd given this some serious thought. Yet, there was still one thing —the critical issue—the one thing that could melt her dreams faster than ice cream on a sunny day. She was almost too afraid to ask. Except she had to.

"Where do you see us living?"

"New York, of course." He smiled, taking another step forward. "After all, that's where my practice is, right? You're a fantastic teacher, Alex. Any school in New York would be privileged to have you teach their kids."

And there went her dream, sinking like the Titanic. Suddenly the pain gripping her chest was unbearable, and sorrow gathered like a storm.

She needed to leave.

"I see," she said, her vision blurring as she moved toward the front door where her coat and purse were stored.

"Sweetheart? Where are you going?"

She swallowed down the lump in her throat.

"I'm confused. Are you leaving? What's going on?" Zac's tone held alarm as he questioned her.

She spun around, tears sliding down her cheeks. "Thanks for the perfect night." She swiped at her damp cheeks, saw his confusion and hurt, and gulped down further tears. "But it's not going to be repeated. We want different things."

Shaking his head, he reached out to hold her upper arms. "I don't understand. What are you talking about?"

"I told you not to waste your time, Zac. This time I mean it."

"You're not making any sense. Talk to me, Alex. *Please,* don't go."

Her heart broke, hearing the pleading in his voice, but there was no point. He would always want to live in New York, and she would always want to stay in New Haven. Period.

Drawing on her inner reserves, she looked directly at him. "I'm sorry, Zac, but it's over. We have no future."

A key unlocking the door interrupted his response. Taking a step back, he released Alex as Melanie appeared in the open doorway with Steven right behind.

"I was just saying goodnight," Alex said, forcing cheer into her voice. "I hope you two had a wonderful evening."

Without looking back, she brushed past them and left.

Chapter Twenty-Two

Alex's hasty departure left Zac standing in the entryway, with Melanie glaring at him and Steven shifting uncomfortably by her side.

"What just happened, Zac? What did you do?"

"Nothing, Mel," he growled, raising his hands.

"Shall I check on the kids while you get the coffee going?" Steven gave his wife a pointed look. "I'm sure we could all do with some."

Coffee? A stiff drink would be better. Even so, Zac was grateful for the reprieve. Turning, he high-tailed it to the kitchen before Melanie could bite his ear off.

As his sister bustled around her kitchen, he sat holding his head in his hands, trying to process the recent turn of events.

If Alex loved him, why wouldn't she want what he wanted? Didn't all women want the same thing? To be in a relationship, to get married. What else was there? She didn't mean living together, surely?

No, it had to be something else. If she'd stuck around long enough for them to talk further, he'd know what her problem was. He huffed out a frustrated breath and lifted his head.

"Here you go." Melanie scrutinized him as she passed over a steaming mug and took a seat. "Now, fill me in on what went on tonight. Alex rushed out of here, upset. Considering she only just left, things must've been going okay."

"Everything was perfect until I told her again that I love her."

"She didn't return the sentiment?"

"On the contrary, she admitted she's in love with me too."

Melanie's eyebrows rose so high, he didn't know whether he should be offended or not.

"Wow! So not what I expected you to say." She patted his arm. "So why *did* Alex leave so fast? I could've sworn she was crying."

Hanging his head for a moment, he asked himself the same question again. Why indeed?

"I wish I knew, Mel."

Though the strong aroma of his favorite java offered no comfort, he took a sip, then linked his fingers around the warm mug. "Alex asked where I thought we were headed, and I might've mentioned marriage."

"What? Are you insane? Don't you think you were rushing her just a little? You aren't even dating!"

He huffed. "I know that! But, it's not like these feelings just sprung up between us."

"What do you mean?" Confusion and surprise crossed her face. "The way you feel about Alex isn't a recent development?"

"No. Not really. I fell for her the moment we met."

Melanie's eyes widened. Didn't she believe him?

"It's true. I know you're going to remind me of how I've treated her in the past, but I was only trying to protect myself and not give in to my true feelings. Seems

Alex felt the same way. She just dealt with it differently." He smiled wryly, then added, "She dated Jack instead."

"I see." Melanie's dull tone implied she didn't appreciate his attempt at humor. "But that still doesn't explain why she bolted."

Steven wandered into the room, clearing his throat. "The kids are fast asleep," he said, slipping an arm around Melanie's waist and pressing a kiss to her head. "Thanks for my coffee, darling."

Zac had to look away. He wasn't in the mood to deal with their perfect relationship.

"So, why did Alex leave?" Steven asked.

Melanie smirked at him. "Zac talked about getting married...to her."

Fantastic—now his brother-in-law was going to think he was an idiot too!

"In my defense," he said quickly, "both Alex and I agreed we're in love, and she *had* asked about the future. So not totally inappropriate, I would've thought."

Steven nodded. "I guess you scared her off then?"

"No." Zac shook his head. "We started talking about where we'd live. That's when things went wrong."

"You need to elaborate," Melanie admonished. "Remember, we didn't hear the conversation."

Slipping off the barstool, Zac shoved his hands in his pockets and paced. "I said it made sense for us to live in New York."

Melanie frowned. "What about her job here?"

"It's easy enough to teach in New York."

"But her life is here! Her friends and family are here."

"Melanie has a point," Steven said, taking a seat. "Trust me. I've been down the same road." He glanced affectionately at his wife, who nodded.

"If I hadn't wanted to compromise, we wouldn't be together right now," Steven added. "Let alone married."

"So you're telling me I need to give up my practice in New York—my dream—and come back to New Haven? Start over?"

Melanie shrugged. "If you want to be with Alex, I think that's the only way it's going to work. At the very least, you should talk it through with her." She sipped her drink, then eyed him. "For the record, Zac, if you take my best friend and my children's godmother away, I'll be furious. It's bad enough you're not around." Her face softened. "I miss you."

"I know, Mel." Walking over to her, he pulled her into an embrace. "I'm sorry I'm not here often." Releasing her, he peered between them. "But like I told Alex, I've made some changes. From now on, I'll be able to spend every weekend in New Haven, so you'll be seeing me more."

Melanie beamed. "Oh, that's wonderful!"

"It certainly is," Steven said, smiling. "We'll all appreciate having you around more."

"Thanks. For the advice too." Zac forced a cheerful expression despite feeling despondent and beat. "I don't know about you two, but I'm ready to hit my pillow."

"Me too. Ben still has a two a.m. feeding." Melanie strolled over to the sink and abruptly swung back around. "By the way, I promised Sophie we'd take her ice skating tomorrow, assuming she was well behaved."

The planned activity had completely slipped Zac's mind. He gave a brief nod. "She mentioned it, and I can vouch for her exemplary behavior."

"Brilliant." Melanie grimaced. "Oh, and FYI, Alex is coming too."

***

Angry tears streaked down Alex's cheeks as she lay in her bed. She felt so stupid. How many times was she going to do this to herself? Zac had never kept how he felt about living in New York a secret! Did she really think he'd suddenly change his mind? And why had she admitted her feelings to him?

Time she learned from her mistakes. Time she moved on, even if it would be a struggle.

Switching off her bedside light, she sank under her bedcovers and attempted to go to sleep.

The following day, she woke up tired but determined to make the most of her day. Unlocking her phone, she dialed Michael's number. He answered after the first ring. "Hey, Alex! I didn't expect you to call. Weren't you busy today?"

"Not anymore. I'd like to spend the day with you...if you're still free?"

He chuckled. "Absolutely! You up for some ice skating?"

"No!"

"Oh. I thought it was one of your favorite things to do." He sounded confused.

"Normally, but if you don't mind, I'd rather do something a little warmer and more romantic."

"I love the sound of that." His voice held a smile. "I take it you have a suggestion?"

"I do. Pick me up at ten?"

"Sounds perfect. "

Hanging up, she closed her eyes. Now she just had to forget about Dr. Danvers and the fact he was down the road, going ice skating with their goddaughter.

Michael arrived on time, terrific-looking in tan cotton trousers, a black polo shirt, and a black leather jacket.

When she stepped out of her apartment, a hint of appreciation sparkled in his blue-gray eyes, and heat crept up her neck as his warm gaze traveled her length.

She'd taken her time choosing her outfit, deciding on silver trousers, a black silk shirt—worn untucked—with a knee-length black suede coat. With the belt untied and the buttons undone, it completed the smart yet casual effect she'd been going for.

"You look amazing," he said, clasping her hand in his. No sparks or tingles, but it felt comfortable.

"Thanks, Michael. So do you."

On the way to his car, they chatted about the weather and where they were going. All the while, she wondered whether going on this date was wise. Last night she'd been declaring her love to one man, and today she was out with another. A man who was very interested in a relationship and wasn't the sort to have a casual fling.

Honestly, neither was she.

She peeked at Michael's relaxed expression. Before she could look away, he caught her gaze and squeezed her hand. When he smiled, she did the same.

They got along so well, and he ticked all the right boxes. The most important one being he lived here and not in New York. Besides, he had a great sense of humor, was the perfect gentleman, and hadn't ever made her even think about crying.

A win, win, win situation, as far as she was concerned.

During the long drive to the theater, Michael's mood turned pensive. Was he waiting for her to take the initiative? Or—

"What do you prefer, Alex, dramas or musicals?"

His sudden question took her by surprise.

"Um...a combination, ideally," she replied. "What about you? Do you prefer action to romance?"

He smirked. "That's not a trick question, is it? I'm a man. Obviously, I like action, but if I'm honest, I like a little romance too."

"An honest man. I love it. Makes you more manly."

Flexing the muscles of his right arm, he sent her a wide smile.

"Show off!" She pushed his arm down, her hand landing on his. He immediately linked their fingers. Momentarily flustered, she spoke without considering his circumstances. "So, do you use the school gym, or do you have one at home?"

"I have my own gear in my basement; set up the way I prefer."

Of course! "Nice. I forgot money isn't an issue."

The one side of his mouth lifted. "And it is for you?"

She shook her head. "I'm not rolling in it, but my folks had a fairly decent life insurance policy. I managed to pay off my apartment, and my salary covers living expenses and vacations. I'm lucky, really. Most women my age are desperate to find a man and get married, so they don't have to worry about getting into debt."

"I'm grateful I don't need to worry about that with you." He grinned mischievously, making her frown.

"Rest assured, Michael, the size of a guy's checkbook is the last thing I'm interested in. Love, friendship, shared beliefs, and mutual goals are way more important. Though I don't plan on marrying a pauper either."

"Glad to know it," he said seriously, then his teasing tone returned. "For a minute there, I worried you were only after me for my money."

"Haha."

A comfortable silence ensued.

"I'm glad we're doing this," Michael said, caressing the top of her hand. "I did wonder when I thought I couldn't see you this weekend."

"I'm sorry about that. I promised Mel I'd babysit for her ages ago. Anyway, that might not be a problem for us anymore."

His brow arched. "She's found another sitter?"

"Sort of. Her brother, Zac, plans on spending weekends here."

Michael shot her a sideways glance. "He's planning on commuting every weekend? From New York?"

"Apparently."

"I can't imagine him doing that for long."

"I told him the same thing last night." She sighed. "He didn't think it would be a problem."

"You *saw* him last night?"

Great. Why did she have to go and mention Zac?

"He arrived while I was feeding Ben," she said. "Mel hadn't mentioned anything about him visiting, so I don't think she knew."

"So you left early?"

"No." She dragged out the word.

"You stayed with him?"

"Yes," she said, without meeting his eyes.

"I thought you didn't get along with him."

"We don't normally, but..." her voice trailed off as Michael's hand left hers. His jaw clenched, and a knot formed in her stomach. Michael was a good man. Hurting him was the last thing she wanted to do.

"You don't need to worry about Zac," she said gently. "I've no intention of entertaining the idea of a long-distance relationship ever again. Especially not with someone who lives in New York."

"So you've thought about it?" he asked, his eyes never leaving the road.

"About what?"

"A relationship with Zac?"

"No. Not really. He seemed to think..."

Alex pursed her lips. Talking about this was a waste of time, totally unproductive.

"You know what? Zac's my best friend's brother, nothing more. Please let's talk about something else," she said, somehow managing to sound more sure of herself than she felt.

The silence lasted ages.

Finally, Michael said, "Sounds good to me," and she released a long breath.

"Thank you."

When she slipped her hand tentatively onto his thigh, and he covered it with his own, her unease lessened further.

A few hours later, as they stood to leave the theater town's trendiest restaurant, Alex clutched her stomach and groaned. "The food was so tasty, but now I'm stuffed!"

"It sure was. So, how about a walk?" Michael gave her a playful smile, then winked. "Because I definitely need to work off all the delicious calories I ate."

She laughed. "You sound just like a woman."

He pretended to scowl.

"I'd love to," she said. "Fresh air is just what I need."

Threading his fingers through hers, Michael led them outside to where the earlier clear sky was now overrun with cotton-ball-shaped clouds.

They strolled along the sidewalk, admiring the Christmas decorations in each store window as well as the pretty lights decorating the street lamps on the way.

The small-town feeling was evident. They passed people who smiled and greeted them as if they knew each other.

"They're so friendly." Michael waved at a few. "I bet they all know we're only visiting."

"You're probably right." Chuckling, she peered around at the couples and families dotting the opposite sidewalk. "I bet they're making up stories about us to use at a town meeting later. They'll say, 'You know that young couple who walked hand-in-hand? They came to see a show in our theater and dined in our finest restaurant. Let's hope they liked it so much they visit again soon'."

"Would you want to do this again?" he asked, his expression earnest.

Tilting her head, Alex lifted a finger to her mouth. "This *has* been a most pleasant day. I think I would. "

"Most pleasant?" He laughed, though it sounded more forced than naturally joyful. "I was hoping for thoroughly enjoyable or to be repeated as soon as possible."

"Okay," she relented, squeezing his arm and batting her eyelashes at him. "What you said."

The toothy smile he gave her said it all. Now all she had to do was make sure she didn't break his heart.

Chapter Twenty-Three

It took Zac a while to gather his bearings when he awoke the following morning.

His sister's guest room. Right.

Wiping his brow with his pajama sleeve, he recalled his dream, rather his nightmare. He'd been desperately running, trying to catch Alex, who'd somehow eluded him. Every time he stretched out his hand, thinking he could touch her, she moved just out of reach. Shouting her name hadn't stopped her fleeing, nor had his declaration of 'Alex, I love you, give us a chance'.

Throwing off the bedcovers, he swung his feet to the ground, pushed his fingers through his tousled hair, and took a deep breath.

Shower first, then coffee.

Exhaling slowly, his thoughts ran to last night's conversation with Alex. Tightness gripped his chest. They needed to talk.

Again.

If he could just get to the bottom of her concerns. With that said, if Melanie was right, and the issue was Alex wanting to stay in New Haven, then he'd make a plan. He'd darn well have to!

After ice skating, he was having lunch with his parents—the perfect time to chat with his dad. '*Danvers' Family Practice*' had a nice ring to it, and Dad would be happy to have his successful son working beside him, right? Zac would get to live near his family again *and* have the woman of his dreams.

What more could a guy ask for?

An hour later, he stood with Melanie and Sophie inside the rink entrance while Steven pushed Ben around in the stroller. When Melanie checked her phone for the tenth time in so many minutes, Zac's gut tightened.

"Still nothing?"

"I'm gonna give her a quick call, make sure she's alright," she said, walking off to a quieter area.

He couldn't decipher her expression given the distance, but she shook her head at one point and a pit formed in the bottom of his stomach. Alex wasn't coming.

Sophie tugged his hand. "Uncle Zac, do you think Miss Alex is okay?"

"I'm sure she's fine. She's probably stuck in traffic." He wished that were the case; deep down, he knew it wasn't.

"Alex can't make it after all," Melanie confirmed, rejoining them.

Sophie's shoulders slumped. "That's not fair, Mommy! I wanted to skate with her."

Zac squeezed her hand. "How 'bout we play tag, Sophie-girl? See if I can finally catch you."

Blue eyes, so much like her father's, lit up. "Can we, Uncle Zac? You won't get a work call and have to leave?"

Her wary expression tugged at his heart. "I promise, I'll be here the whole time."

"Yay!"

At least he'd made his niece smile again.

That made one of them.

Whizzing around the rink with a child hot on his tail kept Zac's mind occupied. Time passed quickly, and before he knew it, they were packing up their skates.

When he was done, he sat next to Melanie, who was feeding Ben discreetly. She regarded him closely, her brow furrowed. "You're going to ask about Alex, aren't you?"

"Why isn't she here?"

"I thought you'd figured it out."

"She told you it was because I'm here, right?" He heard the dejection in his voice but couldn't help it. He'd planned on spending as much time as possible with her this weekend, but somehow—he wished he knew how—he'd gone and ruined everything.

"No. Her actual words were, 'I had a change of heart, so I've made other plans for today'."

"So it *is* my fault she's a no-show."

His sister's sympathetic look said it all.

Leaning his elbows on his knees, he stared at where all the skates had scuffed the flooring over the years. "I'm sorry, Mel. I didn't mean for Sophie to be disappointed."

"It's fine." Her soft hand touched his. "Alex promised she'd take Sophie skating later this week. Besides, look at the bright side; Sophie had a wonderful time with her uncle. That likely wouldn't have happened if Alex had been here."

He smiled tightly. "I suppose."

Would Alex avoid him every weekend from now on? Because he *was* going to keep coming home, now he'd made the time. He wasn't giving up on them.

Another thing Alex missed out on that day was his mom's home-cooked meal. Beef pot roast with carrots and potatoes, along with a delicious dessert of pecan pie and ice cream.

Once lunch was over, and the dishes were cleared away, Zac turned to his father. "Any chance you and I could talk, Dad?"

"Of course, son." He smiled warmly. "In my study?"

Zac nodded, his palms clammy.

A long time ago, it was the place where they'd talk about Zac's future, or Dad would share advice about some girl Zac was crushing on in high school. His study was still the same—bookcases filled with medical journals, walls covered in landscape paintings by his favorite artist, and an antique wooden desk marked with unique nicks and stains. The only difference was the new, trendy, light gray paint on the walls.

As Dad reclined in the overstuffed armchair across from Zac, the desk lamp's light reflected off his lightly wrinkled skin.

"How are things going in New York, son?"

"Good. Really well, actually."

"That's great. I'm so thrilled and so proud of what you've accomplished. You've set the bar very high. I truly believe you did the right thing moving to New York. Not staying here under my shadow was a wise move. One I'm sure you'll never regret."

Zac wasn't so sure about that. Rather than voice his doubts, he offered up a tight smile that lasted all of one second. "I appreciate the vote of confidence, Dad," he said. Then, trying to organize the jumbled words in his brain, Zac massaged the back of his neck. He'd never wanted to disappoint his father.

Would this conversation do just that?

"Are you still happy running your practice on your own?" he asked, leveling his gaze on Dad, his hero.

After a slow nod, Dad rubbed his chin as if measuring his response carefully. "I find working for myself, with no one to dictate how I do things, works well for me. I've been doing it alone for thirty years, and I've never had any complaints from any of my patients." His eyes twinkled. "Except for Mrs. Dotty. She's a hypochondriac who complains about everything, even the fresh flowers I have in reception."

Zac managed a nervous laugh. "I guess why change what isn't broke, right?"

"Exactly."

They both remained quiet while Zac peered out the window. He fixated on the fluffy white patches punctuating the sky. They fit the scene, their presence expected on a winter's day in December. The same way he fit in New York. And Dad had made it perfectly clear —New York was the right place for him.

So what now?

Would he be able to persuade Alex that they could have a good life in New York and still occasionally see everyone? Convince her she could easily make new friends there? That when they had a family of their own, their life would change again. Improve for sure.

"I hope I'm not interrupting." Mom's voice brought him out of his musings.

"Not at all, darling." Dad beamed at her, then glanced at him. "We're done, right, son?"

"We are."

"I thought you might like something hot." Smiling, she carefully set two large mugs down on glass coasters.

"Thanks, Mom." Zac immediately lifted his drink and stood. "I'll take it outside if you don't mind?"

"Of course not." She gave him a one-armed hug. "I'm so glad you're here. I love you."

"Me too." He pressed a kiss to her cheek and left.

Slumping over the porch railing, he took in the view. Subtle garden lights, accentuating the evergreen plants, showed off his parent's well-maintained back yard.

The scene was the epitome of their life—well-ordered and disciplined. Their children were meant to be an extension of that. Melanie hadn't always emulated that ideal, but now with Steven, she did.

Zac had thought he was adhering to the mold—you know, the perfect son. Yet, it wasn't true. Only when he had a family would he feel whole, complete, like he belonged in this perfect picture his parents portrayed.

Just over two weeks ago, he'd been in this exact spot telling Alex he loved her for the first time. He wasn't sure what he'd expected from her right then, but now he did. He needed her in his life, permanently. Whatever it took, he had to make it happen. Pulling his phone from his jacket pocket, he hit number one on speed dial.

"Hi, this is Alex. I can't—"

He'd already left two messages; he wasn't going to leave a third. Tapping on the message icon, he sent her a text: ***Sweetheart, we need to talk. Please call me.***

As he sipped his peppermint-flavored coffee, he made a decision. Twenty minutes later, he was knocking on Alex's door. After his third knock with no reply, the door to the right opened, and an elderly lady stepped into the hallway.

"Are you looking for Alex, dear?"

"Yes."

Kind gray eyes looked him up and down. "Never seen you around here before." Her wrinkles increased as she frowned. "Are you a friend of Alex's?"

"Kind of. I'm Melanie's brother, Zac Danvers."

She gave a slight nod. "Nice to meet you, Mr. Danvers. I'm Mrs. Lewis. I've met your sister. Melanie's a lovely lady. Her children are cuties too."

"They are. So, Alex?"

"Yes, sorry, dear, her boyfriend picked her up hours ago in that fancy car of his. I'm not sure when she'll be back."

"Oh," he said, burying his disappointment. He needed to go, and he had a feeling this lady would keep talking if he didn't make a run for it. "It's alright. I'm heading back to New York anyway."

"I'll let her know you came by."

"I'd appreciate that, Mrs. Lewis."

Turning, he strode back toward the elevators, his fists clenched by his side. Alex was out with another man! That explained why he hadn't heard from her. Mrs. Lewis had said 'boyfriend', which meant it wasn't the first time this guy had visited. It couldn't be Jack, so it had to be Michael, the person she'd been on a date with last weekend.

At home, a couple hours later, Zac stepped out of the shower to hear a text tone alert. Rushing into his bedroom, he grabbed his phone and sunk onto his bed to read Alex's short message.

There's nothing left 2 talk about.

Is that what she thought?

His fingers rushed over the screen: ***I disagree. You said we want different things, but you never explained. I thought love would be enough to overcome anything.***

Her reply was prompt: ***I'll spell it out 4 u. My life's in New Haven; yours is in NYC. End of story. No future. Clear enough?***

His heart plummeted.

Melanie was right; Alex wouldn't give up her home for him. And he couldn't give up his practice, not after the conversation he'd had with his dad today. If he did, he'd have to live with the guilt of failing his father. Instead, he'd have to live without the one person he believed he was meant to spend the rest of his life with.

The lobbing between him and Alex had come to an end with no winners.

Game over.

Chapter Twenty-Four

Dusting off her hands, Alex's gaze swept across the classroom. Yep, the cleaning crew would approve. Gathering her belongings, she slung her purse over her shoulder and turned out the lights. After her recent jam-packed days, she looked forward to heading home and recharging for the final week of school.

Countless Christmas activities with her class had kept her hands busy this past week. Unfortunately, none of it had fully occupied her mind. No matter how hard she tried, Zac had pushed his way into her thoughts at the most inopportune of moments.

Like when one of her kids had fallen in the playground during recess and needed to see a doctor—Alex couldn't help comparing the poor man to Zac. In addition to their ice skating trip, she'd also taken Sophie home twice after school, during which all Sophie talked about was her uncle, causing Alex further heartache.

Zac had remained surprisingly silent, implying he'd accepted their state of affairs. Which meant she was right; New York had won. He couldn't love her as much as he claimed since he'd chosen his work over her. It showed exactly where his priorities lay.

Good thing she'd discovered it now. It was the right call. She didn't want to play second fiddle. If she wasn't number one in his life, the relationship wouldn't work, no matter how much she missed him. Missing his incredible kisses and how he made her feel when she was with him would be a small price to pay for protecting her heart long term.

Besides, Alex mused as she shut her classroom door, who was to say Michael wouldn't be just as great a kisser anyway? If she worked up the courage to actually let him kiss her.

He'd been wonderful and patient. Thoughtful too—sending her exotic flowers, handmade chocolates, and collectible teddy bears—doing his utmost to be removed from the friend zone.

The issue was, she compared everything he did to the only man who got her heart racing. When Michael rubbed his chin, she pictured Zac. When Michael held her hand, she imagined it was Zac. Of course, it didn't help that both men had brown hair and blue eyes. Except Zac's were a deeper blue, especially when he was about to kiss her.

Stop thinking about Zac!

Giving herself a mental shake, Alex put one foot in front of the other and strode down the hallway toward the school exit.

That evening, Michael held the door as she stepped inside the pub. She knew she shouldn't be nervous about them joining Melanie and her work gang, but butterflies swirled in her stomach nevertheless.

"It's rather cozy in here," she said, shrugging out of her stuffy coat. She turned to find Michael's hand outstretched, a smile on his handsome face.

"Let me hang that with mine on those hooks."

Following his line of sight to the far wall, she sighed gratefully and handed over the heavy garment. "Thank you."

The smell of fried food assailed her nostrils along with the stench of alcohol as she scanned the crowded room. Judging from the rowdiness of several customers, they'd been at it for a few hours. Hopefully, Michael would protect her from any unsavory characters.

As if reading her thoughts, his hand looped around her waist, drawing her closer. The spicy scent of his aftershave drowned out the other less pleasant aromas. She breathed it in willingly.

"So, drinks first?" he asked. "Or would you prefer to find everyone else beforehand?"

She pointed to the bar counter, where a few rows of customers were lined up. "I'm thirsty. Let's fight our way through that first."

"Suits me."

Armed with a drink each, they found Melanie and her group, and Alex made the introductions.

Jack gave Michael the once over before offering his hand. "Nice to meet you, Michael. We've heard a lot about you."

"You too, Jack. I'm looking forward to hearing you sing," Michael said. "And your beautiful partner, of course," he added, his gaze shifting to Julie.

Smiling proudly, Jack placed a hand on Julie's shoulder. "The brains and the beauty behind our act, Julie Rolland."

"A pleasure to meet you, Miss Rolland." Michael's natural charm flowed out in his voice.

Blushing, Julie stepped forward and shook his hand. "Please, call me Julie," she said, batting her eyelashes.

Could she be more obvious? Alex rolled her eyes.

"We'll talk to you guys later." Alex dragged Michael to the other end of the table and slid onto the bench seat.

"They seem like a lovely couple," he said in a hushed tone as he settled in next to her.

She stifled a snort. "They're not a couple. They just sing together."

"Oh." He frowned. "I could've sworn I picked up on some serious chemistry there."

"You mean the chemistry directed at you?" She huffed in exasperation. "Julie's the biggest flirt there is."

Leaning in, he whispered in her ear, "You're not jealous, are you?"

"What, of Julie? Of course not!"

"Pity." He sounded disappointed, but his eyes were dancing. "I was rather hoping you would be."

She laid a hand on his arm and smiled warmly at him. "Let's just say she's not my favorite person and leave it at that. Deal?"

"Deal." Covering her hand with his, Michael smiled back. A gorgeous smile that didn't reveal any dimples. Not like—

Feeling like she was being watched, Alex took a large sip of her white wine and glanced casually around the crowded table. Disconcerted by Jack's questioning gaze, she stared back at him for a few seconds, then broke eye contact.

Later, when they walked over to the karaoke venue, she managed to get him alone. "Do you have a problem with Michael, Jack?"

"Nope, I don't. In fact, I'd say he's a great guy."

"Really?" She eyeballed him. "Then why do I get the feeling you don't approve? Not that I need your approval, obviously."

"He's not Zac."

She felt like screaming but kept her voice neutral. "What's Zac got to do with anything?"

Jack pulled her back, halting her steps.

"Do you remember what you told me when we broke up?" he asked, his expression earnest.

Scrunching her brow, she shook off his hand and crossed her arms.

"You deserve someone who turns your world upside down, were your exact words."

"So?"

"Does Michael do that for you?"

"Seriously? You think Zac turns my world upside down? Where exactly is Dr. Danvers right now?" She paused for effect. "In New York, miles away from here. How is he going to turn my world upside down when he isn't even here?" Hearing how bitter and angry she sounded, Alex bit her lower lip and battled to meet Jack's eyes directly.

"You just answered your own question. I've seen the way you look at Zac, the way he looks at you. It's pretty obvious you two are madly in love. You just aren't prepared to admit it."

"I'd be most grateful," she said, glowering at Jack, "if you kept your opinions to yourself in the future." Her gaze shot ahead to where Julie chatted with Michael. "Maybe you should worry more about what's right in front of you than worry about who I'm dating."

Her ire rose as Jack threw his head back and laughed. Then, his expression suddenly became tender. "You can deny it all you want," he said, "but mark my words; you and Zac belong together." He touched her arm. "Everyone else can see it, Alex, except you."

The truth he spoke made her heart stumble. But—

"Seeing it and being able to act on it are two very different things, Jack." She drew in a breath and expelled it slowly. "It's just not that simple."

***

'Flu epidemic. All hands on deck.'

Zac stared at the Friday morning alert from Dan and struggled to contain his frustration. The timing of the overnight outbreak couldn't have been worse! His amended work timetable meant he couldn't leave work at lunchtime, and today's hospital shift would have to be rearranged for tomorrow. So, visiting New Haven this weekend? Out of the question. He could just imagine his conversation with Alex if she'd agreed to date him.

"I'm so sorry, sweetheart, but my patients need me."

"You promised, Zac, and yet you couldn't even make it for two weekends in a row! I knew it was too good to be true. How did you ever think this would work?"

Alex was right. It was hopeless. It never would've worked between them. He belonged in New York, and she clearly wasn't interested in commuting. His brain comprehending the finality of the situation didn't remove the weight he felt in his heart. If only he could give it a command: forget Alex, so the pain would leave.

While Zac downed a lukewarm cup of coffee much later that afternoon, his cell buzzed. Checking the caller ID, he grumbled, "Better get this over with."

Still, he counted to ten, then slid his finger across the screen. "Hi, Mel. I was expecting your call."

"Well, you sure took long enough to answer! Were you with a patient? Either way, I'm sorry to bother you at work, but you were meant to be here in person, if I remember correctly? I actually thought you were serious when you said you'd be here every weekend, but I should've known better.

"It's because of Alex, isn't it? I'll admit I haven't managed to speak to her much this week. I got the impression she's avoiding any deep conversation with me, and I'm sure it has everything to do with you. You better not have ruined a perfectly wonderful friendship! Don't forget, she's Sophie's godmother. Your niece would be devastated if Alex decided to give us all a wide berth because of you."

Melanie stopped for a split second, and he jumped in. "Are you quite finished, Mel? I have about a minute before my next patient arrives."

"Sorry. I'm just disappointed. Mom said you wouldn't be coming home today or at all. She mentioned the flu problem, so I understand. Sort of, but we'll still miss you."

"I'll miss you too, but honestly, I was having second thoughts about coming anyway. Alex made it crystal clear there's no future for us, so I'd rather not risk bumping into her right now."

Not exactly the truth—

"Oh, Zac! I'm so sorry." She sounded genuinely sad for him. "I did warn you, though. I know that's not what you want to hear."

"No, not really." The clock on his computer screen caught his eye. "Mel, I need to go."

"One more thing, then I'll let you get back to work. Tell me you're coming to our Christmas party next Friday." It wasn't a question so much as a demand.

He groaned. How could he have forgotten about the party?

"I don't suppose, by some small chance, Alex declined your invitation?"

"Seriously, Zac?!" The outrage in his sister's voice made him feel bad.

"Okay, okay. I'll come if I can bring a date." No way would he show up on his own when Alex was sure to be there with Michael.

"I'd love to meet Emma, so yes, of course. Though... I'll have to keep Alex out of her way. Otherwise, it may be a little awkward, you know, introducing them. I mean, what would I say?" Melanie paused. "Don't worry. I'll figure it out."

"I'm sure it'll be fine, Mel."

After ending the call, Zac held his head in his hands. *Great.* Now he had to persuade Emma to come to New Haven as his date—without her getting the wrong idea. Because if he couldn't be with Alex, he was swearing off women. For good.

The following afternoon, the rush on the office petered out, and Dan insisted Zac leave early.

At home, he pulled up Emma's number and hit dial. What if she refused to talk to him? Halloween *had* been six weeks ago. He wiped his hand over his jeans, his stomach in a knot.

"Hello, stranger," was Emma's greeting after taking ages to answer.

"I deserved that." He took a deep breath while she kept quiet, no doubt waiting for an apology.

"I'm so sorry, Emma. It's...things have been crazy around here."

"Hey, I'm happy to hear from you, Zac. And I forgive you." She chuckled. "Even if you waited forever to call, and any other sane woman would've blocked your number by now."

He laughed nervously, then swallowed hard. "I was wondering... are you free for dinner tonight?"

"Dinner? With you?" She sounded outraged.

"Never mind, I'm sorry—"

She let out an amused laugh. “Zac, I’m teasing! Of course, I’ll have dinner with you.”

“So, should I pick you up at seven-thirty?”

“Perfect. See you then, Dr. Danvers.”

He released a long breath. *This had better not be a mistake.*

That night, not too long after their eight o’clock reservation time had passed, Zac and Emma were shown to their table by a frazzled hostess—unsurprising, given the place was buzzing.

Trevor had mentioned he’d been served ‘the best pasta ever’ at a new Italian restaurant on the Upper East Side, and Zac decided he had to try it for himself.

As he dropped to his seat, his stomach rumbled. Thankfully not loudly enough for Emma, who sat across from him, to hear. She was casually sipping the red wine they’d managed to order during a short wait at the overcrowded, noisy bar. Their gazes connected, and she smiled prettily.

He smiled back. “It’s really good to see you, Emma,” he said, reaching for his wine glass.

“Ditto. Don’t wait another six weeks before you call again. Okay?”

He nodded, grateful at the wistfulness, rather than accusation, he heard in her voice. He missed having someone outside of work to chat with. Julie, his only other friend, was so busy nowadays.

“I’ll endeavor to keep in touch more regularly.”

“Good,” she said with a firm nod. Her gaze traveled to a couple at a nearby table who were leaning in close, whispering to each other.

Not keen to be reminded of what he was missing out on, Zac lifted the wine glass to his lips and savored the fruity, smooth flavor of the merlot.

When had he last had such an outstanding red? Thanksgiving? Alex had barely touched her wine that day. Didn't she like red wine? He shook his head. What did it matter?

He focused on the beautiful woman in front of him. Relaxed and happy, Emma's eyes twinkled. He cocked his head. "Is there anything you want to tell me?"

Blushing, she avoided eye contact. "I might've met someone."

"Might've?"

"Alright." She chuckled, looking at him shyly. "I *have* met someone. But it's early, so we're taking it slow."

"That's great!" He reached out to squeeze her hand briefly, then scowled. "What's he up to that you're not out with him?"

"A family dinner. More precisely, his father's fiftieth birthday."

"You didn't want to go?"

"I wasn't invited, and honestly, I'm glad. We've been on a few dates, but I'm not ready to meet his family. They're all anxious for him to settle down. He didn't think either of us needed that kind of pressure just yet. I agreed."

"Wise man. I hope he treats you well. You deserve an amazing guy."

"Thanks." Tilting her head, she laid a hand on his arm, but the tingles Zac felt when Alex did the same thing weren't there. "I thought that might've been you," Emma said softly.

He sucked in a breath. "I'm sorry. I should've told you a long time ago, my heart was taken, and I definitely shouldn't have kissed you. Friendship was all I was able to and can offer."

"It's okay. I've forgiven you, and I've moved on." Patting his arm, she looked away for a moment. "She's a lucky woman, Zac, the one who's captured your heart."

Groaning, he rubbed his hand over his face. "If only she agreed."

"What? She's not interested?"

"If I move to New Haven, maybe."

"Wow." Emma shook her head. "A big ask. You can't exactly compare the two places, can you?"

"It's not that. I'd have no problem living there, but my practice is here."

"I understand. I also know if she truly wanted to be with you, she'd move in a heartbeat. I know I would."

"Emma," he said gruffly, narrowing his eyes. He thought she understood.

A slow smile spread across her face. "I meant I would have moved, you know, when we were seeing each other before. Before I realized I was way more interested in you than you were in me."

He shifted uneasily in his seat. "I hope you're not under any false illusions about tonight?"

She held up her hands in surrender. "I promise you, I'm not."

"Okay, good."

He picked up the menu lying neglected on the table, then put it down again and scrutinized her instead. Satisfied she meant what she said, he figured it couldn't hurt to take a chance.

"In that case, would you accompany me to my brother-in-law's Christmas party in New Haven next Friday?" he asked. "As my friend?"

Emma grinned. "I'd love to. Carter's visiting his folks for Christmas, so that would work perfectly. Oh, and a friend of mine, in Beacon Falls, just had a baby."

"That's only a half-hour from New Haven."

"Yeah, so I'd get to visit her too," she said excitedly.

"Brilliant."

At least now he'd have a friend by his side when he came face to face with Alex.

Emma fingered her napkin. "Um, Zac? What do you plan on doing if this woman you love is there? Won't it be awkward if she sees me with you?"

"No. She's made her position very clear."

Chapter Twenty-Five

Zac opened the online medical journal on his work computer and scrolled through the articles until one caught his eye: *Poisonous alcohols - do you know everything?*

He certainly hoped so, but the idea of a patient dying because he wasn't up to date was inconceivable. Checking his schedule, he noted his next appointment time, then clicked on the report.

Fifteen minutes later, satisfied his knowledge was absolute, he leaned back in his chair and threaded his fingers behind his head. He glanced up at his wall clock. If he was right, his office phone would buzz in three, two, one.

Smirking slightly, he answered the receptionist's call with, "Tell Mr. Jones to come right in."

"Zac, it's me."

"Mom?" His heart rate quickened. She never called the office. "What's wrong?"

"Your Dad. He had a h-heart attack."

What? How? His dad was fit and healthy, so why? Struggling to catch his breath, Zac's throat went dry.

"He's in surgery," Mom said, sniffling.

His breath returned in a rush. "I'll be there as soon as possible, Mom. Don't worry, he'll be okay."

Going into crisis mode, Zac dialed reception. "Reschedule my non-emergency appointments for the rest of the day, and refer any emergencies to either Dr. Wilson or Dr. Johnson, please."

"Yes, of course, Dr. Danvers."

Cell phone and medical bag in hand, he strode down the hall to Dan's office. After rapping on the door, he walked straight in.

Dan jumped to his feet, his brow furrowed. "Zac! What's up?"

"My dad had a heart attack. He's in surgery."

"Go. We have you covered," Dan said, grasping his shoulder. "We'll be praying for a full recovery."

"Thanks. I'll let you know what's happening." He turned to leave, then swung back around. "Would you let Trevor know?"

"Of course. Drive safe."

Two hours later, he marched into New Haven hospital's emergency department.

"Zachary Danvers," he said to the nurse at the welcome desk. "My father was admitted earlier after a suspected heart attack."

"Mrs. Danvers said to expect you, Dr. Danvers. She's in the waiting room on the fourth floor. Elevators are on your right."

"Thank you."

Zac hurried to find his mom and sister. Would Steven and the kids be there too?

A momentary panic gripped him. What about Alex? Was school out yet? No. Winter break began Friday—the same day as Melanie and Steven's Christmas party—so Alex would still be teaching her class.

Part of him was disappointed; the logical part, relieved. He needed to make sure his father would be okay, not worry about running into the love of his life.

"Zac, you made it!" Melanie's wobbly smile greeted him as he rounded the corner into the waiting room.

After they shared a swift embrace, he asked if she'd spoken to the doctors.

"Yes. Dad's in the Coronary Care Unit, and someone will be here to take us to him any minute."

"That's helpful." Forcing a small smile, he peered over at his mom. "Hey, Mom."

"I'm so glad you're here, Zac," she said, closing the distance and hugging him tightly.

Easing back, he looked into her shimmering, slightly swollen eyes. "He's going to be fine, Mom."

"I'm praying so, Zac."

A few minutes later, they were gathered around Dad's hospital bed with Dr. Taylor, the doctor assigned to the case. Usually so robust, his father lay hooked up to heart monitors and blood pressure equipment. With his eyes closed, the white sheets matched his pasty face. He'd obviously been given some strong pain medication.

"Dr. Danvers underwent a PCI—"

Melanie raised her hand. "Sorry, Dr. Taylor, what exactly does that mean?"

"A PCI is a percutaneous coronary intervention. A procedure that treats blockages within one's coronary arteries and restores the blood flow to one's heart. The procedure was necessary to stop Dr. Danvers' heart attack and relieve his chest pain." He shot their mom a look of admiration. "Your mother's quick thinking and medical experience saved his life. Thankfully, he had minimal damage to his heart muscles and won't have to undergo any open-heart surgery."

"That's a relief," Melanie said.

"He'll need to rest and be closely monitored over the next twenty-four to forty-eight hours. Only immediate family may visit until he's transferred to a general ward. If all goes well, he'll get to go home in four to five days."

Dr. Taylor rubbed the back of his neck, then glanced between Zac and his mom.

"Given there are two medical professionals in the family, I'd be inclined to let my patient go home earlier if our tests come back clear."

Both Mom and Melanie's expressions brightened marginally.

"My father's in excellent hands, Dr. Taylor," Zac said. "But if there's anything I can do, let me know."

The man nodded briefly, shook Zac's hand, then left.

Mom's stomach suddenly complained loudly, and she grimaced. "Sorry, I missed breakfast."

"I need a snack, too, Mom," Melanie said, giving her a side hug. "And some coffee."

"Why don't you two head over to the cafeteria?" Zac suggested. "I'll stay with Dad, and you can grab me a coffee."

"Deal," Melanie said.

After they left, Zac pulled up a visitor's chair. He stared at his dad's grayish-blue eyes and the thin lines around them that seemed to have multiplied overnight. His mop of salt and pepper hair was noticeably thinner too. Was that even possible in just a few weeks?

Dad's eyelids fluttered open. "Zac. You're here."

Leaning forward, he laid a hand on his dad's arm and smiled reassuringly. "It's good to see you awake, Dad. How're you feeling?"

"Like I've run a marathon."

"That would be a first."

Dad chuckled; well, he tried but ended up coughing.

Grabbing a glass of water from the nightstand, Zac lifted his dad's head so he could take a sip, then gently lowered him back onto the pillow. "You okay?"

"Yes, though probably best you keep your humor at bay, son."

Saluting, he smiled. "Duly noted, sir. So...Dr. Taylor talked about only slight damage to your heart muscle, which is good news. You know you're going to need to rest and take it easy for the next week, don't you?"

"About that..." Clenching his jaw, Dad closed his eyes for a second.

"What's hurting?"

"Nothing." Unidentifiable emotions crossed his face. He looked away, swallowed, then resumed eye contact. "I wondered, son, would...would you be able to cover for me? Or are you going back...back to New York?"

His heart swelled. "I'd be honored. I can stay as long as you need me to. And, if you like, I'll head over there as soon as Mom and Mel get back from the cafeteria."

Dad's eyes glistened. "That would mean so much to me. I really don't want to leave my patients in the lurch."

"Anytime." He patted his dad's lower arm. "I mean it, Dad."

***

After parking his car outside Danvers' Family Practice—in the designated spot for a visiting MD—Zac climbed out and tightened his coat around him. His gaze roamed over the tan brick building which housed the practice, as well as the pharmacy. It had freshly painted black gutters, a gleaming red roof, and large glass windows. Evergreen bushes and trees planted out front made the building look colorful and inviting.

"Nice job, Dad," Zac said to himself.

He pushed open the glass entry door to the practice and stepped inside. The warm, modern decor filled him with a sense of pride, and the maroon padded chairs in the waiting room appeared comfortable and clean. Indoor plants were spread about the space, giving it a homey feel. Paintings of landscapes covered the walls, much like they did in his parents' home.

The difference here was his dad wouldn't be waiting to welcome him into his office, nor to give Zac a lollipop from the jar he kept on his desk. A momentary sadness engulfed him. Breathing deeply, he gave himself a mental shake. Dad would recover and be back at work in no time. He was a strong man, and this was a little bump in his life journey.

Shrugging out of his coat, Zac approached the welcome desk where a familiar woman talked on the phone. What was her name again? Mrs. Baxter, if he remembered correctly.

The second she spotted him, the corners of her lips lifted, and her brown eyes sparkled.

"Correct, Mrs. Lewis, Dr. Danvers is not available," she said. "I'm afraid you'll have to go to the hospital if you need urgent care. Otherwise, we'll see you for your next regular checkup in March." She nodded, listening to Mrs. Lewis's reply, then said, "Thank you, I'll tell him. You have a good Christmas too."

Smiling broadly, she pushed to her feet and rounded the long desk. "Zachary Danvers! My, my, you *are* a sight for sore eyes!"

She pulled him into a bear hug, her ample bosom squashing his chest and making it hard for him to breathe. Just before he ran out of breath, she finally let go of him.

"What's it been, fourteen years since you last stepped foot in here, son?" she asked, looking up the six or so inches necessary to see him.

He chuckled. "Yes, Mrs. Baxter, I believe it's been about that long."

"Please," she said, touching his arm. "You're a grown man now *and* a distinguished doctor. Call me Sue."

"Okay, Sue." It was at that precise moment that Zac had the strangest feeling he'd come home. He buried the emotion quickly but knew he'd recall it later.

The next few days settled into a comfortable routine. Each morning, he enjoyed his mom's cooked breakfast, then drove the short distance to his dad's office. Afterward, he would visit the hospital. Within twenty-four hours of being admitted, Dad had been moved to a general ward with Dr. Taylor reporting he should be home for Christmas.

Zac couldn't have been more thrilled.

Spending time in his dad's office was an eye-opener. Photos of Mom, Melanie and her family, and Zac were proudly displayed on the desk. It filled him with warmth to see how important family was to his dad.

And working with Sue? Well, it felt like they'd been working together forever. She was as lovely as he remembered, just older. After twenty-odd years, the woman sure knew all there was to know about the practice.

Only in the evenings, after saying goodnight to his mom and before closing his eyes, did he allow himself to think about Alex. When he did, his heart ached. They were in the same city, but they couldn't have been further apart. Every time he went to see his father, he half expected to bump into her, but he hadn't. According to Melanie, Alex had visited, just not at the same time.

He desperately wanted to call her. But what would he say?

"Hey, Alex. Want to meet for coffee? Or a kiss or two?"

Yeah, right, more stolen moments.

It was over, they had no future and wanted different things, or so she claimed. Best he get used to being alone with this gaping hole in his chest and a cracked heart. If his sister was right and everything hinged on him moving to New Haven, then it literally was over, and *that* realization brought him zero comfort.

By late Thursday afternoon, Zac had seen all the scheduled patients and was contemplating packing up when the smell of freshly brewed coffee changed his mind. He gave Sue a grateful smile as she passed over a steaming mug and sank into a visitor's chair.

Despite her calm demeanor, his heart rate sped up. "What's up, Sue?"

"I bet you're missing your busy New York practice right about now."

He shrugged.

"Could you ever see yourself settling here?"

Biding his time, he sipped his drink. New Haven *was* different. Busy, yet less rushed. People here came in eager for conversation, inquiring after his dad's health. They cared. In New York, Zac's patients lived hectic lives and came to see him when their health was affecting their performance—for no other reason. They didn't want to know about him personally, only what he could do for them.

He glanced around his current workspace. He could see himself coming in here daily, chatting over patient cases with his dad, living a marginally more relaxed but just as fulfilling life.

Except, their recent conversation served as a stark reminder—Dad didn't want or need anyone's help, including his. This was a once-off until Dad recovered.

The earnest expression on Sue's deeply tanned face told him being honest couldn't hurt. "It's great being here, Sue. Not the same as back home, but somehow it feels like home—if you know what I mean?"

"I do." She nodded. "Before joining here, I worked in a big city practice, and although I enjoyed it, I never really felt at home until I started working for your father."

A faraway look crossed her face, and he sensed she had more to say.

"He talks about you all the time, you know. From what he tells me, it's obvious he couldn't be prouder of all you've accomplished in New York."

"Good to know."

"But...I also know he wishes the two of you could work here together."

"He told you that?"

Worry clouded her features, and she laughed a little nervously. "I probably shouldn't have said anything," she said with a shake of her head.

"I appreciate your candidness." He reached out and patted her hand, giving her a reassuring smile in the process. "But I spoke to him recently and got the impression he was very happy working alone."

Sue fidgeted with her mug, then looked him straight in the eye. "I've caught your father, on more than one occasion, daydreaming while holding your photograph. When I eventually plucked up the courage to ask about it, he told me he'd started this practice hoping to have his son work alongside him one day. Take over from him, ultimately."

Shock spread through him.

Why hadn't Dad ever said anything? Instead, he'd allowed Zac to assume he wanted to keep doing it all on his own. Dad had even encouraged him to open his own practice in New York. Yet all the time, he'd wanted him here?

Well, that certainly changed things!

His heart rate accelerated at possibilities for the future. He needed to talk to his father again, and Dan too. Depending on the outcome...

Hope suddenly blossomed as memories flooded him. Alex, in his arms, like she belonged. Her desire-filled eyes staring intently into his. His hungry lips on hers. Their declarations of love.

They *did* want the same things. He was sure of it. If it turned out he was right, he could broach the subject of a relationship with her once again.

A smile grew steadily on his face as his mind raced.

"Judging from *that* look, I'd say you just had an epiphany."

Sue's voice startled him, drawing his attention back to her amused expression.

He nodded. "Sue, I think you might just be right."

Chapter Twenty-Six

Alex stared at the dark shadows under her eyes in the bathroom mirror. And at her lips pressed together. In just three days, it would be her favorite time of the year. Christmas.

Why wasn't she more excited?

Yanking open her makeup drawer, she scratched for some concealer, swept blusher over her cheeks, and added eyeliner and a splash of mascara. Then she outlined her lips in crimson and painted the rest in red.

There. The color matched her dress perfectly.

She tried to reason with herself. What could she possibly feel sad or discouraged about? School was out, and her class had behaved beautifully. Unless you counted their spirited behavior when she doled out the gifts she'd promised them at the beginning of the week. But the bribe had worked, so she couldn't really complain.

And Michael? He was another blessing in her life, and he'd be arriving soon.

Dating him should make her happy. The man was amazing—attractive, attentive, so patient, and great company—a good friend.

A good friend?

Yeah, that was the problem. If she was being fair, she shouldn't be seeing anyone right now. Not when her heart constantly yearned for Zac—his touch, his smile, his kisses.

Back in her bedroom, she twirled in front of the full-length mirror. The skirt of her fitted dress swung around her thighs, barely reaching her knees. The three-inch heeled, black suede ankle boots she'd chosen to wear weren't her favorite, but tonight they'd give her some sorely needed confidence.

Other than Melanie and Steven's wedding, Alex couldn't remember when she'd last gone to a party. The MacAlistars' Christmas celebration would be the perfect place to kick back and relax.

Except...her heart gave a little lurch...Zac would be there. He'd arrived on the day of his father's heart attack and hadn't left yet.

The few times she had visited the hospital, she'd gone straight after school. Thankfully, the chances of Zac being there at the same time had been slim. Melanie had mentioned he was volunteering at their dad's practice, so Alex hadn't purposefully avoided him. Not really.

But now...

The knot in her stomach grew tighter. How was she going to ignore her feelings and not throw her arms around Zac's neck and kiss him?

Michael would have to be her buffer. If she refused to let him out of her sight, she'd be able to stop herself from doing something she'd regret.

The first couple she and Michael ran into that evening when they entered the MacAlistar home was Jack and Julie.

Both were dressed to kill—Jack in his tailored dark suit with a white shirt and red tie, and Julie in her skin-tight black velvet dress. Amazingly, Julie barely gave Michael a passing glance while Jack had no problem throwing unsubtle glares Alex's way.

Clutching Michael's hand, she jiggled the bag in her other hand. "I'd better get this to our hosts."

Jack gave a curt nod, and Julie smiled sweetly. "Of course."

Dragging Michael away from the intimidating pair, Alex quickly located Melanie.

After they shared a warm embrace, she gestured to the colorful Christmas decorations. "You've gone all out, Mel. The place looks great!"

"I agree with Alex," Michael said.

"Aw, thanks, guys. Sophie helped a lot."

Laughing at Melanie's smirk, Alex held up her gift bag. "Is Steven nearby? I want to give him this."

"He's in the kitchen. With Zac." Melanie's eyes glinted mischievously as they transferred to Michael. "Would you like to meet my brother? He's also from New York. You might've heard of him? He's an MD."

"I think you'd be hard-pressed to find anyone who hasn't heard of Dr. Danvers, at least in New York. So yes, I'd love to."

Alex felt the blood drain from her face, and she automatically leaned against Michael. He peered down at her, concern knitting his brow. "You okay?"

Could she do this? Yes. She had to. It wasn't like she'd be able to avoid Zac the whole night or the rest of her life, for that matter.

Inhaling a deep breath, she plastered on a half-smile and nodded in reply.

***

Zac had no idea where Emma was at this precise moment, but he knew she was fine. Not long after they'd arrived at the party, his date, clearly a social butterfly, had happily flittered around on her own.

On the other hand, the woman he needed to see like he needed air to breathe, hadn't shown up yet. And unfortunately, when she did make an appearance, getting her alone would be a challenge.

His stomach churned.

Melanie had already warned him, Alex wasn't coming alone. Anxious to check out the man she was dating, Zac had hung around the front entrance for a while until Steven requested help in the kitchen. Now, isolated from the crowd, Zac clenched his jaw and focused on his brother-in-law.

"How can I help?"

"If you don't mind buttering the burger buns?" Steven pointed to the bags on the granite counter. "I'll turn the beef patties and get the pizzas into the oven."

Zac started spreading butter on the bread. "Remind me again why this is our job and not Mel's?"

Steven shrugged. "When my wife asks me to do something, I do it, no questions asked."

"I guess you're still in the honeymoon phase. Either that or Mel has you wrapped around her little finger. I'm not sure I'd be standing in the kitchen flipping burgers while other men gawk at my gorgeous wife."

"What do you mean?" Steven paled. "Tell me that's not what's happening?"

Throwing back his head, Zac laughed. "How would I know? I'm stuck in here with you. But seeing how hot she looked tonight, I wouldn't be surprised."

"You about done with those buns?" Steven asked a little brusquely, his color restored.

Grinning, Zac nodded. It was fun seeing his brother-in-law wound up.

"Good. Take over for me. I'm going to rescue my wife." Steven handed him the oven mitts and strode out the kitchen.

"At least you have a wife," Zac muttered.

When the meat was cooked and the pizzas sorted, he grabbed a beer from the fridge and went to find Emma. Instead, he was confronted by Alex in a red dress. His heart skipped a beat, and he couldn't take his eyes off her, despite her wary expression.

"Dr. Danvers, I believe. I'm Michael Smith," a deep voice said, forcing Zac's attention to Alex's date. He tried not to glare at the man or his outstretched hand. "It's an honor to meet you, Dr. Danvers. Your reputation precedes you."

"Mr. Smith," he said gruffly, making sure to look him straight in the eye as he gripped his hand. "What exactly are you referring to?"

"Your name on the Top Doctors of New York list for the past three years, of course. I'd say that's quite an accomplishment."

Alex turned to Michael, her eyes wide. "I didn't know that."

Bowing his head, Zac muttered, "I'm only doing my job."

Michael chuckled. "That may be, but if I still lived in New York, I'd make sure you were my doctor."

Zac scowled. Was that supposed to make him feel better? Like some sort of compensation for stealing his woman?

"There's an exceptional doctor right here in New Haven, Mr. Smith. My dad." Zac knew his tone was anything but friendly, but seriously?

He didn't need his ego stroked; he needed to talk to Alex. He stole a glance at her, but before he could analyze the conflict of emotions there, Michael's earnest voice drew him back.

"Yes, of course. I'm sorry to hear about your dad's heart attack."

"Thanks." The word came out clipped. Attempting a softer tone, he added, "He's doing much better now and assuming the tests on his heart tomorrow come up clear, he'll be home for Christmas."

"I bet that's a relief," Michael said.

Zac nodded, his eyes seeking Alex's once again. From her unsmiling face, one thing was apparent—she wasn't happy to see him. Feeling defeated, his gaze dropped, snagging on her hand in Michael's. Suddenly, his blood boiled, and he had an urge to break them apart. Using great restraint, he fisted his hands at his sides and silently counted to ten.

He'd googled Michael Smith—an ex-hedge fund owner worth hundreds of millions who now taught Math to elementary school children. Impressive and good-looking, it was no wonder Alex was dating the guy. In financial terms, Zac couldn't possibly compare. But, she'd confessed her feelings to him, not Michael. That, on its own, gave him hope.

"I don't suppose you'd consider setting up a practice here, would you, Dr. Danvers?" Michael's question refocused Zac on the current conversation. Not the one he wanted to have with Alex. Alone.

"Never going to happen. Zac loves New York, don't you, Zac?" Alex's overly sweet voice belied her steely gaze.

Crossing his arms, Zac huffed. This was neither the time nor place to have this conversation.

"I need to find Steven," he said, "Know where he is?"

Michael gestured behind them. "I believe he's in the living room, wisely rescuing his wife from a group of single men." He smiled possessively at Alex, who seemed to be paying him an awful lot of attention while pointedly ignoring Zac.

Tightness gripped his chest. Sharing his plans with her would have to wait. He needed to escape. About to step around the couple, Zac heard his name called. He swung back to Emma, who really did look like a million dollars in her fitted, silver sequin shift dress.

Holding out his hand to her, she took it with an easy smile. "Emma," he said, drawing her beside him, "I'd like you to meet my sister's best friend, Alexandra Masters, and her boyfriend, Michael Smith."

Emma's grip on his hand tightened. "Michael," she said in a strangled voice.

"Wow! Emma," he responded, beaming, "I can't believe it! You've grown up into a beautiful woman."

Incredulous, Zac stated the obvious. "You two know each other." His mind whirled. Emma knew the man currently dating the woman he loved. This was a twist he hadn't foreseen. Maybe even one in his favor.

"This is Sarah's sister?" Alex asked Michael, looking just as surprised.

He grinned. "Small world, isn't it?"

"Lovely to meet you, Emma," Alex said warmly. "It's good to be able to put a face to a name." When Emma frowned, Alex added, "Michael's mentioned you."

"Oh."

Interesting. Definitely a story there, Zac decided.

Alex's gaze flittered over to him, narrowed, and went back to Emma. Her smile appeared forced. "You two make a beautiful couple."

"Oh, we're not—" Emma began.

"She's not—" Zac said, but Alex cut them both off.

"I just remembered. I promised Mel I'd help her with...with snacks. Again, nice to meet you, Emma." Dropping Michael's hand, Alex left abruptly.

Judging from Michael's perplexed expression, he was just as confused as Zac.

So why didn't the man follow his girlfriend? The question was answered a second later—Michael couldn't keep his eyes off Emma.

Zac peered between them. Obviously, they had a history, which gave him an idea.

"I'm going to talk to Steven about the food." He waved a hand between them. "Do you two want to catch up?"

Emma's head bobbed up and down while Michael's smile widened. "Sure, that'd be great."

"Brilliant." In that case, he'd go find Alex. He needed to set the record straight.

Chapter Twenty-Seven

The MacAlistar's TV room was empty and, therefore, the perfect place for Alex to hide.

Even with her heart aching and her stomach muscles in a tight twist, she managed to admire the gold and silver tinsel streamers hanging from the ceiling corners and the multi-colored lights flickering above the fireplace.

A cinnamon fragrance filled the air, likely from the mantelpiece's scented candles. A miniature fir tree, adorned with many homemade decorations and haphazardly strung white twinkle lights, had Sophie's stamp all over it.

After rubbing the nape of her neck, Alex rotated her shoulders and forced herself to loosen up. She took a deep breath, releasing it slowly.

Who would've guessed Michael's Emma was also Zac's Emma? And why did it matter so much? It's not like Alex was in love with Michael, just using him to try to get over Zac. Admitting *that* truth made her feel guilty. Michael deserved so much better; he deserved a chance at true love.

And Zac?

Well, he seemed different tonight. Happier, more carefree.

Because of Emma?

It was no wonder he found her attractive. The complete opposite of her, Emma was petite, with chestnut hair and sparkling chocolate eyes.

Tears pricked Alex's eyes, but she forced them back. Maybe she should hunt Melanie down, say she was feeling ill, and leave.

About to turn, she stiffened when strong arms surrounded her. It took a split second for her to recognize Zac's musky scent and feel his warm breath tickling her cheek. "You look absolutely incredible, sweetheart," he whispered.

Leaning back against his firm chest, she raised a hand to her racing heart. His lips brushed her neck, and goosebumps flooded her skin.

"Zac, stop," she said quietly.

"Make me," he murmured before trailing a row of kisses up to her jawline, causing further shivers up and down her body.

Her resolve weakened, and groaning, she turned in his arms. Warm eyes regarded her briefly, then darkened like the sea before a rainstorm. His mouth descended on hers, and, similar to a wanderer in the desert, she finally found her oasis.

The intensity of the kiss grew, and, pressed up against his body, she trembled. His hungry lips explored her willing ones, and when his tongue sought a playmate, she happily obliged. Her determination to stay away fled with every touch, every caress. She needed him the same as she needed to breathe.

If moments, stolen like this, were all they could have, then so be it.

The sound of silverware tapping loudly against a wine glass brought an end to the kiss. A challenge arose in its place—to slow down her breathing and calm her racing pulse.

"Alex." Zac's husky voice revealed his own battle to gain control. He tipped her chin up so she'd meet his gaze. "We *need* to talk about us. I have news that will—"

"No." She cut him off, pursing her lips. "We've been over this, Zac. Nothing's changed." She glanced toward the door. "Steven's doing secret Santa. We'd better get in there, or we'll be missed."

Zac's arms fell away, his lips twisting in either frustration or annoyance. "Yeah, your boyfriend's sure to be missing you by now. Unless Emma's worked her charm already."

She frowned. "Michael's not—"

What was the point?

Side-stepping Zac, she marched out the room as smoothly as she could in high heels.

In the living room entrance, she halted. A large semi-circle had formed around Melanie and Steven, who stood beside the enormous Christmas tree. Michael was chatting with Emma on the far side of the room, and Alex made her way over to them.

She slipped in beside Michael. "Sorry I ducked out. Are you okay?" she asked softly.

"Yep." He linked their fingers and leaned in close, whispering, "I had an interesting catch-up with Emma."

"Good." She peeked over at Emma, who looked a little flushed. From the champagne? Or—?

Zac's return to Emma's side disturbed Alex and kept her attention riveted on them as they exchanged a few quiet words. The tender expression on Zac's face, in particular, created a physical pain in her chest.

Squeezing her free hand into a fist, Alex gritted her teeth, then sighed. She had no right to feel this way since she was the one who'd said they had no future.

She tore her gaze away from the happy couple and concentrated on the gifts being handed out instead.

"Last but not least...Alex," Melanie said, offering her the gift with a curious smile.

"And now, for the fun part," Steven said. "You may open your gift, and if you think you know who gave it to you, you're welcome to say thanks." He eyed them all and chuckled. "Or, if you don't like your gift, you can pretend you don't know who it's from."

Laughter filled the room, and everyone talked at the same time.

Alex led Michael over to a loveseat, saying, "I'm not sure I want to open this now."

"Why not?"

Fiddling with the beautiful red bow tied around the silver wrapper of the small box, she had an absurd thought—he wouldn't be crazy enough, surely?

A quick glance across the room showed Zac's gaze fixed on her. Blushing, she dropped her chin and stared at the gift. No doubt about it, he was her secret Santa.

"I'll open mine if you open yours," Michael coaxed, his hand covering hers.

"Okay." With shaking fingers, she untied the bow and pulled off the paper. A black box. She sneaked another peek at Zac, who was still staring at her.

She huffed. He was being so obvious! Didn't he have a gift to open?

Ducking her head, she took a deep breath and prayed she wasn't about to be put in an extremely awkward position. She snapped the lid open and let go of the breath she'd been holding.

A silver heart-shaped charm, perfect for her bracelet, lay on a bed of red velvet. A smile crept onto her lips as her eyes lifted, colliding with Zac's.

"That's gorgeous and rather generous." Michael's low voice reminded her she wasn't alone. "You said there was a twenty-dollar limit."

"I guess my secret Santa ignored the instructions," she said, focusing back on Michael. He didn't look pleased.

Searching for a distraction, she snatched up his gift—a clever choice of Batman socks—and giggled. She waved them in his face, saying, "Oh, I like these. Your secret Santa nailed it. The kids already think you're a superhero."

"Haha." Michael's mouth twitched briefly as he retrieved his present. When his attention then shifted to Zac, a muscle in his jaw jerked. "So, Alex..."

"Yes?" She touched his hand, and his intense gaze swung back to hers.

"Any idea who *your* gift's from?"

***

Zac couldn't watch the intimate scene any longer. He turned to Emma. "You hungry?"

She glanced at her wrist. "Yes, but I can't stay much longer. Can you still drop me back at my hotel?"

"Of course," he replied, guiding her across the room toward the food table. "Are you excited about meeting your friend's baby tomorrow?"

Biting her lip, Emma stuck a pepperoni pizza slice on her plate and then picked up a paper napkin. "Yes, though I haven't exactly had a whole lot of experience with babies."

"Pity my nephew's at my mom's tonight. Ben's so cute. You could've practiced on him."

"Honestly, I'm glad I won't have an audience when I hold a newborn for the first time. I'm kinda terrified." She scrunched up her nose. "What if I don't hold it right?"

"Emma, you're a capable, intelligent woman. You'll be fine," he said, using his best bedside tone.

"I can see why you're so in demand. A kind, compassionate, *and* hot doctor. What more could one ask for?"

"Now, now, flattery will get you anything you ask for," he teased, grinning at her.

"About that..." He followed her line of sight to where Michael was dishing food onto two plates. Alex was nowhere to be seen.

Zac's lips straightened.

"Think you could sweet talk Michael into moving back to New York?" Emma asked.

"Ha!" Zac suppressed the urge to laugh hysterically. "That would solve all my problems. Sadly, I'm not a genie. If I were, I'd gladly grant your wish. Except I have it under good authority that Mr. Smith very deliberately moved away from the city."

Tilting her head, she peered at him quizzically. "How would that solve all your problems?"

Helping himself to a second slice of pizza, he searched for a plausible explanation. "I guess Michael Smith returning to New York would be bigger news than me being the top MD in the state."

"Huh?" She shook her head, clearly not quite buying his answer. "I'm not sure that makes any sense, but I'll let it slide if you pour me half a glass of wine."

He did as instructed and handed her the drink.

"Thanks. Let's find a place to sit." She inclined her head toward her food. "I don't fancy spilling tomato sauce on this dress. If it has to be dry cleaned, it'll never be the same again."

"Sure."

He shook his head—women and their obsession with keeping their clothes pristine. One night in an ER, working without scrubs on, and he quickly got over worrying about his favorite Armani suit.

By the time Emma had said her goodbyes and Zac had delivered her safely to her hotel, he was getting itchy feet. Alex had been elusive ever since she'd opened his gift, and he really needed to find her.

Breaking a law or two on the way, he raced back to the dinner party, which had become a dance party. The guests swayed to loud music in the dimly lit living room, and he carefully scanned the small crowd for Alex. Locating Melanie instead, he headed her direction.

"Where's Alex?" he shouted when he got closer.

"She left a while ago."

What?

He'd only been gone half an hour! Retrieving his phone from his jacket pocket, he sent her a text: ***Can I come by so we can talk?***

Her response was immediate: ***Sorry. Not alone. Thx 4 beautiful charm. Talk 2 u another time.***

Michael's with her at her apartment? Seriously?

Anger bubbled up inside, and Zac was grateful he wasn't holding a wine glass because he probably would've broken the stem. How could she share passionate kisses with him, then leave with another man? Even if the man *was* her date!

Disappointed she hadn't stayed, his temple suddenly throbbed. He needed to find somewhere quieter, like the patio. Melanie had mentioned arranging some special heating for outside.

Bracing himself against the cold air, he slid open the patio door and immediately spied the heater as he stepped out. After pulling up a seat as close to the artificial warmth as possible, he closed his eyes. Cloud cover prevented stargazing, but at least he was able to imagine the stars.

Why wouldn't Alex give him a chance to explain?

She was so stubborn!

After a while, he blew out a breath. Perhaps he needed to see it from her point of view. Bringing Emma as his date had sent the wrong signal. It implied he missed New York. But the truth was, although he'd come for his dad, he was happy to have been summoned to New Haven.

And thankfully, the scare was over. Dad would be coming home Sunday, at the latest. After a necessary period of adjustment, Dad would return to work, and they would finally be working together at the practice.

Zac still couldn't believe the conversation had been so easy—not when he'd been dreading it.

The courage to speak up had come once his dad had looked a lot better in his hospital bed.

"Dad, I'd like to stay here; join you full-time at the practice. What do you think?"

Dad's beaming face and bright eyes had given Zac his answer. The arguments he'd expected about how much sacrifice had been involved in his moving to New York, how inconsiderate it'd be to leave his patients behind, and how difficult to give up the practice in his name—none of them had materialized.

He'd expected his dad to reiterate how much he enjoyed doing things alone in New Haven without interference. But nothing. No resistance at all to his idea. The tears in his father's eyes had been tears of joy.

Dan had been just as supportive. "You're absolutely not letting me down," he'd said. "Trevor will be a great partner. Not perfect like you, but close enough. You needn't worry about reaching for your dreams, Zac. You can achieve them."

So far, a working relationship with his dad only fulfilled half of Zac's dreams. The missing half was the woman he loved by his side.

As elated as he was with the other changes he'd made, he wanted the final piece of the puzzle to connect. The desperate desire he had to feel whole would only become a reality once he and Alex were on the same page.

Chapter Twenty-Eight

"Where on earth are you going?"

Slowly, Alex turned back toward the Danvers' house and found Melanie staring at her in confusion.

"I-I was about to knock. But...I forgot my coat." She made a show of rubbing her hands up and down her silk-clad arms.

"Well, don't just stand there! It's freezing out, and Mom has a roaring fire inside."

After giving Alex a quick hug in the cozy entryway, Melanie stepped back and eyed her thoughtfully. "You must've been standing outside for a while. Whatever possessed you?"

Shrugging, Alex tried to calm her nerves by taking a deep breath.

"Fine, follow me," Melanie said.

She led her to the TV room, and when they didn't run into anyone else on the way, Alex's clenched muscles relaxed a touch.

Melanie gestured to the dark gray sofa with its oversized red and orange cushions. "Take a seat in front of the fire, and I'll get you a hot drink."

"I-I'll be fine, Mel."

"Don't be silly! Your lips are blue, and you're shivering all over."

What? Had she really been standing outside the front door for that long?

Aware of her precarious position, Alex gravitated toward the yellowy-orange flames dancing in the hearth. With her hands outstretched, she leaned forward to soak up the heat.

Melanie held out a blanket. "This will help speed up the process."

"T-thanks," she said, sinking onto the sofa with a grateful sigh.

"In case you're wondering where everyone is, they're in the kitchen," Melanie informed her as she tucked the blanket around Alex's shaking body. "Sophie's helping Mom with food prep, and Zac's feeding Ben." She straightened and gave a closed-lip smile. "Last I heard, Dad and Steven were having a heated conversation about football."

"I can just imagine."

"Right." Melanie clapped her hands, then narrowed her gaze. "Don't you dare move. I'll be back."

By the time she returned, mug in hand, Alex's shivers had subsided. Smiling sheepishly, she accepted the drink. "I'm sorry for causing all this trouble, Mel," she said before taking a tentative sip and feeling the hot liquid slip down her throat.

"Why didn't you just come in earlier?"

"I was thinking through some things...coming to a decision. Or at least trying to."

Hope sparked in Melanie's eyes. "About Zac?"

After a brief nod, she took another few gulps of her hot chocolate. Gradually, the chill was chased away.

"Are you going to tell me what you decided?"

Alex studied the crackling fire for a few seconds. "Do you mind terribly if I speak to Zac first? In case things don't work out." And because...what exactly was she going to say? She thought she knew, but—

"Okay. But you have to know, the poor man's been driving us crazy—like a jack-in-a-box. Constantly pacing and muttering to himself. I've lost count of how often he's picked up his phone to call you, then changed his mind. My brother's hopelessly in love with you. You know that, right?"

Blushing, she nodded. It made sense Zac was torn. Since the party, she hadn't heard from him. He knew she wouldn't answer his calls, and he wouldn't want to present her with an 'all or nothing' scenario by text. He would want to tell her in person that she needed to choose either a life with him in New York or nothing.

No more stolen moments.

The idea terrified her.

If she loved Zac, she should be prepared to compromise—to support him in his career and agree to be wherever he was. Suddenly settling on her answer, she felt giddy with excitement. She could do it. She could say yes to Zac, agree to his terms.

But, she'd have no friends or family in New York, only him.

Was he enough?

'Yes!' her heart screamed.

What about Emma? The woman was already living in New York. She was gorgeous, perfect, and precisely what Zac should expect in a wife. Except, he didn't love Emma, and apparently, he 'had news'.

Whatever could it be?

It didn't matter. She was determined to make this work—his way. She couldn't live without him.

She'd tried, and it wasn't working.

With her stomach in a flutter, she met Melanie's inquiring gaze. "Do you think you could send Zac in here? When he's finished feeding Ben, of course."

A grin broke out on Melanie's face. "I'll be praying like mad that you guys work everything out so I can call you my sister for real."

"Please don't expect that!" Alex said, shaking her head, though secretly thrilled her best friend felt that way. "As much as I would *love* to be your sister, Mel, I've no clue what's on Zac's mind."

"Oh, but I do." She winked before waltzing away.

***

Zac groaned. Alex had arrived, but his sister had whisked her off to the TV room, claiming she needed some nursing first—whatever that meant!

Tapping his fingers on the bottle Ben had sucked for a solid ten minutes, he waited for Melanie to return. Eventually, she entered the kitchen with a knowing smile and just looked at him.

He wanted to shake her.

"What?" he demanded, startling Ben.

Without a word, Melanie marched over and gently lifted her son out of his arms.

"Hey! I was feeding him."

"Not any longer," she smirked. "Alex sent for you, and I know you want to talk to her."

He couldn't argue with that.

Pausing in the TV room's doorway, his heart raced. Alex sat on the sofa, cradling a mug, her legs covered. She didn't appear ill. Maybe just a bit chilly?

When she noticed him, she set her drink and blanket aside and pushed to her feet. She inched toward him, and he did the same, his gaze traveling her length.

Dressed in a deep green silk shirt and straight black skirt, she was stunning and totally clueless about it.

Swallowing hard, he dragged his attention back to her gorgeous face. The one he couldn't get enough of.

They halted, barely two feet apart, their gazes locking. Zac's heart pounded in his chest while blood rushed around his body. In the background, glowing embers hissed, crackled, and popped.

To keep from pulling Alex immediately into his arms, he fisted his hands and smiled hesitantly.

"Merry Christmas," she said softly.

Completely immersed in her emerald depths, he struggled to find his voice. A few beats passed, and he managed to clear his throat.

"Merry Christmas, sweetheart."

She smiled, her eyes sparkling like gemstones caught in the sunlight. She looked so beautiful, so angelic. All that was missing was her halo.

"I wanted to talk—" he started.

"You wanted to talk—" she said at the same time.

After an awkward laugh, Alex glanced over at the flickering Christmas tree. Her brow creased. "Sorry, you go."

"I wanted to talk about us."

"Us?"

With his knees threatening to buckle, Zac motioned to the large sofa. "Mind if we sit?"

"Sure."

They faced each other, their knees nearly touching while Alex's hands clasped and unclasped in her lap. Zac reached over and enfolded her hands in his, ignoring the tingles that shot up his arms as he did.

"So, I wanted to talk about my dad's heart attack...it put things in perspective," he said in a measured tone.

He watched her closely, adding, "It made me reconsider the future...our future."

Unease floated across her features, making him wonder what was running through her mind.

"I've done some thinking too, about what you said at Mel's," she said before he could ask. "About visiting here every weekend, and...I-I want that, Zac. You're way more important to me than any issues I have with New York or the eventual possibility of leaving my friends and work behind." She smiled tremulously. "Besides, assuming us dating works out the way I hope it will, I'll still see Mel, Sophie, and Ben when I move to New York, right? They're your family, too."

Wow! She was willing to move away from everyone and everything she loved, just to be with him. Although his heart soared, he frowned because she had it all wrong. He should've gone first.

Drawing in a long breath, he shook his head. "That's not what I want, Alex. I—"

"Oh!" Her face colored, her smile fading fast. "You've changed your mind. It's okay, I understand. It's a really big commitment, and honestly, an impossible arrangement."

Without warning, she stood, her expression pinched and her eyes glistening.

He leaped to his feet. "Alex, you don't—"

"I-I should go," she said, starting to turn away.

"Wait!" He snatched her hand and held on tightly, feeling her distress as her tears escaped. "You don't understand."

"You're right! I don't." The anger in her voice surprised him.

She yanked her trapped hand, but he kept his grip firm. He wouldn't let go. Not this time, not ever.

Her mouth set in a hard line. "Let go."

"Sweetheart," he said, giving her an imploring look, "I tried to tell you this at Steven's. After Christmas, I'm going back to New York to pack up my belongings."

"What?" She blinked a couple times, then swiped at each of her cheeks with her free hand. "Why?"

"Dad still needs me to cover for him until he returns to work. When he comes back, I'll join Danvers' Family Practice as a partner, and once he retires, the practice will be mine."

Her mouth dropped open, then snapped closed. "You're moving here? Permanently?"

He nodded.

"What about your partner in New York? I can't believe he's okay with you leaving him high and dry."

He loved that she cared so much. "Sweetheart, Dan's the one who's been encouraging me." He gave her hand a quick squeeze, then let it go. "Dan spoke to Trevor—the other doctor working for us—and he agreed to be a partner."

"Oh, wow."

"Needless to say, Trevor's thrilled to take over my position."

Nibbling on her lower lip, Alex went quiet for a short while. "So...you're doing this for me?"

"Yes. No, I'm doing it for us. I've always dreamed of working with my dad as his junior partner, but I thought he'd be disappointed. I stayed away because he was so proud of me running my New York practice." He smiled smugly. "Turns out I was wrong."

He held his breath as she edged closer, her intense gaze searching his. Then his pulse skyrocketed when her hands rose to gently frame his face. "This is what you really want, Zac?" she asked in a breathy voice.

"Yes," he replied instantly, tenderly sweeping his knuckle over her cheek. "This is what I really want. You are what I really want."

Her whole face lit up. "Me too."

Grinning, he lifted her off the ground and spun her around. She gasped, then laughed freely, the sound soothing the last bit of nerves still lurking in his body. He laughed too, and as he lowered her, their bodies molded as one. Having her in his arms felt like home. He never wanted to let go ever again.

"Best Christmas present ever," she murmured, sliding her hands to the nape of his neck and brushing her fingers through his hair.

"I agree," he managed before her steamy gaze had him almost losing all coherent thought. He stifled a groan. Did the woman know what she did to him?

Maybe she'd consider eloping?

Breathing in the floral scent he loved, his attention dipped to her kissable, red-stained lips. His mouth hovered over them as he whispered, "I love you so much, sweetheart."

"And I love you."

Their kiss was brief, passionate, and filled with love and longing. It had him wishing they were alone, yet grateful they weren't.

"I don't want to waste any more time without you," she murmured.

Before he could respond, her lips were pressed to his again. The kiss they shared was long and lingering, and when they eased apart to catch their breath, the joy in his heart almost overwhelmed him.

"Me neither, sweetheart," he said. "I want to spend the rest of my life with you. Only forever. No more stolen moments."

Acknowledgments

Phew, this second book came together much more quickly than the first. Maybe because the first draft was written a few years ago but had to be put on the back burner while I got my act together to publish *Bad Reputation*!

I'd like to say a huge thank you to my friend and editor, Eve. Without your encouragement and fantastic feedback, I wouldn't have had the confidence to continue writing and publishing my stories.

To Ansie, my awesome friend, you're a multi-talented woman! Thank you for being one of my faithful beta readers, even while setting up a new business, and for spotting those pesky little typo's :)

Thank you to Kris, my wonderful author friend, who has been so supportive in my writing journey and helped catch those non-American terms in my work. You're a star!

To my amazing family, who have endured endless conversations about my books and have put up with being ignored for hours on end while I write or edit, thank you—I love you.

Lastly, thank you to my heavenly Father for all His incredible blessings. He is the giver of every good gift in my life.

About the author

SAMANTHA J. BALL never thought she'd be a writer. An accountant by qualification, she used story-telling to help her sleep. A dear friend heard one of the stories she'd composed in her head and insisted she write it down. She didn't. Years later, her husband, after hearing yet another 'make-believe' romance from his wife, encouraged her to put pen to paper. She did. Writing has since become her passion, with ideas and inspiration coming from movies, books, and real-life characters. She lives in London with her husband, two beautiful grown-up daughters, and a gorgeous Tibetan Terrier.

Printed in Great Britain
by Amazon

16348039R00163